The Archer

Book Two in the Arrow of Artemis series

K. Aten

Yellow Rose Books
by Regal Crest

ISBN 978-1-61929-370-0

First Edition 2018

9 8 7 6 5 4 3 2 1

Cover design by AcornGraphics

Published by:

Regal Crest Enterprises

Find us on the World Wide Web at
http://www.regalcrest.biz

Published in the United States of America

Acknowledgments

Let's get the important people/organizations out of the way, shall we? Regal Crest and those wonderful folks within the publishing house deserve my utmost respect for their guidance in this process. Cathy, Patty, and Micheala, your continuous effort and instruction have been invaluable on my path to becoming a respectable writer. I also want to thank Ted for his sensitivity, insight, and indulgence to my writing whims.

Dedication

Ah, this one is dedicated to Kari. She only read the last chapter while I was writing it and declared that it was a d*** ending, but that it also looked good. I think that description will stay with me for life. As for the ending, I apologize. It wasn't Kyri's fault, but then again it wasn't mine either. There are some stories I don't write, but rather there is a voice dictating inside me and the tale writes itself. And as an author, I've learned to listen to that voice when it tells me it's time to stop.

The Archer (Arrow of Artemis book 2) Cast

Telequire Tribe

Orianna – Telequire Queen and Artemis' Chosen
Basha – Regent to the Queen
Steffi – Economic Advisor (Queen's Left Hand)
Margoli – Military Advisor (Queen's Right Hand), overall leader of all scouts and army
Gerta – Head councilor for Telequire
Shana – Telequire Ambassador
Kylani – Training Master and Trunk Leader for the Army
Cyerma – Training Master, Second in Command
Coryn – First Scout Leader (Morning Shift) and Trunk Leader for the Army
Sheila – First Scout and Branch Leader for the Army
Petrice – First Scout
Deka – Second Scout leader (Afternoon Shift)
Dina – Third Scout Leader (Moon shift)
Kyri Fletcher – Fourth Scout Leader (Perimeter Scouts & Hunters)
Certig – Fourth Scout Leader, Second in Command
Deima – Fourth Scout Leader, Third in Command
Geeta – Fourth Scout
Maeza – Fourth Scout
Malva – Fourth Scout (Veteran)
Pocori – Fourth Scout (Junior)
Degali – Fourth Scout
Shelti – Fourth Scout
Iva – Steffi's Assistant
Milani – Branch Leader for the Army
Kasichi – Branch Leader for the Army
Mitsah – Council Guard and Geeta's cousin
Thera – Master Healer
Kerdina – Master Carver
Achima – Master Fletcher
Iphigeneia – Master Blacksmith
Semina – Healer, Second Level
Gata Anatoli – Kyri's rescued leopard cub

Macedonia

Jordan – Master Fletcher

Romans

C. Caecilius Isidorus – Freedman and Slave Owner, one of the richest Romans of his time

Allectus (Allecte) – Son of Isidorus

Della – Slave healer in Tarentum

Aureolus (Aureole) – Captain of Isidorus' guards, former Tesserarius in the Roman Army

Lucius – Villicus (chief slave over Isidorus' Villa) and head administrator

Caecina Severus – Roman Senator

Galianus – Slave Owner

Gaius Claudius Marcellus – Slave Owner

Aelia – Slave Gladiator Attendant

Cassia – Slave Gladiator Attendant

Drusus – Whip man on the slave ship

Berren – Sailor

Gnichi – Sailor

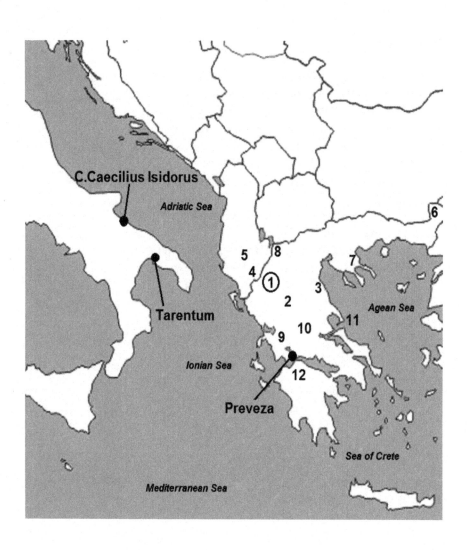

Chapter One

Secrets Shared

I HAD ALWAYS thought midwinter trees were a bit like monsters with their reaching black branches and rough bark. My hands were so cold that they could barely grab on as I moved from tree to tree. My patrol was finally complete for the day and there was nothing I wanted more than to soak in the hot baths back at the village. It had been a full moon since winter solstice and I was nearly finished with my newest cloak. I started with woven white wool fabric and then created patterns and lines with charcoal before washing the material again. The outer portion was complete but I still needed a few more winter white rabbit skins for the liner.

The white wool was expensive and I was forced to use the remainder of my archery contest winnings to pay for it. I thought perhaps my friends Shana or Coryn could suggest ways for me to earn more silver coins as an Amazon. The only issue that remained with my cloak was that if I put the rabbit liner in, it could not be shortened like the last one my mam made for me. I could have a long fur-lined cloak, or a short double thickness wool one. Clearly the design still needed work. In the interim, I was stuck using the shortened outer liner alone. It was not as warm but at least it blended nicely with the bare trees and did not tangle my feet when I ran. A voice called out my name as I approached the scout hut near the edge of the village proper.

"Kyri!" I sighed as I saw Coryn coming from the opposite direction. While I was always happy to see my friend, I knew my hot bath was going to be postponed if the First Scout Leader wanted to speak with me. Perhaps I should have been more grateful since I had not seen her for almost a moon. She had been on outer rotation nearly the entire time since midwinter. It was unusual but she never said why.

"Heyla, Coryn! How is life on the edge?" It was common understanding that the interior scouts that went out and came back to the village each day had it significantly easier than the perimeter scouts. Outer rotation ran along the perimeter of Telequire and it was too long a distance to justify running back and forth to the village center at the end of each shift, so the fourth scouts would spend three full days and nights as part of their scout rotation. When they were relieved by a new batch of perimeter scouts they would take two days to hunt for game on their way back to the village. Then the scouts would have two rest days before doing it again. The rotation differed greatly from the first, second, and third scouts who patrolled the forest around the village. The three shifts of scouts covered morning, afternoon, and moon times while the fourth scouts were on duty night and day. With posted sentries, forward scouts, and runners, it was just a different way of guarding the village. More unpredictable, more exciting, and less dull was how many described it. So "life on the edge" was really just a euphemism for the dangerous Amazon duty as a fourth scout.

The First Scout Leader grabbed a convenient rope that was hanging near and swung safely to the ground. My branch was lower so I simply flipped down to the dead leaves below. "Life is like it always is. I'm glad I caught you though, I have something important to ask. Do you have time to talk right now?"

I immediately grew concerned, not having a clue what she might want to speak with me about. But my time with the Amazons had finally taught me how to school my face to neutrality. I smiled at her and held up my red and chapped hands. "I can be free if you want to talk now. But if you are also finished with shift, I would make a suggestion that we take our discussion to the smallest bathing pool because I desperately need to warm up."

Coryn noticeably brightened at my suggestion. "Goddess, Kyri, that's a great idea! How about I meet you in a quarter candle mark?" I nodded and the tall blonde took off at a fast lope toward her hut. I watched her until she disappeared around one of the supply huts then I made my way back to my own. It had been a difficult moon. Shortly after winter solstice, messengers from our two nearest northern sister nations came in reporting skirmishes on their borders. Much to my great worry, my sister-friend, Shana, had been sent to the nearest one to act in her duty as Telequire Ambassador. While Shana went to Kombetar, the Queen's Right Hand, Margoli, was sent further up to Ujanik to assess the situation there.

Even though I was not in the official correspondence, Shana had found time to send me a few notes of update. She said they were not sure who was behind the attacks, just that they were well organized. Meanwhile our queen had been with the Centaurs for a fortnight attempting to get them to help since the skirmishes were near their northern border. I was not sure what upset me more, that my best friend was away in a dangerous place or that my queen was also away. Both facts touched me deeper than I cared to let on to the rest of my friends and Amazon sisters.

I had the foresight to stop for some food and wine on my way to the smallest bathing pool. I was hungry and suspected that Coryn would be as well. Thankfully she was already submerged in the water up to her neck when I arrived. I may be walking in the footsteps of the goddess but I was not dead. My friend was beautiful and athletic and never failed to turn heads wherever she went. But she was also a notorious feather ruffler and not who I truly wanted deep within my heart. We settled our attraction for each other before I had even become an Amazon. So I certainly was not interested in anything except friendship from the First Scout Leader, but I could not help my reaction to her beauty. I was only human after all.

"Figs, cheese, and wine! Goddess but I could kiss you right now!"

I laughed at her. "Settle your feathers over there first scout, you are not worth my wander." As Shana once told me, Coryn was like a flame. If you were not used to the heat and fire, you could easily get burned. I knew my path was not hers, we both knew it, but she liked to tease me all the same.

Coryn gave me a thoughtful look. "I wonder, who is worth your wander, Kyri Fletcher? There has to be someone who has caught your eye by now. You can't be arrows and trees all the time."

Her words prompted an immediate image of green eyes and I could not stop the blush from creeping up to stain my cheeks. "There is no one, you nosy scout. I have told you before that I am very focused on settling in with my new Amazon family right now." I tried to deflect. "What about you? We have not really spoken since solstice and your confession of stones. Did you and Shana ever speak?"

She held up a hand. "Whoa there, hold that horse of yours. You don't turn that red by thinking about no one in particular. So who is the lucky lady that has caught your pretty blue eyes?"

I could feel my face get hot again and I stalled with a drink of water from the nearby skin. My voice was a mumble when I could finally bring myself to speak. "There is no one, Coryn, now leave it be." A fig bounced off my head and I snagged it out of the water before it could sink. "Bent arrow and broken string, but you are infuriating!"

"Let me guess, is it Tilda?" Tilda was the head of agriculture and there were rumors about her preferring the company of the oxen to most of her Amazon sisters. I could feel my face scrunch up in disgust and I shook my head. "Come on, you can tell me." Her grin was just a little too smug.

"I cannot. It is not something I can speak of."

Perhaps she sensed the subject was sore for me and she grew serious. "Heyla, Kyri, it's not that bad. I've told you about my greatest regret. You can trust me with your secrets. You do trust me, right?"

I nodded. "I do trust you, Coryn, it is just..." I lost the words, fear having stolen them.

"Kyri, whoever it is can't be so bad." A strange look washed across her face then and before I could ask her about it she spoke again. "It's not Shana is it? I mean, I could understand if it was, she's certainly beautiful—"

"Oh gods no!" I could not help being horrified at the thought of having romantic feelings for someone I considered as close as family. "She is my sister. I could never think such a way about her!" I could see her exhale with relief and I stored the information away for future reference. I had a feeling that Shana and Coryn's story was not nearly written yet, but only time would tell the ending of it.

"Kyri." Her soft voice prompted me to meet her eyes. "Whoever it is has caught more than just your gaze, hasn't she?"

Tears pricked my eyes against my will. My brief words with Ori barely skimmed the context of our conversation to come. Sadly we never got a chance to talk before she was caught in the new threat to our sister nations, so all the feelings that I had been pushing down for moons had to be pushed back down once again. I thought I knew how she felt but there was still so much doubt. After all, I was nothing more than the newest member of the tribe. My fur was still drying on the rack, so to speak. Nearly a master fletcher, casual scout, huntress, and budding seamstress, it seemed like I had no path in front of me. Not to mention the fact that I still walked in the goddess's footsteps, meaning my sexual experience was as empty as a quiver at the end of hunting day. My insecurities were only natural given the circumstances. And Ori, goddess! Ori was my queen. Queen Orianna of the Telequire Nation. Defeat slumped my shoulders. "It does not matter, Coryn. There are no chances with her and I am fine with things the way they are."

A candle drop passed between us, and then another. Coryn's

voice was soft when she spoke again. "I've never known you to be someone that would lead a false trail. You can lie to me, but I don't think it's good to lie to yourself. Who would make you think you didn't have a chance? You're Kyri Fletcher, the woman who shot the impossible and newest star in the Amazon sky. Tell me sister, who could make your arrows miss their mark, or at least make you think they would? We're friends, you know you can trust me."

Sadness welled up inside me and I bit my bottom lip to keep from speaking. Trust was a strange bird. I once trusted that my parents would raise me to adulthood. I once trusted that I would follow in my father's footsteps as a master fletcher. But I learned that when you lose those closest to you, it becomes much more difficult trusting in the hearts of others. "I—" My voice cracked with the weight of my words. "It is someone who is not available." I sighed, hating to admit the things that hurt most. "No, that is not right. She is just not available to me."

Coryn passed me the clump of soap and gave me a strange look. "Not available just to you? I don't understand, who wo—" She broke off as realization washed through her mind. "Oh Artemis. It's the queen, isn't it?" I could not meet her eyes when I nodded yes. Finally someone besides Shana held my secret. I took stock and was surprised to find myself only mildly nauseous. "Does she know how you feel? Does she feel the same way?"

The hot water sloshed as I shrugged my shoulders. "I do not know. I mean, sometimes I think so and sometimes I am not so sure. I know she is drawn to me. She admitted as much moons ago. But beyond that I have no idea if her depth matches mine." I could feel the tears come and I pulled my hands out of the water to cover my face.

"Oh Kyri, it's going to be okay." I felt the shift in water as Coryn moved next to me. While the touch of her bare skin to mine would normally have me feeling things unfamiliar and exhilarating, at that moment it did not. Instead, I took comfort in the arm that wrapped around me and I turned to cry on her shoulder. After a handful of candle drops I calmed and I pulled back slightly and felt her palm on my cheek. When my eyes met hers I could see concern. "Better?"

As I nodded at her question we were both startled by another voice in the cave. "I can see this pool is taken. I'll find another."

I knew that voice as sure as my own and I felt the biggest smile come over me. "Shana, you are back! Come join us!"

Wearing a strange look on her face, her voice sounded flat.

"You seem busy. I don't want to intrude."

Confusion took me for a heartbeat until I figured out why she seemed angry. "Heyla sister, we are not busy. Coryn was pestering me about Amazons catching my eye, and I, um, I admitted my feelings for Ori. And my fears."

She walked up then, understanding that she had not caught me in a private moment with one of the most notorious rutting stags of the village. Once she was undressed she slipped into the pool with us. I kept my eyes averted, still shy around Amazon nudity, but I noticed that Coryn looked enough for both of us. Shana interrupted my stray thoughts once again. "You still haven't spoken with her?"

Looking back and forth between her and Coryn, I answered with frustration. "When have I had the chance? She has been gone for multiple seven-days. And even if she were not, the last thing she needs to deal with is my clinging heart."

I was surprised when Coryn spoke up. "Kyri, sometimes it's when things are most dangerous, most uncertain, that we need to hear that someone holds us in their heart. Your feelings may be exactly what the queen needs right now. I've known Ori as long as Shana, and even I can see that she's been lonely since taking on the Monarch Mask. She needs someone to help shoulder the burden of all those hard choices."

Shana shot the first scout a startled look. "Holy Artemis! Is that Coryn, mighty huntress, first owl friend and feather ruffling rogue, preaching the way of love?" Coryn's answer was to grab another fig from the stone ledge and fling it at our comedic ambassador. And just like that, the heavy mood was dissipated.

Coryn made a face at her. "You act like I have no more depth than a puddle after a hard rain. There is a lot more to me than you think, Ambassador."

"I have no doubts about that, First Scout Leader." I held my breath, not wanting to interrupt what felt like was a moment between them. Shana broke eye contact first and turned to me. "Where is Gata?"

I smiled at how my sister had finally come around where the leopard was concerned. It took a while for her to warm up to the cat but eventually they accepted each other. "She hates it in the caves. It is too hot for her so I sent her out to hunt when I got back from patrol. That is when Coryn found me and wanted to speak. So, here we are."

The tall scout jumped slightly, causing water to slosh. "Oh, that's right! Before Margoli left for Ujanik she assigned me the task of filling a new position."

Shana and I answered at the same time. "What position?" We looked at each other and giggled. Coryn just rolled her eyes.

"The position is for Fourth Scout Leader. We need someone over the Perimeter Scouts full time, not just being covered in a rotation by the other leaders. We're exhausted trying to cover two areas each. She gave me her recommendation and suggested I speak with the other scouts and shift leaders to get their suggestions as well."

My mouth opened in surprise. "Oh, that makes sense. The position would cover perimeter scouts and the scout hunters?" She nodded. "So do you want my suggestion as well?"

She shook her head slowly. "No, Kyri."

"Oh goddess!" My head swiveled toward Shana at the tone of her voice.

"What is the matter?"

Shana ignored my question and leveled a serious look at Coryn. "Does the queen know about this?"

The blonde once again shook her head. "Margoli gave me her name, a name that kept coming up over and over again as I asked for suggestions. And I wasn't surprised because you and I both know that our sisters have always been impressed by a calm soul and a competent fletch. It also helps that she's a hunter of the highest caliber."

Feeling more confused than ever, I finally snapped. "Bent arrow and broken string, who are you talking about already?"

They both looked at me at the same time and Coryn answered simply. "You."

My stomach dropped as I felt the blood leave my face. They wanted me to be Fourth Scout Leader? On one hand I was pretty bored with the daily patrols. I barely got to do any hunting unless I took Gata out in my free time. My routine consisted of walking the same tree paths day in and day out. On the other hand, I would be away from the village for days at a time. I would barely see Ori. No, I reminded myself, I would barely see my queen. So maybe my absence would be for the best. My musings were interrupted by Shana's shout of displeasure. "No! Pick someone else, Coryn. She's no fighter and you know it."

The First Scout Leader, head of all the other scouts went quiet. I knew that look well for she wore it when she was most stubborn and determined. "Margoli wants her, as do all the other scouts. She may be new to us, but she's highly skilled and she has killed plenty."

Fear washed over my sister's face. "Please, you can't ask her to do this—"

"I am right here! Do not talk about me as if I am not!" I turned to Shana, my sister and closest friend in the world. "Sister, I know you worry for me but I have to do my job. And you do not have more control over me than First Scout Leader or Margoli, the queen's Right Hand." I turned to Coryn then. "I will do it, if this is what you wish. And I will admit that I have been bored lately with interior scouting." I took a deep breath and let it out slowly. "And maybe some distance from my heart will help give me some direction."

"Oh little one." I ignored Shana's whispered plea. Eventually we all had to grow up. It was time I continued my journey.

Once again addressing Coryn, I voiced my questions. "I will need to know when you want me to start and what my official duties will be."

"How about you take two rest days then start? We have a handful going out in two days to rotate in with the current group. You'll have to pick a Second-fourth and Third-fourth once you get to know your team members. I can make some recommendations but you should be the one to choose who you feel most comfortable with." She chuckled slightly. "Your cat will be most displeased to spend her nights sleeping in the trees."

I was anxious at the thought of picking my second and third commands for leading the fourth scouts. But the anxiety cleared as fast as it came and I smiled affectionately at the thought of my rescued cub, Gata Anatoli. "First of all, she is not my cat. Second, she spends as much time with the queen as she does with me. And I can always bring her a hammock to sleep in, like the rest of us." The image of the half grown leopard cub even got a laugh out of Shana.

Once the moment passed Coryn spoke again. "I suppose that's true. Anyway, meet at dawn near the scout hut, two mornings from tomorrow. I'll introduce you to some of the perimeter scouts and let you take it from there. And don't worry, Kyri, I have full confidence in you."

I acknowledged her words with a nod and let my eyes glance at Shana. She was angry, and worried, and a myriad of other emotions that she did well to keep to herself. Just as I knew her, she also knew me. And she was aware that once I had made up my mind I was not one to be dissuaded. "Well, I am clean as I will probably get and I am ready for real food now." I stood and made my way out of the pool. "Shana, maybe we can catch up tomorrow? Will you still be here or are you just in for a night?"

She shook her head and spoke as I dressed. "No, I'm here for a few days at least. The queen is supposed to be here in a day or two and we're to go over the notes and correspondence from Margoli concerning our situation. Then I'll probably be sent out again, though I'm not sure where at this point."

My heart stuttered at her words. Just as she felt worry and responsibility to me, I held the same for her in return. I did not like the thought of Shana in the middle of a conflict. And while she was raised as an Amazon and subsequently better trained, she was no warrior either. "Okay. How about morning meal?" She nodded and I walked out the door. I did not want to spend any more time in the bathing hut, guessing the direction that conversation would turn after I agreed to the Fourth Scout Leader position. I understood the reasoning of why they chose me. Despite my newness to the nation, I rivaled Coryn for tree running. I was also one of the best hunters in the tribe, only partly due to the fact that I was the best archer they had ever seen.

I could thank my departed da for all of those qualities and more. He pushed me throughout my childhood to always be better, always do better. Many times since coming to Telequire I had felt that he raised me somehow knowing what I was to become after he was gone. The only thing I lacked to make me their ideal Amazon was faith in gods and goddesses, or one goddess in particular. Even though I followed in the virginal goddess's footsteps, I still could not bring myself to truly believe in my heart that she existed.

Nevertheless, I would fight to the death to protect all those things Artemis guarded as her own. She was the goddess of the hunt, wilderness, and all the wild things within. I respected the trees and animals of the forest and all the life they brought to the world around. She was the virginal goddess and the sworn protector of women and children so I could be no less.

On the day I became an Amazon I swore to serve the nation in whatever way they needed. Be that as a shield, or a weapon, I would rise to the challenge in exchange for my family and home here. They honored me and I would honor them in return.

But despite my actions after coming into adulthood and my pledge of fealty to the Amazon nation, at five years her junior, Shana considered me a little sister above all else. My first Amazon friend and I had been through a lot together. It seemed like a lifetime ago that she was attacked outside my homestead in a faraway kingdom. She would have died that day had I not killed for her instead. We each continued to live with scars on our hearts from our first meeting but as she had pointed out before, we both lived and that was what mattered most.

I FOUND GATA in my hut taking up a good portion of the bed. She learned how to use the latch on my door moons before but I quickly got tired of her leaving the door open when she would exit and enter. With it being winter, I knew I had to come up with a different solution. A fortnight previous I got special permission to cut a hole near the floor in the far wall of my hut. Risiki, one of the tribe woodworkers, helped me make a door out of woven reed and grasses. The door hung from the top of the opening by a heavy strip of leather. It was not as complicated as the hinges on the doors to our huts but it did not have to be. As long as Gata could easily push her way through and have the door swing back in place when she was done, that was all that mattered. While it was a little chillier with the extra entry than without, it was still better than coming back at the end of the long shift and finding my main door wide open. I even found a stray chicken on my bed once. I also did not have to worry about larger vermin just because of the nature of my hut mate.

I thought about what kind of leader I would be to the fourth scouts while I ate my meal. Coryn had given me very good training when I went through my initiation. I spent my share of rotations on the edge so I knew all the basics of what the perimeter scouts dealt with on a day-to-day basis. She also showed me how she set up the scout schedule, but that would not be one of my duties. First Scout Leader always had that pleasure. Before going on my initial fourth scout rotation I had assumed that there would be a shortage of women who would want to serve in such a dangerous and remote capacity, but it was just the opposite. Many of the younger Amazons seemed to love the duty, enjoying the challenge and freedom of it. That alone meant I would have my work cut out for me. Scouts were a cocky bunch and despite the fact that my name had supposedly been suggested multiple times, I had no doubt the perimeter scouts would test me. At twenty summers old, I was extremely young for such a position in the tribe and I knew it well. Their trust and respect would have to be earned before they would truly consider me their leader.

While I was tired from a long day in the cold, I would not be able to sleep with the weight on my mind. I turned to the one thing that I knew could soothe me, fletching. Even though my

Amazon trials were complete I found that I could not stop making arrows. It was a skill seared into my blood practically since birth. Daughter and granddaughter to fletchers, I knew that task best. So after clearing away my meal dishes I brewed some tea and set out my tools to work. The nation already had a master fletcher and bower, but I knew my arrows would be welcome should I choose to donate them to the stores. There was another reason I liked to fletch beyond the comfort it brought me. I still had the far away dream that I would someday receive my master's mark and I did not want to fall out of practice before the time could come.

Candle marks later, while gluing the fletching on an arrow, a knock sounded at my door. Not wanting to lose my focus on such a delicate placement, I called out without turning around. "Come in!" I had a feeling I knew who it would be. Shana entered and stopped to stare at the newly added Gata door. "What is this? Were you getting too hot in your hut this winter?"

I snickered. "On the contrary, I was getting much too cold. This one—" I gestured with my thumb toward the slumbering cat "—does quite well opening the door to let herself in and out as she pleases. However, she has not taxed herself to close it again after. I got tired of finding leaves on my floor and chickens in my bed."

"Oh goddess, you didn't? And I'm surprised she didn't eat the chicken!"

I made a face. "I did and I am too but she never bothers the village animals. She does all her hunting in the wood. But anyway, I made a door that she can push through and it will swing shut again. Then I put a better latch on the door for people." With my fletching properly placed, I motioned toward the other chair at my table. "Have a seat. I can clear this stuff away."

She waved away my actions. "No, you can keep working, it's fine. I just wanted to see a friendly face this evening and I feel like it's been ages since I last spent time with my sister." I looked at her then and knew her visit went beyond wanting to catch up. There was a look in her amber colored eyes that I had not seen before. So instead of listening to her words I put my tools and arrows away and got out a skin of wine and two mugs. She raised an eyebrow then nodded her assent. Pushing the full mug toward her I looked into her eyes. Though she had not admitted it, I could see the sadness lurking beneath the surface.

"Something troubles you." She nodded and stared at the mug in her hands. "Is it the attacks to the northwest?"

Her eyes slipped closed at the end of a long sigh. "Yes."

Shana's hand trembled beneath mine. "Sister, what is it?" I waited while heartbeats thumped by. I knew that whatever it was, she could not be rushed.

After emptying nearly half her mug, she finally spoke. "Do you remember in one of my notes that I said things weren't too bad yet because they told us only a few of the Kombetar sisters had been killed in the skirmishes?" I nodded, creeping dead crawling its way up my throat. "Well I was wrong. The reason that there have been so few killed is because the raiders are trying to take our sisters alive. They've taken at least twenty from Kombetar, and another eleven from Ujanik. Some of the girls haven't even had their menses yet."

I stared at her in shock, confused. "But why? I mean, I am assuming they will be slaves, but what use are children when you want people to work for you? You would think they would only want the adults." She stared at me sadly. I simply did not understand. Were children easier to train to slavery?

"Oh, little one." Tears filled her eyes then and my fear grew. What could be worse than a life of slavery? "Kyri, sister, they use them. They use them the same as they would adult women. Some men, some pigs, prefer the sexual company of young girls and boys. There are truly evil people in this world, Kyri Fletcher, and I'm sorry I was the one that had to tell you."

I slid my chair back from the table as if that alone could distance me from the words she spoke. "No." I had been called tenderhearted too many times in my life but I had never taken issue with it. I saved little Gata Anatoli from sure death when it was suggested that I should let the wild things be. I killed her mam and felt responsible for the little cub. I also saved Shana from sure death, though not before she was savagely beaten by soldiers. I carried the guilt of that day and she carried the nightmares. But her words, the horror that was happening just northwest of our border, the knowledge left a stain on my heart so deep that I feared I would never be clean.

My mind and heart whirled in a kaleidoscope of emotion. Shana watched as fear, denial, and disgust raced across my face. And finally when nothing else was left, I felt the familiar burn of anger. It was not hot like I had heard other people speak of it. My anger had always been cool and clean with determination. "We have to stop them. Why are we doing all this talking and negotiating instead of going to get our Amazons back?"

She grabbed my hand and brought me back close to the table. "Peace, sister. We are doing all we can right now. We can't just rush in not knowing the situation in full. We aren't sure who is responsible and the trackers that have been sent out never returned. We need more information and more support in this. Make no mistake, there will be a battle. But we want it to be on our terms and with minimal losses to the Amazons and our allies." She sat back in her chair and took a deep breath. "I didn't come here to upset you tonight, but I did want to ask you a favor."

I unconsciously leaned forward, wondering what she could be asking of me. "What is it?"

"There will be a battle, of that there is no doubt. And when the time comes they will send the warriors of the tribes after them. But if they need more, if the battle goes poorly, they will ask for volunteers among the tribes. Sister, I don't want you to volunteer."

"What?" My shout was loud enough to wake Gata but I could not help my reaction. "No, you cannot ask me to stay at the village and wait while my sisters risk their lives! This is my family now and I took a vow to defend them in every way possible." I drew in a ragged breath. Just the thought of danger to those I love was enough to set my head spinning. "If you are there then Ori will be there as well, and I cannot sit idly in my hut while you fight and die to a stranger's sword!"

She leveled a stern look at me. "You will if the queen orders you to."

Anxiety blossomed in my chest. "Please do not do that, Shana. Do not ask her to keep me home. That is unfair."

"Oh Kyri, I don't think I'll have to. I think Ori will choose to keep you home regardless of what you or I want."

Her words echoed through my head and the more I thought about them the truer they felt. Abruptly I stood and walked to the sheathed sword that hung from a peg set in the wall. I ran my fingers along the detailed eagle's wings that shaped the cross guard. "She gave this to me just a moon ago. Do you think she assumed I would never use it?" I turned back to Shana and she started to speak, but I cut her off with a wave of my hand. Stalking to my quiver next, I pulled one of my forest fletch arrows from within. "I came into this nation with skill and determination and I have not once hesitated with my shot. Do you think I would do any less against a more organized foe?" When I looked away from the arrow toward my friend, she was crying. "I lost my parents and my home because I spent my life being nothing but a girl who did not understand the world. I am no longer that girl and I learned much since leaving the homestead. There is no way I will let another person be taken from me without a fight."

"And if the queen orders you to stay behind?"

I knew my eyes would be stormy blue. Determination and anger always turned them from the light. "I will find a way." She stood and before I knew it I was wrapped in a strong hug. I could not prevent the breath from hitching in my chest, nor could I stop the warm tears that slowly made their way down my face. All I could do was return her embrace with all my strength. "I will not lose you too." She left shortly after and I found that the only energy I had remaining was for sleeping. Maybe I should not have taken the Fourth Scout Leader position. I had a feeling that in the coming moons my concentration was not going to be completely with my duties.

Chapter Two

Pushing the Limits of Silence

THE NEXT MORNING found me subdued. I considered my options for the day ahead. I could hunt for those last few winter white rabbits I needed or cut more small staves for arrow shafts. I could even head to the training grounds for some much needed practice. Instead I remained in my bed. I had promised to meet Shana for first meal and I knew if I did not show up she would come to my hut and roust me out. So it was with much reluctance that I crawled out from under warm blankets and an even warmer leopard. Gata twitched an ear and opened one eye to look at me. I snorted at her laziness. "If you are hungry you need to come with me for scraps. Otherwise you are on your own to hunt." She gave a little rumble and her furred muzzle split wide into a great yawn. Then with as much grace as only a cat could have, she stretched and leaped from the bed. Her feline expression seemed to say, "well, are you coming?"

When I entered the meal hut I was surprised to see the queen sitting with Shana. I stood in the doorway for a heartbeat, taking in her appearance. She looked tired, circles evident beneath her beautiful green eyes. Shana saw me and waved me over so I stopped to fill a plate on the way. I no longer fetched scraps from the kitchen for Gata. She had gotten too big to lay at our feet in the dining area so the cooks started leaving a bowl outside the door for her. Though truthfully, most of her meals she hunted for herself. When I sat down Ori immediately placed her hand on mine. "Heyla, Kyri, it's good to see you this morning. I've missed my home and friends."

I gave her a small smile in return. "It's good to see you too, Ori. Gata has really been lonely since you've been away."

"Just Gata?" Her eyes held humor that I simply could not feel in that moment. I shrugged and started shoveling food into my mouth, pushing those feelings down once again. However, I was not so clueless that I missed the look that passed between my queen and my best friend. Conversation was kept light while we ate though most of the words spoken were between Ori, Shana, and Basha. The regent had joined us about halfway through the meal. When I was finished I stood to take care of my dish but was frozen in place by calloused fingers against my wrist. The goose-bumps that followed were my usual reaction to Ori's touch. Intimately conscious of her hand, I met Ori's expressive green eyes. "Are you busy this morning?"

I thought about her question, wondering how I wanted to answer. There were a quiver's full of things that I would and could do on my rest days but there was nothing I really had to do. I shook my head. "No, not really busy. I was going to shoot a quiver or two of arrows then maybe get some sword practice in. Why do you ask?"

We were interrupted when Basha and Shana left the table and said their quick goodbyes. "Well I could do with both of those if you're interested in company."

My heart stuttered at the thought of spending candle marks in the busy queen's company. No, my heart was *clamoring* at the thought of spending candle marks with Ori. I gave her the only answer I had within. "I would love some company. Would you like to meet at the archery range in a quarter candle mark?"

Her hand still had not moved from my wrist and when she smiled she gave it a little squeeze. "That sounds good. I'll see you then."

I closed my eyes and said a prayer to a goddess I did not believe in. How could I put distance between us when clearly neither of us wanted distance?

Our first quiver of arrows met their targets in relative silence. Ori finally spoke while we were retrieving them downfield. "I heard about the new scout leader position from Coryn last night. She also mentioned that you accepted it." She looked at me and there was a weight to her gaze. "Did someone pressure you, Kyri? I thought you had no interest in a leadership role."

I inspected my arrows as I pulled each and put them one by one back into my quiver. I expected questions when she suggested we practice together, but as usual I had no understanding of her reasoning. Once I had finished filling my quiver I turned my eyes toward hers. "No one pressured me, and I never before had any desire to be a leader."

"Then why?"

I sighed as we started walking back to shoot again. "I think I have been bored with the daily routine of interior scouting. If you remember, I made an oath in front of the nation to be whatever was needed, to do whatever was required. If Margoli requested that I be Fourth Scout Leader and I had no reasons why I could not or should not fulfill that role, then how was I to say no?"

Once we reached the shooting lines we moved back to our original stations. "Margoli, Coryn, and the other scouts trust that I can do this job." I did not need to add any words to my statement but it was obvious what was left unsaid.

Ori gave me a hurt look. "You think I don't trust that you're capable?"

I simply shrugged because it would not be wise to put words in her mouth, nor was I willing to voice my fears.

"I do trust you, Kyri, I hope you know that. But this is serious scouting that is done on the perimeter, and dangerous. It is especially dangerous now. It's only a matter of time before the raiders come our way."

Insight crept in like a draft. "Are you worried for me?"

She jerked her head around. "Of course I'm worried for you! You've only been an Amazon for a few moons and many of the scouts who will be with you are also young and unseasoned."

I drew an arrow and took aim at my target once again. "I am fully capable of my duties and I can take care of myself." I shot my arrow and knocked another as she got ready to shoot.

"I know you can. It's just that you're not a warrior, Kyri." Anger once again washed over me as she spoke those words I had come to hate. She made to release her own arrow and my temper snapped. From one moment to the next, my arrow dashed hers from the sky as a second buried itself in the kill zone of her target. She turned to me in shock. "How did y—"

Lowering my bow I cut her off before she could finish her question. I turned to her and it took all my willpower to hold my anger in check. "I may not be a warrior but I am an archer. I can and will take care of myself and all those put under my charge. Clearly you misspoke when you named me worthy at winter solstice. Now if you will excuse me, I have to prepare myself for my coming duties as Fourth Scout Leader. Good day, my queen." Without even a backward glance at my arrows downfield, I took off at a lope toward the trees. Each step farther away drove a thorn into my heart. But I needed some time to think. I needed to be alone. And the only place I could be guaranteed both was the forest.

THE TREES WERE cold to me after a few candle marks. At least I had four more winter-white rabbits for my efforts in solitude, though I was no closer to understanding my own state of mind. I had planned to make a stew with the rabbit meat but I was not sure if I would be up to eating it given the cramping in my stomach. I did learn one thing about myself while in the forest around Telequire. Until that moment on the archery range, I had never disagreed with the queen. I had never been angry with Ori and I did not like the feeling at all.

I decided to start the stew anyway and maybe see about giving an apology. Ori was just worried about me. But if I was going to grow to be a contributing member of the tribe I would have to learn to fly on my own. Food over the fire, I left in search of the woman who held so much of my attention. Her hut was empty so I headed for the council chamber. Instead of my queen, I found Shana and Basha inside, deep in conversation.

My sister looked up from their scrolls. "Heyla Kyri, are you looking for me?"

I shook my head. "I am actually looking for the queen. Have you seen her?"

Shana's dark curls bounced lightly when she shook her head. "No, but I just got here a few candle drops ago."

"She left to go spar near the training hut. Take your sword, I suspect you'll need it." Shana gave her a sharp look and she shrugged. "What? She was in a foul mood is all."

I sighed loudly, accepting the fact that Ori's mood was most likely my fault. Shana turned a concerned gaze my way. "Kyri, is everything all right?"

I just shook my head at her and walked back out the door. As Basha suggested, I stopped by my hut and grabbed my sword before heading to the training circle. Ori was alone going through a solo sword routine. It was unusual to not have multiple pairs practicing. Perhaps the other sisters were afraid they might be asked to spar with her. The look on Ori's face told me they probably would not have liked it.

Instead of interrupting her I removed my cloak, bow and quiver, then began stretching. Ori had been training me in the sword for moons. My own sword was a gift from her and consequently one of my most treasured possessions though I willingly admit it was barely used. I stopped my routine as she came to the end of hers. I could see anger in the set of her mouth and brows and knew with certainty that my words earlier had hurt more than any arrow I could shoot her way. Instead of re-sheathing her sword she turned her angry eyes toward me. "Are you here to tell me more of what I do and do not think of you, Kyri Fletcher?"

I looked around to make sure no one was near enough to listen, then held my hand palm up toward her. "Peace Ori. I will not apologize for wanting you to trust in my skills and abilities when others seem to have no qualms. However, I am deeply sorry that I hurt you and that I did not respect your worry for me. I have never wanted to hurt you, my queen."

She looked at me for an entire candle drop before speaking. Or maybe it was a heartbeat that felt overly long. "You did hurt me, but I also hurt you by not giving you the respect you were due as a member of this tribe. I will admit that I hold a lot of frustration and anger over the situation in the West right now and I'm afraid I may have taken some of it out on you."

And just like that, some of her words and motivations made sense. "Would you like to spar for a bit, to help burn off all that angry energy? I normally run through the trees in times of turmoil but I will admit that it is cold for even me right now." I gave her my best contrite smile. "While I will not be much of a challenge for you, maybe it will help just a bit."

Ori swallowed and looked away from my gaze. "I don't know if that would be such a good idea right now."

I cocked my head, trying to understand the words unsaid within her words. Was she still so angry? "Why do you say that? Are you afraid that you would hurt me in anger?"

Her eyes widened. "No, never that! But Kyri—" She paused, seemingly weighing her words. "There are things you simply don't understand. And yes, it has to do with the fact that you are not a warrior, you are not a fighter."

I pleaded, with frustration at being coddled still coloring my words. "Explain them to me then, please! Help this green Amazon to understand."

She did something unexpected in response. Ori smiled at me, and it was not altogether friendly. "If you really wish to understand then draw your sword and step into the circle."

Trepidation fluttered through my belly. "Ori?"

"I said step into the circle, Fourth Scout Leader, and show me what you're worth!"

I had been training with her for moons so I thought surely it would be nothing I could not handle. Despite my internal reassurance my mouth was dry and my guts knotted mercilessly. I held my sword in the first defensive position as I entered the circle. There was no warning when she attacked. Usually I could expect a yell, false step, or even the revealing flicker of the eyes, but Ori had none of those tells. She came at me like fire in a dry forest and it was all I could do to stay with her. I never even got a chance to go on the offensive as she ran me around and around the ring.

After a particularly vicious kick to the midsection I spun
away to catch my bearings. I sucked in a breath at the look in her
eyes. They were hard and calculating, not at all the woman I had
sparred with on so many occasions before. They were not the eyes
of my trainer and friend of the last few moons. I was looking into
the eyes of a warrior and that warrior was fast. From one heartbeat to the next she came at me again. It took all my speed and
reach to parry blows but she grew faster still. I lasted only a few
more candle drops before she completed a twisting motion with
her blade and mine went flying through the air. Rather than yield
I dove and rolled away, coming up with a boot dagger in each
hand.

She gave me another smile only that one seemed equal parts
proud and predatory. "Very good, Fourth Scout Leader. Now that
you have two blades to my one, what are you going to do with
them?" I did not speak, instead parrying blow after blow each
time she came at me. Every single time I strained to hold her
sword on the cross guards of my blades. Tiring, I knew I had to
think of a way that would bring the match to an end. On her next
downswing, I did something completely unexpected. Instead of
blocking with both blades, I blocked with one and threw my second blade at the ground toward her feet. Momentarily distracted,
she had no defense when I stepped close and wrapped my suddenly free arm around her midsection. The grip on her sword was
lost when I picked her up and slammed her down onto her back
in the dirt.

My body pinned hers to the ground and both of us were left
breathing hard. Green eyes gone dark, I assumed my move had
further angered her. Instantly aware of my body lying on hers
with my groin pressed between her legs, I was as far from angry
as a person could get. Heartbeats went by as we remained immo-
bile in the cold dirt, panting into each other's faces. When a pink
tongue emerged to run across her lower lip I was gone. I lost control over my actions and leaned toward her, eyes never breaking
contact. The first touch of my lips to hers nearly left me undone.
But when she fisted a hand into my hair to pull me closer I was
unraveled from the inside out.

With a whimper I followed her lead and my body fell to its
natural instinct to grind into hers below me. But it did not last, it
could not. By the time she pulled back from me, pulled me back
from her mouth, my breaths came fast and heavy. It was no prop-
osition in the bathing pool. It was no fleeting kiss to the corner of

my mouth. It was me wanting her and her giving to me in return. "Kyri." I felt unfocused and it took me a heartbeat to realize she was calling my name.

She pushed my shoulders lightly to move me away and I looked at her in confusion. "Ori?"

Her voice was rough but her gaze was the most tender I had ever seen. "If you don't get off me I'm going to take you right here. In the cold, in the dirt, and in front of anyone who may be watching." I did not believe her, or maybe I just did not completely understand. "Kyri! You need to back off. I'm on the edge right now and I can't be on the edge like this with you."

Hurt blossomed in my chest and I quickly scrambled to my feet. "No? But you can be on the edge with someone else?" I made to turn away to pick up my knives but was stopped by a firm hand wrapped around my bicep.

"That's not what I meant!" Her green eyes seemed to burn into mine. "But we haven't even spoke of anything yet. You haven't told me of all your reasons and I haven't told you of mine. We can't go from that place of emotional ignorance to what we were doing just now. It—" She looked away then, perhaps finding it too hard to meet my eyes. "It is too far a leap and I don't think I could bear it if you pushed me away again."

My jaw sagged in shock. "Pushed you away? I have done nothing but want you nearer and nearer for moons now!" I blanched when I realized the depth of my admission. I tried to turn away again but she continued to hold my arm tight.

"Truth?" I could not speak anymore, my traitorous mouth had already said too much. A nod was all she got. Ori's stare lasted a few heartbeats longer before she nodded back. "Then I think it's time we had our conversation, isn't it?"

I was simultaneously overjoyed and panicked. I had known for a while that the time would come when we would open ourselves bare but it was still a frightening prospect. Maybe food would help. I knew Ori would walk over hot coals for my rabbit stew. Analyzing my actions I also understood that I made the stew for her, no matter how much I did not want to eat earlier. "If you truly would like to talk we could do it over dinner. I, um, I have a pot of rabbit stew simmering in my hut."

She laughed and I could not help the shiver that raced through my body when she moved her hand up to cup my cheek. "You already know the way to my heart, Kyri Fletcher. We're halfway there." When she removed her hand again I became achingly aware of just how cold it was outside. I could not bring myself to move and I think she sensed it so Ori gathered my daggers and handed them back to me hilt first. "I have a meeting with the council after I clean up but it won't take long. We can't make any real decisions until all the facts are in so we'll have to wait for Margoli. She's due in tomorrow, provided she runs into no delays on the way from Ujanik. What all that means is that I should have my evening free. So I will meet you for evening meal at your hut?" I nodded and continued to stand with knives in hand, long after she walked away. Before I could fully collect my scattered thoughts a voice sounded next to my ear. I whirled around, knives at the ready. The blades barely missed precious skin as my best friend jumped backward.

"Whoa sister, I didn't realize that you were armed!"

I shot Shana an irritated look for scaring me. "Is there a reason you had to sneak up behind me?"

She laughed. "Is there a reason you were standing there swaying like a sapling, deaf to the wind in the trees?" I sighed and bent to sheath my knives but she stopped me with an outstretched hand. "You may as well leave those out. I came here to spar. That is, if you're not too tired?" Just as Ori had been instructing me in the sword, Shana had been doing the same for me with knives. She actually started teaching me long before I officially became an Amazon.

I shook my head. "No, that is fine. My lesson with Ori was short but interesting." I gathered my fallen sword and re-sheathed it on my back and shook the kinks out of my neck. The barrage of questions would come as quickly as Shana's knives so I made myself ready for both. She did a few loosening up moves before we started circling each other.

"So, what is going on with you and Ori? First she is in a foul mood and you are upset. Then I find you here after sparring with her, looking like a red leopard has leaped into your path."

There were times that Shana was hard to follow. "Red leopard?"

She chuckled as she swiped at my ribs on the left side. "Yes, you looked both frightened and perplexed. So what has been said or done to put the red-leopard look on your face? Did you work out your differences or did you just spar?"

I tried a combo move with both knives at the same time I tried a leg sweep. It did not work of course. There was a reason that Shana was one of the best at knives in our tribe. "I think we did both?"

"Are you asking me or telling me?"

A kick to the midsection and a knife coming from the outside sent me into a diving roll just to get out of her reach so I could recover. "She, um, we..." It was too much for words. I could not focus on Shana's moves in front of me at the same time I was trying to explain all that was said between Ori and I, or rather all that was left unsaid. I tried one of the tricks that Kylani, the training master, had shown me. I received the lightest of cuts on my cheekbone for my efforts.

Then while I was momentarily distracted she kicked out and divested me of one of my knives. I thought it strangely humorous that it was the one she had given me the previous sun-cycle. I tried to parry with the single knife to her dominant hand and grab her wrist just as I had seen her do once before. Of course while I had seen the exact move win Shana the statue during fall equinox games, I was unaware there was a countermove. I pushed my height down onto her and she quickly collapsed her knife side and spun out of the way. After that she twisted her wrist out of my grip. Before I could recover my rapid fall forward, I felt an elbow drive into my back as she swept my legs out from under me. I was face down and winded from the blow so it was nothing for her to place the knife tip against the base of my skull.

My face was in the dirt by that point so I had to spit in order to clear my mouth enough to speak. "I yield you the match."

Laughing she stood and helped me to stand as well. Then with careful fingers she wiped the small amount of blood from the cut on my cheek. "Sorry, I got you there."

I shrugged. "It is fine, I can barely feel it. I am more upset that you downed me so fast."

Her smirk caught me off guard, though it should not have. "Well, I've had a lot of practice downing women." I punched her arm and we both laughed. When the laughter finally tapered off, the pride in her smile caught me off guard. "Seriously though, you shouldn't be upset. That's the first time I've come at you fully. Despite the short loss you did well, Kyri." She held out her hand and I gripped it palm to forearm in the way of the warrior. Her admission left me feeling better. Clearly I must have been doing well in the knife for her to trust me enough to not hold back. Once our blades were sheathed she wrapped an arm around my waist and gave me a quick embrace. "Now, tell me what is going on with you, sister. Did you push Gata out of your bed to make room for owl friends at last?" She laughed again, always entertained by herself. "Now you just need to convince Ori to come visit you some night!"

I ignored her jibe and innuendo. With Shana it was always so. Instead, I opted for truth that would quiet her tongue. "I kissed her."

Her screech turned several nearby Amazons our way. "*What?*"

I put my hand over her mouth, not wanting my private feelings announced to the entire tribe. "Shh, be quiet you! I need to check on my stew. Would you like to talk in my hut?" She nodded and did not say another word until we were back in my hut with the door closed.

"Okay, did you kiss her this morning? Is that why she was in such a foul mood? Or did the kiss happen later?"

I shook my head. "No, it happened just a little bit a go while we were sparring."

Shana tilted her head slightly and my eyes were drawn to the way the sunlight played through her dark curls. "Oh, well that's good then!"

Hope blossomed in my chest like a warm spreading pool. "Really?"

"Well yeah. If your kiss had been the thing to put her in a foul mood earlier, that wouldn't be a good sign for your future romance."

I could not stop the growl of frustration as she once again aimed a barb my way. "Shana! I am trying to be serious here." I ran a nervous hand through my hair, careful not to dislodge my Amazon feather. When I dared glance at her again, the look of sympathy in her amber colored eyes opened me wide. The familiar prick of tears would not be stopped as I sank onto my bed and put my face in my hands. "What am I to do?" She comforted me as only a near-sister and best friend could. She knew of my fears and of the depth of my feelings for the beautiful Telequire queen. She was also close with Ori, so presumably she also knew how that same queen felt about me in return. But I accepted that it was not her place to say and never asked her to break Ori's confidence.

She rubbed my back and let me cry. Only when my tears ran dry did she prompt me to speak. "So what happened?"

I took a deep breath and slowly let it go. The words followed of their own accord. "She went to the archery range with me to shoot. Once there she questioned me about taking the Fourth Scout Leader position. She was upset and had many of the same reasons as you. She told me she was worried for me, being so new an Amazon. We argued and she reminded me that I was no warrior, implying I could not take care of myself and I lost my temper."

"Oh goddess, Kyri, what did you do?"

My sigh was heavy with regret. "As fast as she could release her arrow, I released my own and knocked it from the sky. Then before she could say a word I buried a second one in the center of her target."

"Artemis! From your shooting station?" I nodded. "Then what happened?"

Mouth suddenly dry, I got up from the bed and retrieved my water skin. "I, um, I told her that while I may not be a warrior I was still the best archer the nation had and that I could take care of myself. Then I accused her of not speaking truth when she named me worthy at solstice."

Shana's mouth was open in shock. "What did she say?"

I shrugged. "She did not have a chance to say anything. I told her I had to prepare for my new role as Fourth Scout Leader and I left her there."

"Holy Artemis, you're lucky that she didn't take you apart right then!" I looked at her curiously, confused as to why she would think Ori would be violent toward me no matter what the provocation. She shook her head. "Ori can have a bit of a temper when her authority or her honesty is questioned. She's strange about it. Was there anyone else around?"

I thought for a heartbeat before answering. "No, it was still early so it was just the two of us on the field."

"Ah, that makes sense then." Shana snorted. "Well it certainly explains the mood Basha said she was in later." She met my eyes again. "So now I understand her foul mood earlier, but that doesn't explain what prompted you to kiss her. Did she kiss you back? Was it just a thank you for her excellent sword technique?" She snickered at her humor though I could not see it.

"I went hunting after I left her standing there. I wanted time to think but I could not figure anything out so I decided to make some rabbit stew. It was then that I realized she was only concerned for my safety. Just as I had been concerned for both of your safeties while you have been gone, even though I am more than aware that you can take care of yourselves. Anyway, I found her and apologized though I could tell she was still angry. I offered to spar with her to work off the anger and she did not want to do it."

Fine dark brows rose as Shana turned to face me. "Oh!"

I squinted back at her, trying to see if there was some hidden meaning or Amazon code that I was not privy to. "What do you mean, oh?"

"Kyri, sparring is not like shooting your bow."

I made a face at her. "I was not birthed of my mother yesterday, Shana! I assume your words have more meaning than what you are telling me so explain them please."

It was Shana's turn to stand up and pace, possibly trying to find the words to explain to my confused ears. "Until now, you've only sparred under controlled situations. But fighting is very high energy. And sometimes when all that aggression and passion comes to an end it, it doesn't end. Does that make sense?"

I stared at her like she had grown antlers. "No, it does not. Bent arrow and broken string, just say it plain, Shana!"

She stopped suddenly and gave a great sigh. Gone was the humor from her eyes when she looked into mine. "Sometimes fighting, sparring, battle, or any of those things can bring high emotions to the forefront of who we are. And sometimes all that coupled with the aggression needed to win will trigger a battle lust of sorts. It can make you excited." I thought about her words and felt a hot blush creeping up my neck to my ears. She smiled at my embarrassed features. "Oh ho, so you do know what I'm talking about!"

I nodded. "She was not going to spar with me but I begged her and that is when she changed. The moment I entered the ring with her she became different, harder. She gave me no quarter, much the same as you today with the knives. When she disarmed me of my sword, I actually drew my knives and continued fighting."

She inclined her head and gave me a smile. "Good job with that. What happened next?"

I swallowed, the memory of those next moments sent sparrows flocking around my stomach. "I wanted to win and I wanted to prove to her that I was capable. Maybe I just wanted to prove to myself that I was worthy of—anyway, everything I tried failed against her. Finally, with no other options I caught her blade on just one of my knives and threw the other at her feet. When she was distracted I stepped close and lifted her, then slammed her down to the ground onto her back. It was then with me lying between her legs and pressed tight against her, with us breathing hard, breaths long gone with the intensity of how we fought, that we kissed."

I shook my head, trying to deny what I did or perhaps deny

the rejection I felt when she pushed me off. "Shana, I looked into her eyes and I could not stop myself. I only meant it to be a quick press of the lips. I do not know what happened from there. The next thing I became aware of was Ori stopping us and telling me she needed space in that moment, afraid of what her actions would be if we continued." I swallowed the lump in my throat. "She is coming over later for stew and that talk we were supposed to have a moon ago."

Shana knew my heart well when it came to our queen. "It's a long overdue conversation too. Is that why you're so nervous? What is there to be scared of, sister? You can't really be afraid that she doesn't return your feelings at this point."

I shrugged. "I am not so naïve about the world. Even I know that sometimes feelings are not enough. I am barely into my feather and a lot younger than all of you. I do not think the nation would ever see me as a good match for the queen."

There was a reason that Shana had been chosen to be Telequire's first Ambassador of Nations. She certainly knew how to talk, and she knew when the most eloquent words were necessary. But what some would consider to be most surprising is that she also knew when just a few words would suffice. Her smile was tender and the fingers that wiped the remainder of salty drops from my face were more so. "Kyri, I think you should let the queen worry about who is a good match for the queen. As a wise woman once told you, just be you and things will happen in their own time."

I was surprised when a laugh tumbled from my lips. "Reusing your old words now, sister? I thought your tongue never tired or ran out of fresh moves."

"Woods weasel!" She lightly slapped my arm, but it did not detract from the perfection of her words. They were exactly what I needed to hear. Her work was done but I had a feeling that mine was just beginning because my head was full of thoughts long after she left my hut. It continued to swirl as I bathed, and even as I sat at my small table before mealtime. Instead of pacing nervously, I began fletching a few arrows for the calm it provided me. The only thing worse than imminent terrifying action was the wait before.

Chapter Three

The Language of Things Unsaid

GATA ARRIVED WITH Ori shortly before dusk. I was surprised to see a large cushion in Ori's arms when I opened my door. It was similar to the one she kept in her own hut for the half-grown leopard cub. On top of the cushion and wrapped in rough cloth was a loaf of morning bread. She also had a distinctive red skin of wine slung over her shoulder. "What is this?"

She smiled as she entered. "You have eyes of your own, Kyri Fletcher. I brought bread and some of Thera's spiced wine to put over the fire. You do have a small pot, don't you?"

She stood in the center of my hut staring at me. I stood there with my arms crossed staring at the large bed that took up most of her reach. "I am not talking about the food and drink, Ori. You are coddling her!"

"Just grab the wine and bread before I drop them, Fourth Scout."

I scrambled to comply and gave her a dose of sarcasm with my service. "Yes, my queen, anything for you." She tossed the large cushion to the floor at the end of my bed. Much to my shock, Gata immediately curled up into a ball on top of it. I pointed at her and shook my head in consternation. "This cat!"

Ori just shrugged. "I thought it was time you had your bed back. Like you've said many times, she's getting too big for all those things she did as a small cub."

I blushed at being called out on my own coddling. "It does not bother me, really. Truthfully, she is very warm in the winter."

The queen who held my future with the Amazons smirked as she walked to the pot of stew I had simmering over the fire. "Well then, perhaps you need something else to keep you warm at night. Or someone."

Words failed me and I felt my blush deepen. It was not about being teased. I had put up with as much almost daily from Shana. It was the fact that my queen was doing the teasing. Until that moment Ori had never said such things to me. We had always tiptoed around with words said and unsaid. Shana had warned me once that Ori's skill at innuendo far surpassed her own but I never believed her. I thought for sure that my queen, sweet Orianna, could never be as bawdy as our very own Ambassador of Nations. I was wrong. "Did you just, um, you?"

My stumbling words and lack of speech were apparently too much for Ori. Her laugher rang out clear and sweet in the quiet of my hut, and my breath caught at the beauty of her. Her voice was full of humor and high spirits when she spoke but her look was serious. "I would like to be myself with you, and I would be honored if you can be the same with me in return."

I nodded with what I knew to be a shy smile gracing my lips. "I would like that very much. Now how about we eat and I put the wine over the fire to warm?"

Dinner was comforting and like so many others we had shared over the past few moons. Her laughter would freeze the breath in my lungs, her small touches to my hand would quicken my heart. When we were finished I put a lid on the pot and set it outside my hut to cool. Ori cleared my bowls and poured two mugs of Thera's wine. In a move that surprised and thrilled me, she sat on my bed and held out the second mug to me. I took a seat next to her, not even pretending I should leave any space between us. "We should talk of those things now, Kyri."

Her voice was low and my heart rose into my throat. I nodded in agreement but it did not seem nearly answer enough. "I am not sure what to say." It was one thing to say that you need to speak to someone about your deepest feelings and desires. It was another to actually do it. But Ori was a queen, and a good one at that. She had a remarkable way of making me feel at ease while at the same time making me feel safe. She was strong, decisive, and kind.

Her face was serious but her smile was warm. In the combined lamp and firelight, the green of her eyes seemed darker, like that of moss growing in the deepest part of the forest. "Are you happy here, Kyri?"

I blinked in shock. I had no idea why she would even ask such a thing and I became desperate to reassure her. "Of course I am happy here! What reason would you have to think I was not? Ori, this is my home. Telequire nation is my family now and I am—" I stopped at the realization of something big. Guilt and sadness rode tandem on the horse of my conscience. "I am happier than I have ever been." The cycles that my mam was alive, I felt most loved. And the time that followed with just my da, I discovered my love of the forest and fletch. But being an Amazon, I felt complete. I had everything I had always dreamed of—love, challenge, and family. The fact that I could feel such a way after the death of my parents was the true source of my guilt.

Always insightful, Ori questioned me. "Do you feel bad for being so happy when you've lost your parents and childhood home?"

I shrugged. "Truth? I never thought about it until just now. And yes, I did feel bad for a heartbeat. But actually looking deeply into it, I think my happiness is always what my parents wanted. When I last saw my da, his only desire for me was to be happy and live free. With the Amazons I have done that." I drained my nearly empty mug and set it on the table next to my bed. Then seeing hers was empty as well, I put it on the table too. Turning back to her, I could not help the goosebumps that raced across my skin as our arms brushed. "Why do you ask me this? Have I done something to make you think I am not happy?"

In a move that was not unfamiliar, she took my hand into hers. Sword calloused fingers traced the lines on my palm, eliciting a ticklish twitch. She spoke without meeting my eyes. "You haven't done anything to make me think this, but I've noticed something about you since you came to us. You have so much potential but you hold yourself back." I started to protest but she squeezed my hand and I held my tongue. When she looked up her green eyes bore into mine and I knew she was speaking words I needed to hear. "I care very much about your happiness, Kyri. I— I care very much for you." I exhaled slowly, savoring the words I had waited so long to hear. But rather than draw a breath to replace the expelled one, I froze. I was afraid to say anything that might cause her to take those words back. I was afraid to move, fearing she might take her hand away from mine. And I was afraid. She shook our entwined hands. "Heyla, Kyri, are you with me?" I nodded, but still had no wind to speak. She smiled and I imagined that my face was quite red. "Breathe, Kyri. You can't kiss me if you die from lack of breath."

Her words were loud in my ears but they made no sense. At last my body took over where my heart had failed. I drew in a ragged breath and words left with it. "Kiss you?" She did not have to speak. She merely lifted her free hand and gently cupped my cheek. She must have found the answers she sought with her questioning gaze because in the span of two heartbeats she pulled my head down and sealed her lips to mine.

Oh goddess, her lips! They were soft and firm and so much warmer than I expected. She parted them slightly and I followed suit, the gentle taste of wine and spices like ambrosia on my tongue. I was unsure how long we sat there occasionally pulling breaths between kisses. She eventually moved her hand to the back of my neck to pull me tighter, then she gripped my hair and pulled me tighter yet. Ori kissed me like the gods were all gone and the world was ending. And I not only let her, but I kissed her the same way in return. When I moved my own hand up to tangle in her short golden hair, she moaned low in her throat. Just that sound alone elicited feelings I had no context for. Desire and passion were small compared to the heat that exploded in my heart and radiated outward and down.

But as with anything in life it had to end. Ori pulled back reluctantly and I let her. It was a lot to take in, almost too much. I needed the break as much as she did. I looked at our still clasped hands and said the first thing that fell down the rabbit hole of my mind. "I have wished for this for so long. My need to be near you was like a great owl outside the window, always watching me, always waiting."

She cocked her head and looked at me curiously. "What has been stopping you?"

I sighed remembering all the stones in our path and pulled back a little more. "The same thing that will continue to stop me, to stop us. The very nation that we hold so dear." I made to stand.

Despite her apparent surprise at my answer she refused to allow the space I was resigned to make between us. "No! No running, Kyri. Now explain why you think the nation has been stopping you from meeting your desires."

Sadness pulled my mouth down. "Ori, you are the queen of a thriving Amazon nation and I am naught more than a novice Amazon. I have never accomplished anything great in my life and you do amazing things each day as our ruler. You deserve so much more than I have to give. And the nation would agree with me if they knew about this thing between us." Ori sighed and my heart dropped with the sound. I thought for sure that she had finally understood what I tried so hard to explain.

Her head shook back and forth and I closed my eyes so I did not have to see. "Oh Kyri, while you have the heart and soul of an Amazon, you really don't understand what that means." Confused, I opened my eyes to see a smile on her face. "Being an Amazon doesn't just mean freedom of the soul and freedom to fly through the trees doing Artemis's will. Being an Amazon also means freedom of thought and freedom of heart. As queen, I can take anyone as my consort. Anyone, Kyri! There are no expectations of me when it comes to who I favor, or even love." She stood then, and I scrambled to stand too. "I don't think the problem here is whether or not the nation thinks you would be worthy enough to consort with the queen. I think the problem is that you don't think you're worthy."

"I, um..." She was right. My fear of my own inadequacies far exceeded anything I had witnessed within the Telequire nation. I was afraid that I was not worthy. That had been my fear since I became aware of exactly how deep my emotions ran for the queen of Telequire. I was going to have to change a lot more than my outlook in order to truly understand my place and my future with the nation. With those thoughts in my head, I dropped to a knee in front of the queen. "Queen Orianna, please forgive your loyal Amazon and friend."

I looked up and she raised an eyebrow. "And what is the queen forgiving you for?"

"I have claimed that your heart is above all others within my own chest, yet I have not done all that I can to honor that heart. Instead I have placed both our hearts in a cage of fear."

She did not say anything for a few heartbeats and I grew nervous. Then she slowly lifted a hand to caress my Amazon feather. As with many times before, I had no understanding of her actions or her silence. It was only when she smiled that hope began to open in my chest like the petals of the sweetest flower. "Stand up Kyri. Tonight I'm simply Ori. I'm not here as your queen. I understand your need to prove yourself. You told me once many moons ago that you needed to do things your own way or you would never consider yourself worthy of honor or praise. That is why I'm honored that you accepted the Fourth Scout Leader position. And why I would also like you to get your Master's Mark and continue with whatever things you do that make you happiest and help you grow." Once I was standing, she tugged me into a close embrace. Her head rested on my shoulder and I never wanted it to leave. "We have a lot of difficult days and moonless nights ahead of us. We need your bravery, your skill, and your heart right now, Kyri Fletcher. I need those things from you. And because of those dark days ahead, this growing spark between us—" She paused and shook her head before continuing. "No. If I'm expecting you to give all your heart and bare your soul, then I can do no less. This growing love between us needs to go at the right pace. I want to do this right and I don't want to rush what feels like Artemis's blessing to me."

I cocked my head at her. "But why, Ori? Why does the pace of this love between us matter?"

Despite the fact that my hands were now both entwined in

hers, she pulled me closer. "Because when this is all done and the dark days are behind us, I want to claim every single piece of you, feather to fletch."

I nodded and swallowed the enormity of what she was saying. Her suggestion that she wanted to claim me feather to fletch had my heart racing. I had not considered something as deep as that, as her claiming my feather for her own. I would never have been so bold as to ask that commitment from her. Though I wanted to. "You would wait for me?"

She caressed the side of my face with fingers strengthened by half a life of sword work and stained with the ink of her many treaties as queen of the Telequire nation. "You fill me like no other. For you, I'd wait an eternity." The kiss she left me with was slower, less rushed. But it threatened to buckle my knees just the same. I could not help sighing her name when she pulled away a second time. She shook her head ruefully and stepped back from me. "Don't sigh at me Fourth Scout. I'm afraid this slow walk of ours will sorely test my patience as well as the stamina of my fingers. I don't need your guileless teasing to make it worse." I laughed with her because I knew exactly what she was talking about. I had a feeling I was going to regret spending my nights hanging like overripe fruit from trees with a dozen other perimeter scouts around me.

MY REST DAYS passed much too quickly and before I knew it I was tree-walking with my new scout group. Just as with the inner scouts, the perimeter scouts covered the nation's outer edge in quadrants. As scout leader I would actually spend a day with each quadrant, only hunting one day on the way back instead of the two that everyone else would do. That gave me a chance to better connect with all the members of my new team.

After my first seven-day as Fourth Scout Leader I had a better handle on all my duties and the people that would look to me for direction. I was pleasantly surprised to see that Certig was a perimeter scout. I remembered meeting her on the boar hunt from the previous sun-cycle. Because the role of Fourth Scout Leader was new, so too were the Second-fourth and Third-fourth roles. Coryn informed me that Certig had already been filling in a lot in various leadership capacities, so she recommended I make her my Second. And after getting to know the rest and assessing their personalities and skills, I chose Deima as my Third-fourth. She was a good friend of Coryn's, though I knew they had not seen

each other often since Deima came to the perimeter scouts. My job
mainly involved assigning sections each day, making sure gear
and supplies were stocked, and generally taking the lead when
any situations arose.

Coryn's last bit of advice before I officially made the trip to
the edge with my team was to trust my instincts. There had been
many discussions with her and Kylani about my unique skills.
They both knew about my actions and tests while at Tanta nation.
If they trusted me and my instincts then I could do no less of an
honor than to trust myself. We had a dozen Amazons per quad
perimeter, and they spent their candle marks moving back and
forth along the line watching for trouble at our border. Even
though I enjoyed my first seven-day as Fourth Scout Leader, I
was still excited to get back to the village and see Ori. My excitement quickly turned to dread when I noticed that preparations
were being made for the leave-taking of a large war party. It
seemed as though runners were constantly crisscrossing my path
as I tried to make my way farther into the village. Wagons
strained with supplies, and despite the chill air, the rest of the village population flitted about like bees in a hive. I dropped off the
roe deer I had taken on the way back from the edge and went in
search of my best friend.

In the end, I did not find Shana so much as she found me. I
was getting ready to go looking for Ori in the council chamber
when my sister slipped out. She nodded to the guard outside the
door and took my arm in hers.

"You can't go in there right now. They're in a meeting."

I pulled her to a stop when we were a decent distance from
the guard and common foot traffic. "What is going on? Did Margoli return to take warriors west?"

She looked at me in silence and I did not like how tight her
amber colored eyes were or the way the corners of her mouth
turned down as if in pain. She shook her head and pulled me forward again. "Come with me to my hut. I have many things to do
and not many candle marks left to do them." Worry was a hard
ball in my stomach and I swallowed the sick feeling down as I followed closely back to her hut. Once inside she poured herself a
mug of wine and went straight for the words she knew I would
like least. "Telequire nation is sending an army of two hundred
warriors west. I will be accompanying the queen, and the queen's
Right Hand. Kylani and Coryn are to come as trunk leaders, and
Sheila, Milani, Kasichi, and Gestia will be branch leaders." I sat in
the nearest chair, sick with her news. I knew from all my sessions

with Margoli that an Amazon army consisted of two trunks of one hundred women each. The trunks then had two branches each. I wasn't reassured by their numbers.

All of them. All the people I cared for most were about to go to war. The ones I loved were leaving me behind. I could not stop my voice. I could not still my words any more than I could still my heart from beating. I stood so fast the chair fell over behind me and I grabbed her arms in my strong and capable hands. "No! You cannot go! She cannot go!" I could feel tears racing down my cheeks as I pleaded with the closest person I had to family. "Please Shana! Please do not let her go! Say you will stay behind."

Rather than try to get out of my grasp Shana stepped close and pulled me into a hug. "I'm sorry Kyri, but I can't. We have to go. The others need us. Our sisters are out there and we need to get them back."

My heart broke. "But I need you too."

"Kyri Fletcher, look at me." I opened my eyes but she was nothing but a blur through my tears. "You are whole and hale. The girls that have been taken, they are at the mercy of men like the ones who attacked me outside your homestead. Would you have us leave them just so we can stay safe at home and save you the worry?"

I was not ashamed by her words as much as I was shamed by the fact that I failed to think of others before my own fear. I shook my head in answer to her question. "No. No one deserves that. It is our duty to protect women and wild things. It is our duty to protect the Amazon nations and right those wrongs against us." I could feel the swollen grittiness of my blue eyes, and I knew they would be red with my shed tears. "Why can I not go with you?"

She shook her head at me in return. "The queen, Margoli, Kylani and the council were up late into the night deciding who would stay and who would go. There is nothing that will change their minds."

"But if I ask Ori—"

"I was there, Kyri. Your name came up but Ori and Kylani both said no."

I ran my hand through my hair in frustration, careful not to dislodge my feather. "But—"

Shana stepped back and shook me to make me see. "Kyri, the queen's word is law and she said no. And before you think they are coddling those who are left behind, that is not why you weren't chosen. They are afraid that once they get the armies together to the west, the enemy will circle more raiders between Kombetar and Centaur lands and go after the Telequire nation. Sister, I promise I will be as safe as I possibly can be. We have fifty Centaurs that will join with us as well as nearly two hundred more warriors combined from Kombetar and Ujanik." She smiled in an attempt to lighten the mood. "Besides, Ori will be there to take care of my diplomatic yap."

I sighed. "But who will take care of Ori?"

"Kyri, sister, Ori can take care of herself. She is the best swordswoman I've ever seen."

Thoughts were racing through my head and I had no answer to her words. Instead, I grabbed her mug of wine and drank it straight down with barely a gasp. It was nice that she liked the good stuff, and that I was finally gaining an appreciation for it. "You do not understand. From the moment I put myself between Ori and that boar last fall, I knew it was my path to always watch hers. How can I do this if I am nowhere near?"

Shana poured more wine and drank it herself. "You will, sister. Have faith in your future and trust in the plan that Artemis has for you. And we need you here protecting the village. All those hotheaded young perimeter scouts are now looking to you for leadership. Can you do this?"

I hated her words but I knew she was right. My one word response was more a resigned sigh than an answer. "Yes."

She gave my hand one last squeeze and started moving around her hut again. "Now, I have to pack, and I'm sure you want to change and bathe after being out in the trees so long. Oh—" My attention left the hands that were busy packing her saddle bags and moved to her face. "Ori says she will come see you later after evening meal. We are leaving at first light tomorrow."

I nodded and slipped out the door when she turned away again. I did my best to avoid people as I walked to my own hut. I felt numb. After eating in solitude at my small table I decided that a bath was the only thing I could do without falling apart. I took my spare leathers and a drying cloth to the smallest bathing cave and hoped I would not have company. I was trying not to think of them being away and in danger. They were all capable fighters, more than capable. But that knowledge did not prevent the fear roiling in my belly. I ducked my head down into the water and held my breath. If only I could have floated like that forever, I could almost believe everything would be okay. My lungs forced me back up long before my heart. As soon as I broke for air I could tell I was not alone. Though I suppose I should not have been surprised to see her. "How did you find me?"

Her voice was low and perhaps a little hoarse. "Gata. She knows your name and she's gotten pretty good at finding you when I ask. She wouldn't come into the cave though. I think it's too warm for her."

"Yes, it is too warm for her. She never comes into the caves with the exception of the temple."

She stepped a little closer. "Would you like some company, Kyri? I will understand if you are angry with me right now."

I sighed and watched the water ripple just below my chin. The torches and oil lamps kept the chamber bright enough for bathing. I looked up at my queen and knew I could not deny her anything. "I think you know by now that your company is always welcome." All I could do was hope that she did not want to actually come into the water because I was unsure what I would do if she came near me with her flesh bared. My fears grew as she unclasped the warm cloak I had given her for winter solstice. The bottom dropped out of my stomach when Ori removed the soft cotton wrap she wore as a shirt. I quickly averted my eyes and found a cake of lavender soap near the edge of the bathing pool. As I washed I heard her slip into the water and dunk beneath the surface. Still avoiding meeting her eyes, I dropped below to rinse my hair as she came up. I stayed under longer than was necessary but not nearly as long as I needed. When I broke for air again she was much too close.

"Kyri, please." The queen's short hair was slicked away from her face and her skin shone golden in the flickering light. Her beauty held me mute and it must have shown on my face because I saw her eyes soften a little bit. I realized then what a burden she had been carrying for the past moon. And with the situation to the northwest she would have to lead her people off to war, most likely leading some of them to their deaths. She would have to leave behind all that was comfortable and safe in order to keep the rest of her nation from harm. Ori needed someone to tell her it was going to be okay.

My next breath felt tight in my chest and I knew that I would have to push all my fears and desires away for just a little while because she needed me. My heart raced with the understanding that my queen needed *me* for comfort. "Turn around, let me wash your hair." I could not tell if she had water droplets on her face or if tears pricked her eyes, but Ori turned around and left me with the view of her smoothly toned back and shoulders.

In the center of the pool where we were, you needed to stand to keep your head above water. Near the edges there was a ledge carved into the stone that ran the entire distance around the small pool. I tried to stay back so that no part of my body touched hers, save for my hands. The short strands were easy to wash, much easier than my own long dark hair. I did not want to stop so I continued to massage her scalp, just as my mam did for me when I was a little girl. I swallowed thickly when she gave a low moan.

"Goddess, but that feels amazing." I continued to ignore the nearness of her bare skin and let my hands speak for me. I could see her relax under the massage so I started working my way down to the back of her head and neck. That was when she started to speak. "This situation frightens me, Kyri."

I cocked my head unseen behind her. "Why are you frightened? You have led people off to war before." I slowly moved my hands down to her shoulders, using strong fingers to dig into the muscles and soothe the tension below.

Her head dropped forward as she answered. "I fear for them, all the women that I lead into battle. I fear for them every single time. I and I alone will be responsible for leading some of them to their deaths and each death breaks a part of me inside."

I continued my ministrations, knowing that my hands were giving her a desperately sought measure of peace. "We follow you willingly, Ori. You are our queen and we trust you implicitly not to lead us into a losing battle, or a false one."

"But what if you die? If any of you die it will be on my shoulders."

I sighed and my breath tickled the drying hairs at the nape of her neck. "Dunk down, you need to rinse the soap from your hair. I will rub your shoulders more when you come back up." She did as I asked, rinsing thoroughly before breaking the surface of the pool again. I lathered my hands and started to work on her neck and shoulders. "Ori, my queen, some of your people will die. And yes, those deaths will be on your shoulders because someone has to lead and take responsibility for the nation. But only the sacrifice of that death will be on you. The death itself, and all the tragedy of it, will be on the hands of the raiders who have taken our sisters. Your responsibility is to give those deaths meaning." I felt more than heard her sigh and knew that she took my words to heart.

She raised a hand and splayed her fingers across the surface of the water. "But what if I lose someone close to me? How could I live with that death, no matter how much meaning it has?"

I shook my head at the same time I spoke. "Truth? I do not know. I am a novice with these things. It took a while for me to come to terms with simply killing ones whose souls were turned to darkness. I have no idea how I would cope with leading an innocent or a friend to their death. But know this, Ori, you are strong and you are a true leader." I shrugged and sloshed the water around me. "At least not all you care about will be in danger. Some of us will be safe and sound, swinging from the trees around Telequire."

She turned her head to look at me over her shoulder. "You are angry."

I sighed again and stilled my hands. Then, before my brain could protest, I stepped close behind her and wrapped her in an embrace. Her back slid smoothly against my breasts and my heart pounded frantically in my chest. But the heat of her and the solid comfort in my soul told me it was the right thing to do. "I am just so very worried. I lost the two most important people in my life before I was twenty summers old. I could not bear to lose more right now." She held my arms to her and relaxed into my embrace. "I am not angry with you. I understand the reasons behind your decision to leave me behind. I am simply scared too."

"Kyri..." She did not finish what she was going to say. Instead we stood in silence with warm water all around. It felt like an eternity though it was probably more like a few candle drops. I simply reveled at the feel of her in my arms. Eventually she sighed and my heart plummeted a little. We could not stay there forever. Before I could step back to give her space, Ori spun in my arms. The gasp came unbidden at the feel of her skin rubbing against my most sensitive areas. I shuddered when her hands came up to tangle in my wet hair and pull me into a deep and desperate kiss.

The chamber got hotter and my heart pounded in my chest as she pulled me nearer yet. There was no room left between our bodies and the water was all but forgotten. I shifted my legs so we did not fall over into the pool. I did not mean to direct it where it would affect her so. She shuddered and her mouth fell away from mine when my thigh brushed her center. She hissed in surprise. "Oh goddess!" The sound made my belly flutter and parts of me began to throb below the surface. Seeing the vulnerable skin of her neck as her head canted away from me was too much to resist. I moved my mouth down to take smooth skin between my lips and teeth. In a move that surprised me she abruptly pulled my head away from her. "Kyri, goddess, stop! You have to stop."

She backed away and I think we both moaned at the loss of contact. I was confused and did not understand why she stopped when everything felt so good. "Ori? Did I do something wrong?"

She ran a shaking hand through her hair and looked up at me. Then as her hand fell back to the water she took another deliberate step back. "No love, you didn't do anything wrong." Her breaths were measured as she tried to gain some semblance of control. I understood because I was doing the same. "Everything felt amazing and so very right. But I meant what I said about moving slowly down this path. And I can tell now that slow is impossible when I'm alone in a bath with you. You test my resolve like no other."

I was pleased that she was as affected as I felt. But I was not so pleased at the way things were left aching with need in my body. Perhaps she was right about not bathing with someone you favored so much. The temptation was too great. "I think you might be right on that. Our bath has left me most uncomfortable." I smiled ruefully and reached up to braid my hair into an intricate pattern my mam had shown me long before I learned to run the trees. Ori averted her gaze as my breasts rose from the water with my actions, and I felt a small amount of pleasure in her discomfort.

Another long sigh. "Yes, that is one word for it. Though I wouldn't mind one of the shoulder massages again. Maybe next time with clothes on, yes?" She smiled but it faltered and her eyes grew wide when I stepped near again.

I held a hand palm up. "Peace, Ori, I am just going to say goodbye. I have done enough thinking in this water. It is time someone else had a turn." Her lips were like silk when I gave her a goodbye kiss. I shivered as I dried with a soft cloth, though I swear I could feel heat from her stare. Once I was dressed I went to leave but her voice stopped me at the large skin that covered the doorway into the cave.

"Will you come see me off in the morning?"

Her words carried more weight than a simple request. They were asking me to make a declaration to the nation at the same time they were promising to me that everything would be okay. I swallowed and pushed my fears and insecurities down. I gave her my smile like a gift. "You could not keep me away." I left then, taking my thoroughly awakened body back to my hut. It would be a long night grown much too short.

Chapter Four

Innocents Lost

MORNING DAWNED DARK with a cold rain turning moods sour. Women were running around making last moment arrangements, moving goods between wagons, and saying goodbye to their families. A few children were around as well to bid farewell to one or another mother. It was against nation policy to allow both mothers to leave for war. One had to remain behind at all times. The intent was not to spare the death of a mother since single mothers fought in battle all the time. It was to spare the death of both mothers at once. Besides the two hundred warriors, there were scores of support staff that would be leaving as well. Cooks, healers, messengers, hostlers, and more would all follow behind the main force as they moved roughly northwest. I was up early enough to catch Shana still in her hut. The bundle in my hands was wrapped in scrap leather to keep it dry. When she opened the door I came inside and held it out to her. "What's this?"

I shrugged. "It is cold and you do not know how long you will be gone. You will need something more than this ratty old thing." I fingered one of the many mends in her cloak to emphasize my point.

When she unwrapped the bundle her mouth dropped open in surprise. "Kyri, this is your winter white. You've been working on it for moons. You can't give me this." She tried to hand it back but I refused to take it.

"I can and I have. If it makes you feel any better, I cannot use it with the fur liner while I am running the trees. I need to work on the design some more. But it will be perfect for what you will be doing." She continued to stare and I merely smiled back at her placidly. "Just say thank you, Shana."

She swallowed thickly and smiled back at me. The twinkle in her eyes came back when she spoke. "Thank you Shana."

I laughed and pulled her into a hug. "Now who is the smart one, huh? Be safe sister, I am going to miss you."

When we pulled apart, her eyes were shining with more than mischief. "I will. And you be safe too, Fourth Scout Leader. Come now, let's go see the queen." Despite her protestations, Shana wasted no time pulling on the warm cloak before shouldering her saddlebags and walking out the door. I carried her bow and quiver and travel pack.

Ori looked stressed as she spoke with Basha and two members of the Telequire council. While I waited for her to finish speaking I loaded Shana's items onto her horse and said my goodbyes to Coryn and Kylani. Both clasped my forearm like warriors, wished me luck, and told me to trust my instincts. I could only try.

When Ori finished with the last of her instructions, I caught her eye. Her smile was warm and reassuring as she made her way to me through the crowd of people. Thankfully the horses were all off to the side, leaving the area where I stood for goodbyes clear. I could see she was wearing the warm cloak I had given her at winter solstice and it lifted my spirits to know she was taking part of me with her. When she was close enough she wrapped me in a tight embrace, her voice nearly a whisper. "You came."

I pulled back so I could see her face in the wet gloom. "I would never let you go without saying goodbye." I could feel tears threatening but swallowed them down as much as possible. "Swear to me, by leaf and by arrow, that you will return."

Her eyes were sad, the green dulled by responsibility and fatigue. I knew she could not make promises to me. The future was a changing thing that no one could predict. I also knew she would say the words anyway to make herself feel better as much as me. "By leaf and by arrow, I will return to you just as I left. As Artemis is my witness, I will hold you in my heart every moment that I'm away." She pulled me down and kissed me, as if sealing her lips to mine were the only way she could make those words real. Then Ori pulled away regretfully and touched my lips with her fingertips as she did. "I have to go, Kyri."

"I know."

She stepped back and I became aware of a few curious gazes around me. "Be safe, Fourth Scout Leader."

I nodded. "Be safe, my queen." I turned to leave the common area at the edge of the village, unable to watch her ride away. My eyes stayed facing the ground to hide my tears and I nearly toppled Margoli as she stood behind me. The surprise on her face told me she had witnessed our private goodbye though her look quickly turned to one of sympathy. She did not say anything, merely nodded in understanding and stepped from my path.

When I made it back to my hut I wanted nothing more than to dissolve into the great wracking sobs that threatened, but I did not. I found Gata curled up on her bed and went over to her. On my knees, I took the opportunity to run my hands through her soft fur. It was a goodbye of sorts. When I was finished, I called her up and rolled a spare blanket into a bundle. The bundle was then wrapped in waterproof leather and lashed to her back. She did not like it but I had been training her to carry items for moons. I also knew it would not stay there long. "Gata, go to Ori." She looked at me curiously, but she also knew the command. I had sent her to the queen many times in the past. I pointed at the door. "Go to Ori, Gata." With a rumbling purr she rubbed the side of her face against mine, drying my tears. I opened the regular door for her so she would not have to fit through the small swinging door with the bundle on her back. She turned her gold-flecked eyes toward mine, intelligence obvious in their depths. "Stay with Ori." With one last rub against my leg she trotted away. The bundle swayed precariously on her back, being larger than what I would normally tie. I watched until she was no longer in my view then went back into my hut. It was done. There was no more I could do to protect the ones I loved. I could only wait for them to come home again.

A FORTNIGHT PASSED before the first messenger arrived in the village. Luckily I was on a rest day when she rode in so I received my messages without delay. I had three in total, from Ori, Shana, and Coryn. I cherished them, reading each one twice before finally writing three short notes in return. Scrolls were expensive and often we had to write on old ones that had been scraped off. The messenger left the next morning after speaking with Basha and the council and getting a good night's rest. My scrolls were sent out with a slew of others. Many women were off to war and being missed. Mothers, sisters, aunts, nieces, daughters, and lovers. While I was not alone in my grief and sadness, I was still alone.

My time with the perimeter scouts had been fairly mundane. We had not seen any real action while living on the edge. I could feel genuine affection and bonds forming with my team and I took joy in it. I received my fair share of teasing of course. It was not even because I was a young Amazon and newer to the tribe. It also was not due to the fact that I was their new leader. It was because I was new to the group overall and no one was safe from their witty comments and loose tongues.

It started with me getting teased about walking in the footsteps of the goddess. Scouts were a notoriously randy bunch so I was a little unusual with my lack of experience. I took it with good nature because that was exactly how it was meant. I got regular challenges in bow and arrow since I had made the impossible shot on the anniversary of my birth. As the rotations passed I found that more and more were asking me to teach them the ways that I had learned from my da. By the end of my first moon nearly all of the fourth scouts could shoot accurately while running through the trees. Most Amazons were taught to shoot from a stable vantage point starting with their very first bow. I explained that a running shot was helpful with more than just scouting. It directly translated to riding on a moving mount as well.

It was reassuring that even though most of them were closer to my age, all were willing and eager to learn, and all gave me the respect that my position was due. I also enjoyed getting to know my Second and Third, Certig and Deima. Deima had a sharp wit and humor about her that could always make us laugh. And Certig was so upbeat that I could not help but feel better in her company, even after the longest of scouting rotations.

Once I had learned everyone's names and got a feel for my teams, I stopped moving each day through a different perimeter group. Instead, I would spend four days with a perimeter group, take a single hunting day and two rest days, then I would spend the next four days with another perimeter group. This allowed me to see different people with each rotation since I was not synched with any one person's schedule. It was also nice having more than one day at a time with each group.

I even survived the gossip about me and the queen when it finally surfaced. Despite Ori's reassurance that no one would judge me unworthy of her favor, I expected a negative reaction from my sisters when news finally made it through the nation. During my second rotation with my northwest quadrant scouts, we were taking our dinner after running the perimeter all day. It was chilly so I allowed a small fire of dry wood to warm us up. Guards were posted in the trees, just to keep an eye out for anything untoward. They would be rotated in every two candle marks throughout the night so everyone got equal amounts of rest. We did not have standard shifts living on the edge as perimeter scouts since we were more likely to be called out at any time to investigate trespassers or other trouble and we had to be ready.

It was during the downtime, when everyone was relaxed and warming, that someone brought up the rumors. Amazons loved gossip as much as they loved their wine and celebrations. Other than the guards, the rest of the team around the fire was grilling the newest birds in our group. They had just rotated in from their own rest days and were ripe with gossip and knowledge of the Western War. The queen and army had been gone for more than a moon and we were all ready for our sisters to come home.

I was sad to learn that another messenger had come and gone, taking with her my chance at sending Ori a letter. But I cheered at the hope that a scroll would be waiting for me on my next break. Certig just happened to be with me in the same group when the latest word came to us. She was first to ask questions, anxious about her lover being away with the other warriors.

"So what is the news, Geeta? Have they heard anything more from the army?" The last word we received said that they were fighting small skirmishes only, waiting for the return of their deep scouts. They could not actively attack the enemy without knowing more about their forces and where the captive Amazons were being held. The biggest fear was that they may have moved the captives straight out to slave ships bound for the lands of Rome.

Geeta was my age but had short legs to my long. Her red-dish-brown hair was barely long enough to tie a feather. She was one of the biggest gossips in fourth scouts and loved being the center of attention. "Well, my cousin Mitsah was outside the council chamber when the messenger came in. She said that according to reports the deep scouts were back. Queen Orianna was given the honor of leading the combined forces and she was making preparations for multiple points of engagement. They sent a group to negotiate with the leader of the raiders but were forced to pull back when one of the Amazons was killed." I sucked in a breath and was not the only one. Geeta stopped talking, perhaps realizing that we were all worried about loved ones. "It's okay, she wasn't one of our Telequire sisters."

Someone mumbled. "Still..." I heard a few more whispered prayers to Artemis at the news of another sister gone. Certig's voice prompted again. "What else, Geeta?"

The small gossipy sister smirked at the group. "Well, that's all I heard about the army that's away. But I did pick up a rumor about a certain Fourth Scout Leader." I could feel my ears heat up in anticipation of whatever rumor she had brought back, but I ignored the eyes that turned my way and continued to eat my rabbit leg and roasted red roots. I allowed the gossip sessions with fourth scouts as long as no harm came of them. And because of that, it was only fair that I take my lumps like everyone else. A few people laughed and one even called out my blush. "Ooh, it must be good if she's turning that color. What is it, Geeta?"

She looked a little too pleased with herself when another of our sisters answered back at her. "Oh come on, we already know Kyri walks in Artemis's footsteps! That's not gossip."

Heads turned from me back to Geeta. "Are you sure about that, Maeza?"

I swallowed at the same time I tried to breathe and ended up choking on my bite of rabbit. I could not stop the indignant squawk from leaving my lips. "What?"

"Well?" Geeta questioned me and faces kept turning back and forth between us, like the pendulum center of our impossible target.

I could feel heat suffuse my entire face, wondering exactly what she had heard about me. "Of course I still walk in the footsteps of the goddess. I think I would know if I strayed!"

One of the newer scouts, who had not been in on the initial teasing and questions when I first started with fourth scouts, spoke next. "Why?"

I was confused. "What do you mean why?"

Back to Geeta. "Perhaps she's waiting for someone, right Kyri?" And so that was when I had the flavor of what she had heard. I was surprised it had taken so long given the fact that my very public goodbye was seen more than a moon previous. Though we were seen mostly by people that had left the village.

When eyes once again turned back toward me I was resigned to my words. "You have already rode the horse this far, Geeta. You may as well put it in the stable and tell us all what you have heard. I will not lie about myself to anyone, or for anyone."

Her eyes took on a playful glint. "So it's true about you and Queen Orianna?"

Voices erupted around the fire. "What?" "Holy Artemis!" I even heard one that took me by surprise. "Nice choice!" I was unsure who that voice referred to, me or Ori.

I held up a hand for quiet. "Calm your feathers, scouts! Ori and I are good friends—" I was interrupted by Malva, one of the veterans of the fourth scout troop.

"Owl friends?" Laughter followed her words.

Though I would have thought it impossible, I could feel my face heat further. "No!" Even more laughter followed in response to my vehement protest so I tried again in a calmer voice. "No, we are not owl friends and we will never be owl friends." They seemed crestfallen with the news. I did not lie to them. I knew in my heart that I wanted more than just the occasional night with my queen. And I had finally come to realize that she wanted the same from me. I was not completely sure how to say as much among my group of notorious feather rufflers, but I tried nonetheless. "The queen and I have grown close. But there is a lot going on right now and the stench of danger fills the air. So we are taking things very slow." A few whistled at my words, teasing with their less verbal innuendo. Others let out little sounds of approval and congratulations. I smiled at Geeta's response.

"Lucky Fourth Scout Leader!"

But I nearly swallowed my tongue when I heard another call out. "Lucky Queen!"

I scrubbed my face with the hand that was not holding food. "Thanks, I think."

The group let out a chorus of muted laughter. Just because they were having fun did not mean they had forgotten their duty. When attention had finally shifted away from me, Certig leaned close. She had been sitting right next to me so her whispered voice carried clear in the quiet night. "How long have you known?"

I thought about that fateful nervous day when I sat outside the food hut nursing injuries and a tiny leopard cub. "Since the moment I met her."

My second in command smiled indulgently and nodded. "Cupid's arrows have struck true my friend."

Feelings of insecurity pushed their way upward and I met her eyes in the firelight. Certig was a good woman and would surely tell me true. "You do not think I am too young, or too inexperienced? I mean, she is our queen."

She returned my serious stare and put a hand on my shoulder. "I think if Artemis wills it, it should be so. Your paths crossed for a reason, Kyri Fletcher. Who are we to shove you in a different direction? Our queen deserves to be happy, and so do you."

Nothing more was said about it. We went back to eating our dinners and readying the camp for the night. And I realized that despite my initial embarrassment, I was glad the subject had been brought up. I also knew that Ori had been right. My fears were for naught. I could only hope that all my fears proved to be as such.

AGAINST MY WISHES trouble found us early the next morning. I woke to bird whistles circling the trees. Any Amazons not already on guard duty grabbed their packs and immediately flocked to the high branches. Bows strung, we sat in quiet and watched the approaching force. I could feel my palms sweat as we witnessed the foot soldiers coming in from the northwest, opposite the rising sun. I sent one runner to the village center to warn the interior scouts, and I sent two more runners out to pull the perimeter scouts from the quadrants on either side of us. That left ten of us to wait and ward off the advance of nearly three score armed and armored men. They followed no road making it clear that their intention was to hit the nation while our warriors were away.

As they drew closer I could see that they carried a variety of weapons. They were either really prepared for any kind of combat, or the force was a group of ragtag bandits and someone else was leading them by the purse strings. They even had a black and red standard, though I could not tell what the image was. I could see swords and sarissas. The swords would only be trouble if we came down out of the trees. The sarissas were long spears that did little good in our forest as they were almost impossible to maneuver in the thickest areas. I was not even worried about the double handful of men who carried crossbows. Those did not have much range and took far too long to reload. No, I was concerned by fact that the rear half of soldiers carried bows strapped over their backs. I had drilled often enough with Margoli and Coryn and knew that we were required to give them a warning. Not everyone coming to Amazon lands meant us harm though I was pretty sure the lot approaching did.

I let out a low whistle and accompanied it with a hand signal. It was often hard to see our fellow sisters in the low light of the high branches, but all would hear the whistle to wait and watch. Unfortunately, in the cold of winter we had no leafy cover to hide us from view. All we could do was pull our masks down and meet the challenge head on. When they were within bow range, I put one of my forest fletch arrows into the field in front of the one man who rode horseback. "You are about to trespass on Amazon land. State your business or march back the way you came."

In response, all the men in the front drew shields from their backs and formed a phalanx of sorts. The mounted leader laughed. "Oh I know exactly where we are, Amazon. We're here to look for some friends. You see, some of your sisters are getting lonely with our army so we're just going to take a few of you back with us to cheer them up. What do you say? Want to make this easy and throw those bows to the ground?"

My next arrow was lucky enough to cut through the thin line that held their banner to the pole. The men below it nervously shifted and I could see their leader's face turn red as the banner fluttered to the ground. My voice was calm and clear to the invading force though my insides shivered with dread. "Your next step forward will mean death." I gave another hand signal and my scouts spread out to make it more difficult for the archers on the ground. They knew those men would be the first targets for our arrows. My saving grace was that with the strength and draw of my Madagascar Rosewood bow, my arrows would have at least another ten paces of distance on them. I waited for the angry man to make his decision and sighed when it came.

"Archers! Kill those gods be damned tree whores! We need to push through to the easy ones in the village."

I made to put an arrow through the leader but he whirled and took off to the back, out of my range. Their archers moved up and were easily covered by the men with shields. Despite their relative safety, I put one man down and knocked another arrow. I called out to the scouts around me. "They cannot hit you if they cannot see you. Aim for their exposed places and try to keep most of your bodies behind the branches."

As the force approached, archers and scouts started shooting at each other. When I noticed the shields facing more my direction, I took off at a run toward the opposite side so that I had a better angle for shooting. I hit two more while I was moving, each time eliciting a trilling cry from my sisters. Every arrow that struck an enemy after that received the same victory cry. The black and red flag archers tried to hit me while I leaped from branch to branch but I was too fast for them to adjust their aim and stay behind the safety of their shield brothers. One came close, but I think I surprised the man by catching his arrow out of the air and firing it back at him. I was deeply concerned for my scouts. There were too many men on the ground and too few of us. The second feather that Margoli had placed in my hair, a little more than a moon before, felt heavier with my responsibility as Fourth Scout Leader.

Difficulty started when Maeza took an arrow to the shoulder. She cried out in pain and clutched at the branch nearest to her head. Sensing weakness, the shielded men shifted and moved in her direction. I ran as fast as I could to her position, knowing she would not be able to hold them off with her injury. Luckily, when I started rotating with perimeter scouts I had packed a larger backup quiver of arrows and I had slung both onto my back as we came up into the trees with the first warning whistle. But we would not be able to hold out forever. All we could do was hope our other scouts got here in time or we would be lost. And there was no telling where the other two teams of perimeter scouts would be while running their lines. The farthest reaches of the next quad were nearly three candle marks away. I made it over to Maeza's position in time to catch another arrow and fire three back the way it came. I yelled at the others. "Do not waste your arrows. Fire only if you have a good shot. Hit any flesh that is exposed! We have to hold the trees until more birds come."

My words gave me away more than any feather in my hair. The mounted man called out to his soldiers. "Hit the one in the tree with the wounded woman. That's their leader!" He spurred his mount around to the other side of his men. "I want her head!"

I cursed, for sure as anything I had trapped myself and Maeza with me. She could not move far nor could she move fast. The enemy force would target our spot more so than before and they would not be shooting to wound. I glanced at the sun that had safely risen over the horizon and was startled to realize we had already been battling the trespassers for at least a half candle mark. "When one runs out of arrows, we all drop down and take swords! No one will fall to these men without all her sisters at her side."

Despite all the preparations fourth scouts made in order to successfully live and patrol on the edge, I knew that even the spare arrows would not last forever. My head whipped to my right when I heard another voice cry out in pain. Another scout had taken a crossbow bolt to the calf. The crossbowman was dead, having come too close to get his shot, but the damage had already been done. "Certig, cover!" I watched as my Second ran the branches to help cover Pocori, one of our most junior scouts. Through it all I continued to shoot. I knew that I injured many, every little bit of flesh that was not armored or shielded I put an arrow in. I killed at least ten with shots to the head. The downside of being the better shot, of being the more prolific shot, is that eventually I did run out of arrows. I even shot Maeza's since she was incapable of doing more than hiding behind me. The time came when the men on the ground sensed my dilemma because they pressed forward quickly. Quicker than my scouts in the trees could compensate.

I caught the next arrow that came my way and handed it to Maeza. If they wanted to give me more ammunition then I was certainly going to let them. Unfortunately, they caught on to my tactic much too fast. Despite all my speed in the trees and my accuracy with a bow, despite my uncanny ability to catch arrows out of the air, I had always been nothing more than human. Understanding what I was doing meant the archer's arrows started to come faster. Until the moment arrived with me standing on a branch, desperate to protect one of my own. I had an arrow in each hand but no time to catch another. Instead I watched with grim fascination as it caught me. The first one hit me in the thigh, and the next seemed to sprout from my arm like a black and red leafed bloom. The third hit me just below the ribs on my left side. I groaned and could not stop myself from crumpling forward. I would have fallen had Maeza not wrapped her arms around me at the last moment. My injured scout, despite her own pain, prevented me from falling to the loam below us. Agony darkened everything around me but I swore in that moment that I could hear a chorus of birds calling in the trees. Maybe it was a dream.

I WOKE IN a familiar place, and a familiar smile looked down on me. "Welcome back to us, Kyri." I tried to sit up and bit back a cry at the fiery lances of pain that erupted in various places on my body. The worst of which was my side just below my ribs. Thera used gentle hands to help ease me back to the bed. "Easy there little one, you don't want to start bleeding again."

My mouth was impossibly dry but I tried to speak my fears anyway. "How are Maeza and Pocori?"

She patted my hand then reached over and handed me a mug of tea. "Drink this." I complied and once it was gone she told me what I needed to know. "They are both fine. Maeza took an arrow to the meaty part of her shoulder. We just cut the fletching off the arrow and pushed it through. She's going to be sore for a while but it didn't hit anything important inside. And the crossbow bolt that hit Pocori didn't even penetrate enough for the barb to catch." She shook her head and clucked disapproval. "Crossbows are such weak weapons."

"And the force, were the scouts able to drive them away?"

Thera scowled. "Lucky for you and your troop, all your messengers found their mark. The perimeter scouts from your southern side arrived first and shortly after them the interior scouts. By the time the perimeter scouts to your north side arrived, nearly the entire invading force had been killed. Third Scout Leader

Dina was still on duty and they made sure to take the leader of those bastards alive."

My eyes felt heavy and my dedication to duty warred with my need to sleep. I tried to sit up again and only hissed in pain. I suspected that she put more than pain killing herbs in the mug. "Please Thera, I need to give my report."

Against my will my eyes slipped closed. "Easy there girl, you need your rest more right now. There will be time for reports later." If she said any more after that, I never heard. Sleep had claimed me once again.

IT WAS COLD as I ran through the trees. It was surprising because Da never made me run on the coldest days, fearing I would fall and get hurt. I wanted to stop but I could hear my mam calling me from farther out. "Mam? Where are you?" I ran on until I got a stitch in my side and my leg started to hurt. My arm also throbbed steadily as I grabbed each passing branch for balance. "I am coming, Mam, do not leave yet. I am coming." I started to get too cold to run and I could feel the tears streaming down my cheeks with my pain.

"Kyri, come back, love." The voice sounded again but I was starting to think it was not my mam. It could not be my mam because she was dead. Right? "You've wandered too far, Kyri, come back to us." I wanted to listen, but I knew I had to keep running. Da would be so disappointed if I did not. If I listened really hard I could probably even hear his voice in my ear. "Never aim an arrow when you do not have complete control." I looked down as the forest blurred by and abruptly stopped. Where was my bow? I could not hope to shoot without my bow. If I did not shoot then how could I be an Amazon? I was a fletcher. That thought made me pause. No, I was an archer and an archer was nothing without her bow. Nothing.

Confusion set in because I could no longer find sense in my surroundings. Where was my family? Where were my friends? The cold grew to be too much and I curled around myself to stay warm. Pain exploded from my leg, then from my shoulder and side. When I looked I could see my forest fletch arrows growing fast from my skin. Fear and nausea battled for control and I cried out for the only person who could take it all away. "Ori!" The voices came back but they were false and full of madness.

"She's taken with fever."

"Can't we do anything for her?"

"She's going to be sick, grab the bucket! And you, go grab

fresh cloths and cold buckets of water from the stream. Hurry!"
Cold burned me and seared the skin from my body. I thought that
I had died and wondered why there was no Elysian Field like my
da and mam had promised. I cried then because I had once again
lost all that I loved. After that, things went dark.

I COULD TELL it was morning when consciousness found
me again. My head hurt like someone was squeezing it between
two large stones. I had yet to open my eyes because the skin
around my brows and nose was warm. It felt as though a shaft of
sunlight were streaming across my face and I knew it would be
too bright. Instead of sight I concentrated on what I could feel
and hear around me. Someone was holding my hand and my own
twitched with the knowledge of it. The air shifted around me and
a voice that was hoarse but still recognizable moved near to my
head. "Kyri?"

I tried to speak but it felt like I had been swallowing sand.
Before I could open my eyes a mug of cool water pressed to my
lips and I drank it down greedily. I had never felt so weak before.
When I had swallowed my fill I opened my eyes. The queen was
slightly blurred to me and my head pounded like a drum, but her
golden hair glowed around her face in the morning sun. My chest
nearly burst with happiness at seeing the queen and her name fell
from my lips like a prayer. "Ori." She gently cupped my cheek
with her right hand and tears came to her eyes. Dismayed I tried
to reassure her. "Do not cry, Ori. Please do not cry."

Her tears fell in earnest then, despite my pleas. "Oh, Kyri, I
thought I'd lost you."

"I am okay. It is naught but a scratch." She laughed a little at
my blatant lie then cried some more. I was curious as to why she
was with me instead of at the Western War. "Why are you here?
Is the war over?"

She dried her tears and when her green eyes met mine they
looked haunted. "Yes, it's over. Their army was no match for ours
in size and we were able to overcome them without the loss of too
many of our sisters and allies. The ones that survived will face
Amazon justice in the village of Kombetar."

I watched those sad eyes for a heartbeat after she finished
speaking. "And the others? The sisters that they had taken?"

Ori shook her head and a look of pain came over her face, one
that I had never seen before. "More than half of them were killed
when we overran their camp. At least a dozen had been shipped

to Rome already. Only about thirty survived to return back to their homes." She swallowed and I knew there was more.

"Tell me."

My heart broke with her words. "Some of them were no more than children. And they abused them, then had the girls killed when they saw us coming. It was monstrous. They were innocents and we lost them." All I could do was hold her to the best of my ability as she sobbed into my uninjured side. My poor sweet queen carried so much weight on her shoulders. I knew that every event like the Western War would chip away at her light. I also realized that my path to watch over her was more than just a physical one. She would need someone to be strong for her when she could not help but be weak. She would need someone to hold her when she was scared or alone. And she would need someone who could walk beside her and tell her everything was going to be okay, even when it did not feel as such.

I held her to me in pained silence and I refused to let her go. "It is going to be okay, Ori. The night will never win over us because the sun always rises to kiss the forest. When things seem darkest I will be your light, my queen."

She quieted and whispered her words. "Not queen, I'm Ori to you."

I shook my head and winced where she could not see me. "No, you are my queen. But you are also Ori, and you are my love."

She turned hopeful eyes toward mine. "Truth?"

"Truth."

Ori turned her head back toward my shoulder but I could still make out he muffled words. "Then I am truly Artemis's blessed."

Chapter Five

The Impossible Dream

HEALING WAS SLOW work. For the first half moon after the attack I was unable to walk around much. My leg was an obvious reason, but surprisingly so was the wound in my side. I did not realize how much I used my middle muscles until I took an arrow to the side. I tried to use a crutch but it hurt too much. I think if it had only been one or two arrows I would have fared much better, like when I was clawed by Gata's mam. But three arrow wounds were frustratingly painful. The queen had ridden ahead and returned half a moon before spring equinox, but the army took longer to catch up.

Even though everyone was back in time for the sacred day, it was a somber mood that hung over the coming celebration. There would be funeral pyres lit for the sisters who fell in battle. And with all the various injuries only half the normal number of women would take part in the equinox games. I was disappointed that I would not be able to participate in my second seasonal competition with the Amazons. But after three days of walking in fever dreams, I was left with less than a fortnight to recover from my injuries, which was not nearly enough time according to the healers. If Shana or Ori were not hovering over me, it was Thera or another healer telling me what I could or could not do. Certig was doing a great service filling in for me with the fourth scouts but I was anxious to get back to my duties there as well.

The morning of equinox eve dawned clear after days of rain. Even though there was a perfectly good cushion at the foot of my bed, Gata had taken to sleeping with me again after I came out of my fever. I wondered if she sensed that I was injured and wanted to be closer. Or maybe she just missed me when I sent her away to protect the queen. Perhaps it was a mistake sending the leopard but I did not regret it. Once she was sure I was safely on the mend, Ori practically stripped my feathers for sending Gata to her. She insisted that if the cat had been with me I would not have been injured. And I told her that Gata may have been killed instead and that was not an option. When I asked if Gata helped her while they were gone, she admitted that the leopard had saved her life. Ori did not bring up the subject again after that.

I groaned as I stood and began to dress. My arm was pretty much healed. The arrow that hit there was very similar to the one Pocori took to her leg. It barely penetrated. The other two were a different story. The one that hit below my ribs missed my lung and Thera said I got lucky that it did not hit anything else inside me, just muscle. The same for the arrow that I took in the big muscle of my thigh. Of course all the arrows hit my left side since that was the way I stood when shooting. The healed skin of my arm was pink and sensitive. The other two wounds were finally closed but still sore. And after gauging my pain level I decided to forgo the tea Thera had been leaving for me. The drink gave me a sick stomach that was oft times not worth the pain relief.

The walk to the meal lodge was most interesting. There was a chill in the air but it did not stop the women from scurrying about, trying to prepare for the evening feast. Decorations and banners were hung from poles and trees, and garlands of flowers festooned everything. Many smiled at me or stopped to say heyla and I laughed in surprise to realize I actually knew quite a few of their names. Coryn was the first of my close friends to enter the meal hut after I arrived. I smiled and waved her over as I ravenously made my way through pan-fried chicken eggs, barley cakes, barley porridge, and some figs. When the attractive first scout sat down with her own food she laughed and pointed at my eggs.

"I thought you said you didn't like them that way?"

I shrugged and swallowed my food with a bit of cool water. "I had never actually tried them when I said that. The first time I saw someone eat them pan-fried I was nursing a sick stomach and sore head from Tanta spirits." I shuddered at the memory of how disgusted I was at the time. "Everyone else seems to like them so I thought I would give it a try. It is actually pretty good."

Coryn snorted. "Oh goddess! I've been morning sick from wine before but never from spirits. I can only imagine how much worse that would be. And I've heard that Tanta stuff is strong, whew!" When Shana walked up a few candle drops later I was intrigued to see them exchange shy smiles with each other. I knew I would have to ask my sister about it later. It was probably nothing more than a fanciful wish, but I was hoping for more than just forgiveness from her toward the First Scout Leader. Time would tell best.

I had been thinking about time a lot, having so many candle marks free and so little to do after my injuries. Time could be like the wind slowly scouring around the stone cliff, letting it stand tall for all to see. Or it could be the raging river taking boulders down to naught more than pebbles and sand. I wondered how time would wear me.

I had been missing Ori considerably. Once she knew my health was no longer in danger she was forced to take a trip to the Shebenik nation, located directly north of us. The Western War had shaken many, all fearing similar attacks to their own from the darker factions of the world. She had been working hard to not just solidify the details for treaties with our closest neighbors, but with all the Amazon nations together. Her reasoning was that if one nation fell, the rest might be seen as easy targets as well.

I knew that she would do her best to be back in time for the festival but if not, Basha would fill in for her as the priestess's right hand. With no Artemis in my heart, I was unsure if it would be the same for me without Ori. I tried not to think about it. I tried not to suffocate under the things that seemed to be holding me down. I began having dreams after the attack. They were similar to what I dreamed of after Shana had been attacked and beaten by the soldiers near my steading. I dreamed that instead of the raider's arrows going into Maeza and Pocori, they were my own. Blue and green instead of the black and red that I saw with my own eyes. Sometimes I dreamed that instead of the armored men it was Ori shooting me down out of the trees. I always woke in a cold sweat.

The previous seven-days of healing meant that not only was I unable to defend myself with knife or sword, but I could not run the trees and my ability with a bow was in question. Archery and tree running were the two constants I held my entire life, the two things that comforted me most. I had already decided that I was going to try my bow later in the day and see how my side felt. The leg only bothered me when I was walking, so it would be fine if I were to try some target practice. Because of my decision and innate impatience, breakfast went much too slowly for me. I was disheartened that the queen had not shown up. I said my good-byes and received a concerned look from Shana. She knew why my mood had been low and I gave her a small smile and nod to show I was okay.

It was still fairly early by the time I retrieved my weapons and found my way to the archery field. Stringing my great bow was a challenge, both painful and long. But I was determined to prove to myself that I had at least something left of me. While a fletcher could be content staying inside making arrows all day, I was no longer just a fletcher. And I was not content with the one thing I used to live for back in my days of naivety. Kylani found me as I pulled my first arrow from the quiver. ·

"Are you supposed to be out here? Has Thera cleared you yet?" Amazons were not allowed to resume weapons practice or active duty after an injury unless they were cleared by a healer. I had not actually been to see a healer in days so I doubted I had clearance. However, the last time I saw Thera she had not actually said I was forbidden from shooting a bow.

"She made no mention of archery the last time we spoke. If she did not want an archer to shoot her arrows, she should have given me explicit instructions. Since she did not, I am going to assume it is permissible."

Kylani raised an eyebrow and I raised one back. Finally the training master shook her head and scrubbed her face with one hand. "Oh Artemis give me strength! What is it about all you hot-headed young scouts, hmm?"

I gazed resolutely back at her and spoke clearly and reasonably. "I am not a hot-head at all. You should know this, Training Master. However, I am an archer and I do not feel like myself unless I can shoot. I want to be me again, can you understand?" It was possible she would not understand because I had never been good with words when things seemed to matter most. But I stood there and waited to see if comprehension would come just the same.

She smiled and I let out the breath I had been holding. "Give me a candle drop, I'll be right back." She took off at a jog down field and pulled the advanced target out. Once the pendulum was moving, she jogged back to me and waited. I stared at her and she smirked at me in return. "Well? What are you waiting for? You hit the pendulum a day after being attacked by a leopard. I have no doubt that you can hit it again after a fortnight of healing from three tiny little arrow wounds. Let's see what you're made of Fourth Scout Leader!"

I could feel my spirits rise like a hawk in the wind. She did understand. My first draw ended prematurely as pain radiated from my side. I took slow steady breaths and tried again. My second draw was much better and I was able to focus on the moving target down field. It seemed strange that only six moons before I had stopped the pendulum. I knew that I would be lucky to make the easiest shot on the three skill tier target. Good archers can hit the regular circle without the round pendulum dashing the arrow away. Masters can hit the moving pendulum as it swings back and forth. The perfect shot, the impossible shot, will go through the hole in the center of the pendulum and bury the arrow tip into the red circle behind it.

The wind was null so I did not have that worry on my first spring equinox with the Amazons. I merely blocked out the sounds around me and the pain of my body. I stopped thinking about my path in the nation and I refused to dwell on the depth of my feelings for Ori. Instead I watched that pendulum swing back and forth, timing the rhythm. When I could do no more for my aim, I released. Shock washed through me as the arrow sank home, stopping the pendulum cold once again.

"By Artemis, but you're amazing!"

I spun around at the sound of her voice and winced as the skin and muscles at my side stretched. "Ori, you have returned!"

Kylani chuckled at my reaction. "Your powers of perception are pretty first-rate for a fourth scout"

I scowled at her and turned back to my queen. Ori stepped forward and pulled me into a gentle embrace. "I've missed you, Kyri."

I whispered in her ear. "I have missed you too, my queen."

She pulled me back and gave me a familiar rebuke. "How many times have I said that it's just Ori to you?"

I shook my head, feeling lighter than I had in ages. "When I am showing off my skills on the archery field, you are my queen. When I show off my skills in my hut, then it is just Ori." She should have known the way my thoughts worked by that point. Because I was a scout, that meant I was an archer. And my skills would belong to the queen. But in my hut where I had been for so much of my time, I could practice my skills as a fletcher or cloak maker. I tried to always keep private and public situations in mind when I addressed Ori. My wandering thoughts pulled up short when Ori's mouth dropped open and Kylani roared with laughter. "What is so funny? You know I have only been calling you Ori in my hut while I fletch or sew. I want everyone to know that despite our feelings for each other I respect you as my queen."

The blonde in front me started laughing then and scrubbed her red face with both hands. "Oh goddess, Kyri, I don't know what I'm going to do with you sometimes!"

I was confused and it easily showed on my face. "Have I done something to embarrass you?"

Kylani tried to help. "Kyri, back up that charging horse your thoughts are riding. Can you not understand why your words were so funny?"

"I just said that when I am showing my skills on the field that

she is my queen and when I show my skills in my — oh goddess!"
The blush that worked its way up my neck to my face and ears
felt as hot as any before it. I turned to her and she started laughing all over again. "Bow and fletch, Ori, I am so sorry. I did not
realize what I was saying —"

She waved away my words and got control of herself once
again. "It's okay, Kyri. Just know this, if you ever do show me
those skills in your hut, you can call me whatever you like." She
threaded her arm through mine. "Come on, I would like to relax
for a bit and talk with you. I feel like I've spent more time in the
saddle than anyplace else.

My face was nearly purple at that point but I tried to remember courtesy on the range. "I have to go down and retrieve my
arrow."

"Just leave it Kyri, we won't have enough competitors at the
games tomorrow to need that one anyway. Besides, I like the fact
that it will prick the other bow-head's pride to know that an
Amazon who is healing from three arrow wounds can still make
the impossible shot. Now I'm going to have to come up with a
better challenge for you." I just shook my head and laughed. I
had come to know some of those bow-heads very well since I
became Fourth Scout Leader, and they would certainly see it as a
challenge.

We went back to Ori's hut because she said she still needed to
empty her travel pack. I was not going to complain because her
hut usually had a fire started, which meant it would be warm and
cozy. We ordinary Amazons did not have the privilege of a runner that filled pitchers, started fires, and ran errands and messages for the queen. Well, her hut would have been warm if the
door had not been left wide open. I started laughing when I saw
Gata lying on her custom made cushion.

"Now you know why I have that special door in the side of
my hut."

Gata twitched her ear at me and Ori smiled ruefully at the
both of us. "Perhaps I should do the same then."

I found the situation supremely humorous. "Look at you coddling that overgrown bag of fur! And to think you have been giving me grief for letting her sleep in my bed at night."

The look she gave me froze the breath in my chest. "Perhaps I
was merely jealous of your furred friend." Before I could make
my lips form a response she winked and turned back to her task
of emptying saddlebags.

I sighed and knelt to pet Gata. "I do not think I was in so

much danger while you were away."

"Danger?"

I watched as she turned toward me with a curious look on her face and gave her a waggish smile. "Yes. Sometimes I think you will kill me a hundred times over with every setting sun. Your words and little looks wind me in circles more than any swirling wind."

Ori cocked her head. "Are you complaining about my little looks?"

I stood carefully and made my way to where she had poured two mugs of cold water. "Never! I would gladly die each day for nothing more than a smile."

She laughed and as always my heart felt like it would beat out of my chest. When she pulled me to her from an arm's length away, the force of it caused us to stumble. I steadied her and she brought us together into a kiss. Her lips were chilled from the sip of water the moment before and I freely traced my tongue over them. When she opened to me our tongues touched and I was unable to stop the whimper that issued forth from my throat. I threaded my hands into her hair, mindful of the feathers, and she did the same.

Heartbeats pounded away, or maybe it was entire candle marks of running wax as we stood there. But sooner than I would have liked I was forced to shift my weight off the injured leg. Understanding my pain, Ori broke from our kiss and walked us over to her bed. Once I was reclined there, she crawled on top of me and straddled my hips. She was careful of my injuries but her smile hinted some mischief I was unsure of. "Now that I have you where I want you, will you tell me more of all your little deaths?"

I smirked back at her. "You only have me because I wish to be caught. I could reverse this any time I like. I am larger and stronger than you, my queen."

"You forget that I too suffered a side wound similar to yours when the boar got me at fall equinox. So I know that you would not like trying to sit up right now. No, I have you snared as sure as any insect in a spider's web." She tapped her bottom lip with her finger. "Now, what to do with you?"

She was right, I had limitations because of my injuries. Sometimes I did not like to admit to such limitations but I was willing to play along with her game to save me some unnecessary pain. The heat of our bodies caused my breath to come faster in anticipation. "Indeed I am yours to do with as you wish." I was extremely conscious of the feel of her resting on my pelvis. The press of her groin to my own was the biggest reason for the tight anticipation that spiraled me out of control. I licked my dry lips and met those heartbreaking green eyes. "Everything I have is yours, Ori."

Meeting my eyes for that moment must have conveyed hidden secrets to her because that was the look she carried on her face after. "Leave your hands at your sides and do not move them unless I say. We wouldn't want you to strain your injuries." My heart felt as though it would skip all the beats and I knew she could feel me tremble beneath her. All I could do was watch as her face came closer. When the delicate tickle of her breath played across the skin of my neck I raised my hands to her hips. It was a small movement but I needed something to hold in order to convince myself it was all real. Her lips, soft and pink as apple blossoms, trailed the length of my neck. My skin flushed at that first contact and spread quickly throughout my body. The heat that suffused me far surpassed any I had felt before. Her hands were on my shoulders as she tasted my skin and her center pressed me to the bed. I was sure those four glorious points of contact were the only things that kept me from floating away.

"Ori." Her name was a sigh from my lips and she pulled away to look me in the face once again. Her eyes seemed especially large and I could tell by the rise and fall of her chest that her breath came as fast as my own. She looked at me curiously and I realized that in some ways she was as tentative about all this as I. Rather than respond to that unanswered question I moved my hands up to pull her into me fully. When our lips met again, so soft and sweet, it was as if someone had turned up the urgency of our desire. My hands stayed in her hair but hers wandered well beyond my shoulders. She touched me in places that I had never had another's hands and it was all I could do not to moan continuously.

By the time her questing fingers moved under my tunic I had started unconsciously thrusting my hips into hers. My nipples had become harder than even the coldest stream could make them and every pinched roll of her fingers shot fire straight to my groin. It was more than I had ever hoped to feel in my life, and the beauty of it struck me deep. She made me feel so much, body and soul. I whispered her name in awe and tears pricked the corners of my eyes at the reverence I felt in that moment. Much to my dismay she abruptly stopped.

"Oh Artemis, what am I doing!" When I opened my eyes she had one hand steadying herself on the bed and the other pressed to her lips.

Fear wound itself into a knot in the pit of my stomach and slowly crept toward my throat. "What is it, Ori? Are you okay?" I was desperately trying to control my breathing and the throbbing that had started where our flesh connected most.

Taking her hand from her lips, she reached trembling fingers down to wipe away the few stray tears. "I've hurt you. I'm so sorry, Kyri. I should have been letting you rest instead I—"

I grabbed that same hand in both of mine. The tips of her fingers were wet with the proof of my emotions. "No, you have not hurt me. These feelings you evoke in me are the best I have ever had. And they are so beautiful, you are so beautiful, and I did not know how to show it. Not sad tears, my queen, they are happy."

She keenly searched my face as if she could discern the truth of my words by value of eyes alone. And maybe she could. "I love you, Kyri. That should be clear to you by now. I love the way our bodies come together and the heat builds between us faster than with any other before." She sighed and I felt a little disappointment start to creep in. "But it is still not the right time to take this heat any further."

"But—" She covered my lips with a single finger.

"I want this, I need it! But you have to be ready, my love. I have to be ready. Because one thing I do know for certain is that it will change everything. And I'm selfish enough to want you whole and hale the first time we give ourselves to each other completely, in mind and body. Do you understand?"

I nodded because I did understand. I wanted to give her everything and I felt like I was not complete while I was injured. Despite what my head and heart wanted though, my body clearly had other ideas. I shifted uncomfortably, knowing the throbbing was a long way from being satisfied. I had to clear my throat twice to speak. "Um, since you are being all noble and polite, do you think you could not sit that way any longer? I am afraid that you are making me most uncomfortable right now."

He eyes darkened with what I had come to understand as desire. That was when I knew that she felt exactly as I did. I did not mean to move my hands up to her hips but once they were there I could not help pressing myself into her. She gasped and rolled off me before I could make the motion more than once. "Goddess! Are you trying to kill me, Kyri? My willpower is only so strong. I am not made of stone, woman!" I really looked at her then and was reassured that she seemed as flustered as I felt. Her lips were swollen and darker than when we started, and I touched my own to see if they felt the same as hers appeared.

Ori's smile was soft. "The look in your eyes right now, it's so full of wonder."

I moved my hand to cup her cheek gently. "Because I am full of wonder. All these things inside me, the way my breath catches and thoughts swirl like eddies in the water. You feel them too, yes?"

"I do."

I breathed a sigh of relief. "Then maybe we are both blessed."

She snuggled into my good side and placed her head gently on my shoulder. "I know it's early, but will you rest awhile with me?"

She was warm against my uninjured side as I pulled her closer yet. "Of course." And that was the last thing I remembered as my eyes slipped shut. Healing was also hard work.

MY EYES FLEW open at the sound of a knock on Ori's hut door. She did not move but I could tell by her breathing that she was awake as well. The candle on the mantle had burned down by a few marks, so I estimated that it was late morning. Ori's voice was muffled against my tunic. "I suppose I have to get up and go be queen now. After all, it is equinox eve and there is much to do." Despite her words she merely yawned sleepily instead of making any effort to rise. I looked closer and was glad to see that the dark circles that were under her eyes when she arrived had all but disappeared.

The knock sounded again and I smiled at her uncharacteristic laziness. "The door will not answer itself, my queen."

She poked me in the ribs on my uninjured side. "Listen to you! Are you trying to get rid of me so soon?"

I shook my head and smiled, then used a peg in the wall to pull myself into a sitting position with minimal pain. "No, I am merely considerate and aware that I have to share you with the rest of the nation."

"Kyri." She momentarily stopped me from getting off the bed. "There is a big part of me, an important part of me, which is for you and you alone."

I smiled and gave her a soft kiss in response. "And I think you know that everything I have is yours for the taking."

Her look was full of simmering heat and it stole the breath from my chest. I found myself back to that place of sharp and immediate wanting and I pressed my legs together in response. I had finally been given a taste of all those things I had heard whispered of before, and I found that my body was ready for a full meal. I think she knew the state I was in because her voice was a little lower and rougher when she found words to speak. "If you think that's going to make me want to get out of this bed then you are sadly mistaken."

I forced myself to stand as the knock sounded a third time. "Mistaken or no, someone has to answer your door." I gave a half-hearted sketchy Amazon salute. "Shall I bid them welcome, my queen?"

She sighed dramatically and threw an arm over her eyes. "I suppose."

Her antics had me still laughing when I opened the door. I was surprised to see that the runner was none other than my injured scout, arm bound in place to save her injured shoulder. "Maeza! How are you? How is the healing coming along?"

She took in my sleep wrinkled tunic and the image of the queen still abed and grinned. She lowered her voice to keep the queen from hearing and leaned toward me. "Not as well as you appear to be doing, Fourth Scout Leader." She winked at me and I could feel the blush begin but no way to stop it.

Ori spoke from her place on the bed. "She's blushing at your teasing, isn't she?"

We both turned to look at the queen in surprise, not realizing she had such good hearing. Maeza looked mortified. "Uh, y—yes, my queen." She back-trailed a little, afraid of offending the woman behind me. "My apologies, Queen Orianna, I didn't mean anything by the comment—"

She was interrupted before she could babble any longer. "Maeza?"

"Yes, my queen?"

Ori stood and walked over to embrace me from behind. "Hush now, no need to worry. I actually found your words quite humorous."

The fourth scout swallowed quickly. "Yes, my queen."

We stood there for a heartbeat or two before Ori spoke again. "Maeza?"

The nervous younger woman actually paled slightly. "Yes, my queen?"

"My message?"

A look of dismay spread across Maeza's face as she realized that she'd forgotten the entire reason for her visit. "Oh Artemis." She whispered to herself under her breath and I did my best not to laugh. "I'm so sorry. Um, the council wishes to speak with you after your rest. At your earliest convenience, of course."

"Tell them I'll be there in a candle mark. I want to spend a little time in the bathing pools to wash off the road dust before we go over the treaties I brought back." Clearly dismissed, Maeza turned away to take her message but Ori was clearly not finished with her. I could tell by the way her body shook with silent laughter behind mine that the queen was going to torment my scout just a little longer. Of course her words were guaranteed to torment me as well. "Maeza?"

The scout's shoulders stiffened before she slowly turned back around. "My queen?"

Also wondering what she had to say, I glanced at Ori and noticed a familiar smirk grace her features. "I can assure you that your Fourth Scout Leader is doing *very well* and I would know best, wouldn't I?" Maeza's eyes grew wide and my own face warmed. Point made, she released the temporary messenger with a wave of her hand. Laugher rang out when the door was once again shut. "Oh goddess! They really need to stop using injured young scouts as temporary messengers. They are so easily flustered."

I ran a hand through my hair and then pointed a finger at her. "That was mean, Ori." My grin told her that I was not serious with my anger and that I enjoyed it just as much as she did.

She moved closer and smoothed the wrinkles in my tunic that our nap had placed there. "Uh huh." She abruptly turned away and dug another set of leathers out of a woven basket at the other end of her large hut. I gathered my bow and quiver and moved toward the door. She stopped me just shy of opening it and gave me a mischievous smile. "Where are you headed now? Can I tempt you to come keep me company in the bathing cave again?"

I thought of the last time we bathed together and was immediately reminded of the untended heat that still throbbed through my body. I swallowed once to try and wet my mouth enough to speak. "I do not think that would be a very good idea. As a matter of fact, I have something to take care of back in my hut." Two could play at her game of teasing.

Ori cocked her head as she gazed back at me curiously. "Oh? And what could be more interesting than keeping your poor queen from drowning in the deliciously hot water?"

I startled Ori when I closed the distance between us and drew her into a kiss. Her arms were trapped between us and the kiss was hot and insistent. By the time I broke away again her lips looked lightly bee-stung and the green of her eyes had darkened perceptibly. "It seems that someone has stoked a fire inside me and I need to spend a little time alone dispelling those flames. I hope you understand, my queen."

I had touched myself plenty over the course of my life, though I had never once spoke of it to anyone. And the look the queen gave me let me know that I had accurately hit my mark with my own teasing. Ori's lips were parted with the increased speed of her breaths and her nostrils flared at the scent of some imagined prey. I had avoided the hunter, if only temporarily. I was happy to note that it was her turn to be speechless. "Until later?" She nodded and I backed out the doorway. Once the door was shut again I hurried around the side of the next hut over and could not stop my laughter at the look on her face as I left. Of course, I also did not slow the walk back to my own hut. I meant every word that I said. There was a fire burning inside of me and the sooner I took care of it the better off I would be for the coming festival.

I made it to my hut with no interruptions. It was chilled inside but it did not matter. The heat was still with me and our actions in Ori's hut had me throbbing uncomfortably. As I reclined on my bed I thought of those beautiful eyes that darkened just for me. I had seen her enough to recognize my thoughts reflected in those green depths. Her looks were of passion and they stoked mine higher than even the greatest Amazon bonfire. Hardly believing the flames my body was capable of, I reached down and cupped myself through the material of my winter breaches. I shuddered and my heart raced at how good it felt. As my hand slid beneath the material and along the taut skin of my abdomen, I could not help imagining that the questing digits belonged to Ori instead.

I tried to be slow with my smooth and slippery strokes. I tried to hold her image in my head the entire time. But my body had decided that slow would simply not do and barely a candle drop in I felt as though my head was filled with a great pressure. I moaned at the thought that I would not last longer. All at once the heat built to a crescendo and crashed through me. Back bowed I threw an arm across my mouth to muffle the scream of my release. It was both guttural and sacred, like my love for Ori. As I pulled my hand free from my girdle I stared at the glistening moisture on my fingers. It looked a lot like the tears she had wiped away earlier.

I thought about all I had learned from life before that

moment. I pictured my path through the forest and who I had become while traveling that path. I had been a daughter before, and a fletcher. For me there was no difference between the two. With the way I was raised, to be one meant I had to be the other. But once I left the safety of my childhood behind, I became other things as well. I was an Amazon and a leader, surprised as I was to be the latter. And despite all my misgivings and sorrow, I had come to be considered an archer of the highest order. I knew without a doubt that all those things and more I would gladly give to the nation in exchange for my life in the trees.

But with Ori it was different. My loyalty to the nation was all about who I could protect, how much the nation could benefit from my skills and knowledge. But my loyalty to my queen went much deeper. For her I would give my future, my heart and soul. Deeper yet, for her I would give my passion and that sacred part of me I had never given another. I sighed as I thought about the coming festival and wondered if I would be cleared for duty soon. As I lay on my bed in the cold hut with passion dried on my fingertips, I could not help hoping that the chance to bestow my gifts upon Ori would come sooner rather than later.

Chapter Six

Honeyed Amber and the Arrow of Truth

WE MADE IT through the temple ceremony where I received the mark of Artemis, just as I had for every seasonal ceremony since coming to the Telequire nation. Ori wore a distinct smirk on her face as I walked by with drying goat's blood on my forehead. I was also pretty sure I heard someone whisper, "not for long," as I walked back to my place next to Shana. It sounded a lot like Coryn. Despite the fact that I had not been able to take the Amazon's belief of Artemis into my heart, I had always felt the ceremonies were beautiful and full of magic. As with the previous few ceremonies Gata was on hand to lend her voice to the event, though I still snorted at the thought that anyone would consider that spoiled beast a sign of Artemis's favor.

It was the rest of the day's ceremony and celebration that was difficult for the entire nation. Nearly a score of our sisters had been lost to the Western War. While it did not seem like a lot considering the number of warriors and support personnel that left on that dark and wet morning, each death left a hole in the nation. And each death took a little piece of Ori's heart. We were in a clearing just outside of the village proper. Perhaps it was their way of putting some distance between the sadder parts of the ceremony and all the things we would be grateful for later. Plus the smell of the funeral pyre—thick, cloying, with the taste of burning death searing the back of my throat—was not easy to forget and was best kept away from the feast.

Women and children were openly crying throughout the gathering, mourning the Amazon spirits that had crossed over to their Golden Mountain. Even though I had not lost anyone close to me in the battle, tears still tracked down my face as Queen Orianna read the list of those who fell and their accomplishments. Once she finished with the funeral all the Amazons moved back to the village center for the Ceremony of Light. There the queen and council honored the bravest of the Western War, which had to be done before feasting could begin. At least a dozen warriors were called up to receive red beads for their rite of caste feather. The red bead was sacred and symbolized a brave action performed by the Amazon receiving it. The beads themselves were slid carefully onto the thong, and rested just above their caste bead.

After the bravery beads, the queen then announced those Amazons who went well beyond their duty to the nation. Their actions were not just brave, they had resulted in the saving of many lives. As the queen explained the actions of each I grew amazed at her ability to remember everything for the sake of ceremony. I was also filled with pride to see Shana and Coryn among the six that received the eagle feather honor. The entire nation watched as the queen tied the new feathers in with the ones already there. The eagle feather was striking next to Shana's jade green Ambassador and her rite of caste. It was just as striking next to Coryn's First Scout Leader and rite of caste feathers.

I knew from my days as an Amazon initiate that names were submitted to the queen and council for them to judge who was worthy to receive such battle honors. Just when I thought the warrior ceremony was complete, the queen announced more. "For their bravery in holding off nearly three score armed invaders while the army was away at the Western War, I would like to call up the following Amazons to receive beads of bravery." She then named all the members of my fourth scout troop that were on duty that fateful day. I was glad that they were chosen because I knew how frighteningly outnumbered we were at the time. Though small, my little troop did a great job of keeping the enemy from the forest until help could come.

As each one walked across the dais, including my two injured team members, I held my fist to my chest in an Amazon salute. I was the one who submitted their names to Coryn when she asked a seven-day before, and I was glad to see the queen and council agreed with me. Expecting the ceremony to be near completion, I turned my gaze toward the bare wood of the bonfire. The sound of my name was startling as it carried over the crowd. "Kyri Fletcher, please come to the dais."

Shana and Coryn had come back to stand by me after they received their feathers and each gave me a nudge to the back. Shana pushed me once more when I hesitated. "Go on, Kyri."

Coryn gave me an impatient look. "Come on Fourth Scout Leader, I'm hungry!"

Unsure why I was being called I limped my way up the steps to stand next to the queen. "For her bravery and self-sacrifice during the day of the surprise attack, Kyri will also receive the eagle feather of honor. Not only did she maintain a calm head while outnumbered, she was willing to sacrifice her life to save a sister. Nearly half the attacking force were found to have Kyri's forest fletch arrows in them." Basha stepped forward with another eagle feather and handed it to Ori. I was not sure what surprised me more, the fact that the queen's hands had a slight tremor as she tied the thong into my hair or the tears I could see glistening in her eyes behind the Monarch's Mask.

When I turned toward the crowd I saw my entire fourth scout troop step forward as one and salute. Then it was my turn to fight back the tears. They were all so brave, and it pulled at my heart to receive such honor from them. The Ceremony of Light continued on as I stepped from the dais. Traditionally the nation would feast after the bonfire was lit then children would be sent to bed before the revelry began.

One of the things that most surprised me when I came to the nation was the presence of so many young children and girls past puberty. I asked Shana about it not long after I arrived and she explained how the Amazon nations usually had a local village that they fostered boys to when they reached puberty. No males past that time were allowed to stay in the village, and they were only allowed to visit with an appropriate escort. The way the nation's women birthed children was due to another arrangement. Some women found temporary mates in the surrounding region and others had permanent mates in that same neighboring village. The ones that had permanent mates usually spent some of their time at the Amazon village and some of the time with their mate. It was a unique partnership that allowed such a division to exist between bonded pairs but it seemed to work for many.

That was why I was surprised at the amount of younglings running around since my only notions of mating were that of my bonded parents. I never realized that people could be so varied in their methods. All the thinking of children and bonding turned my mind to Ori. I wondered what it would be like to form a partnership with the queen. I would not want to have a partnership like the ones that live in separate villages. I would want the kind of bonding that my mam and da had. I would want us to be equals. Or at least, as much as we could be with her being the queen and all. Though my mental wandering took me far afield, my sister brought me back quite quick.

"Heyla, Kyri, what has you dreaming so hard over there? The fire is lit. Are you ready for food?" My eyes widened to see that the flames had gone up while I traipsed through my thoughts. As I was getting ready to answer her question my stomach gave a great growl. Gata, who was sitting at my feet, growled in response. Both Coryn and Shana laughed at the half-grown leopard's antics. "It's good to see that no matter how big your cat cub grows, some things never change." As we loaded clay-fired *skyphoi* with venison, shredded tree fowl, and lentils. I also added roasted vegetables seasoned with olive oil to the top. I switched the deep bowl of food to one hand and snagged a loaf of soft bread to tuck under my arm, then lastly grabbed a handful of olives to take with me to one of the tables nearby. Shana laughed at my juggling act as I arranged myself onto a seat. She could not resist poking fun at me. "You know sister, you can always go back for more or just make a second trip before you started eating. You're getting as lazy as that spoiled cat of yours."

Ears red, I pitched an olive at her head. "Woods weasel! I am not at all lazy. I am simply practical!" Before the olive could hit the ground the cat in question stood on her hind legs and snagged the salty fruit out of the air. She used her paws to pull the olive into her mouth and promptly spit it out again. She wiped at her muzzle and gave me an irritated look, then turned and walked away. That only set off more laughter.

Coryn slapped the table. "Oh goddess, the look that cat gave you! I hope she doesn't leave any wild friends in your bed tonight, Kyri."

Shana chimed in. "Kyri only wants one friend in her bed, isn't that right?"

"Gata's offerings in your bed would certainly be a shame. Do you need someplace safe to hide tonight?" I sucked in a quick breath to hear Ori's voice so close behind me. I glared at both Coryn and Shana for not warning me that the queen was approaching. They just grinned back. I was glad that they were getting along so well but, bent arrow and broken string, I did not need them ganging up on me.

I turned to look at the woman I had come to regard above all others. She had her mask pushed up to the top of her head since the ceremonies of the day were all complete. "Heyla my queen. Would you like to join us at our table?"

"Now what do you think, Fourth Scout Leader?" I smiled and made room for her. As she was sitting down Basha slid in on my other side. Her mask was pushed to the top of her head as well.

Always upbeat, Basha smiled around the table. "Heyla sisters! I don't know about you all but goddess I'm starving!" Since I was starving as well I followed her example and started shoving food into my mouth to avoid any more interruptions. The bread was still warm and the venison had been roasted to perfection.

Conversation flowed despite my busy hands and mouth, and I was struck to realize that those all around me were friends of the truest kind. Not people you say you know but really do not. They were all women who were real friends, women who would give their life for mine and legitimately cared about my happiness. And happy I was.

Candle marks later I found myself sitting on a log watching the dancers move around the fire. Their motions were as sensual and primal as the beat. Ori was like a true goddess among them. I was ashamed to say that despite all my scout training the hand on my arm startled me. I pressed a fist to my chest and turned to look in the eyes of Maeza. "Bent arrow and broken string, do not sneak up on me like that, Maeza!" I laughed to show I was just kidding but her eyes did not laugh with me.

"Scout Leader, can I speak with you?"

At first I was worried that she still carried concern about her words from earlier in the day. "If you are worried about the queen still, it is okay. She was just teasing you. Teasing both of us really. And call me Kyri when we are not on duty."

She smiled and blushed slightly, visible even in the light of the great fire. "No, it's not that. You see, I—" She blew out a breath and ran a hand through her hair. I waited knowing that everyone's words came in their own time. When she was finally able to meet my eyes hers were wet with tears. "I owe you my life, Kyri. You didn't just risk your life for me, you gave it willingly. You stood in front of me and took all the arrows so that I did not have to. You braved pain and risked certain death to be my shield when you could have simply left me there and saved yourself."

I placed a hand on her arm and gently reminded her of more facts than she was remembering. "Maeza, you took your own arrow that day."

The scout shook her head in denial. "No, it's not the same. You came to me when I was hurt and you stood there in the line of fire without flinching despite the agony you felt as each arrow found its mark into your body. There was no thought to it for you. You simply took the arrows and made them your own to keep me safe. You did everything you could to keep me from being hit. And the way you simply caught them out of the air, or even better, when you fired their own arrows back at the enemy soldiers. You were amazing!"

I could feel my face get hot at her praise. "Maeza, we are sisters and more than that you are my fourth scout. I feel protective of all of you and I would take a hundred arrows if it meant keeping you all safe."

"That's what I'm trying to say. You would take a hundred arrows with no thought of the sacrifice. There is no look of fear, no hesitation to you. You simply act in whatever the best manner is to protect the nation." She gave me a sweet smile and held out her hand. When she opened her palm I saw a small carving of a leopard and it looked very much like Gata. It was even stained with something to make it appear more real. The little wooden cat was extremely well done. I had no idea my scout could carve so beautifully.

"What is this?"

Maeza shrugged. "I can never truly pay you for the life you gave me but I created a token of my appreciation. I'll admit that I was skeptical when you were made Fourth Scout Leader. But now I would follow you over all others, Kyri Fletcher. Save the queen, of course." Before I could respond she nodded once then walked off.

I must have had a strange expression on my face as I sat there for the next few candle drops. Ori broke free from the dance circle and sat down on the log next to me wearing a concerned look on her face. "You look bemused, love. Is something wrong?"

I shook my head and held up the little carving of Gata. "No, nothing is wrong. Maeza gave me this to thank me for saving her life. It just surprised me, is all."

She took it from my hand and turned it over to examine the little wood carving. "Goddess, it's beautiful! Does she study with Kerdina, our carver?"

I shrugged. "I have no idea but you are right, it is beautiful."

Ori took my hand into hers and gently pressed the little carving into my palm. When I turned to meet her gaze she gave me a soft smile. "So are you." I blushed predictably.

I placed the carving into my waist pouch and continued to hold her left hand in my right. I decided to change the subject. "Have you entered the usual contests tomorrow, my queen?"

She gave my fingers a squeeze. "Ori."

I cocked my head and looked at her curiously. "Funny, but I do not recall the competition called 'Ori'. How does one win such a thing?"

Ori's blonde hair was soft and damp on my neck where she leaned against me. Her voice was low but I could still make it out over the sound of drums and singing. "Well for starters one has to make the impossible shot."

I chuckled. "Oh ho, so any excellent bow-head could win the prize?"

Our hands together felt warm and I received a little poke in the side for my comment. "No, not just anyone could make such a shot. There are only two whose arrows have penetrated so deep."

I felt my eyebrows go up in surprise, wondering who the two could be. The conversation suddenly felt more serious than intended. "Two, my queen?"

Ori shrugged against me. "Well you know Artemis comes down every sun-cycle to make such a shot and in turn gives the Amazons hope for the coming seasons. As her chosen, I hold her very close to my heart."

I could feel my breath catch at what she was telling me. I understood that Ori would have had plenty of lovers in her cycles with the tribe. But I found it hard to believe that she had not taken another into her heart. "And the other?"

She looked up at me then and I could see her eyes reflected dark green in the firelight. "There has only been one other. Her skill and kindness have won me as sure as any goddess in the pantheon." She must have read the shock on my face in response to her admission because she lifted her palm to caress my cheek. "I've had many lovers, Kyri. Does it bother you that I've never truly taken them deep into my heart?"

My own heart raced at the feel of her warm palm against my skin. My mouth went dry at the mere thought of Ori as a lover. But it was my soul that truly soared at the realization that while there was a vast chasm between our experiences, we were on the same heart path. I was not alone in the new and novel feeling of soul yearning. I tried to bring my thoughts back down from the sky and answered her question honestly. "It does not bother me. I actually feel better for it. But you say Artemis was the first you took into your heart. Does it bother you that I do not carry her there as you do?"

She thought for a candle drop and I waited nervously for her response. "I am Artemis's chosen but that doesn't mean I am blind to all else. Faith is a personal devotion. I think the important thing is that regardless of the driving force behind our beliefs, they remain the same. You have a good soul, you are brave and honest, and you are full of love and laughter. I see you as someone that I would trust with the heart of the Telequire nation, with the very heart of me. So I guess you could say that besides my faith in my goddess, I also have faith in you."

I swallowed the lump in my throat but before I could speak

we were interrupted by Steffi and Shana. Steffi's face was flushed and sweaty when she looked toward Ori. "My queen, it's time to do the fertility dance. You have to prepare."

I had no idea what the fertility dance was but Ori looked to the sky and I followed her gaze. The moon was full and well-risen and her sigh was great. "So I see." She turned to me with a sweet smile. "I have to go. We have one more ritual to perform. But I'll be back later, okay?"

I nodded and she gave me a kiss on the cheek for my understanding. However as soon as she walked away with the queen's Left Hand I turned to my friend. "What is the fertility dance?"

Shana sat down next to me. "Ah the Fertility Dance, or Dance of Blessing, is performed every spring equinox. Didn't you have something in your village that would ask the gods for favor concerning the coming crops, or pregnant livestock, or maybe even asking a boon of lovers?"

I thought for a heartbeat. "Yes, but the day of *Máios* was a moon later I think. I do not believe we ever had it this early."

She smiled. "I know some places have it at different times but for Amazons, solstice and equinox are sacred times of the sun-cycle. It is the time when we would most ask a blessing from our goddess."

I guess that made sense. Everything in the Amazon nations seemed to revolve around the times of seasonal change. "So how is this dance different from the others?" Before she could form a response a distinctive pattern of drumbeats sounded throughout the village center. I looked at her again once they had paused. "Do you not dance to this one?"

Shana's laughter startled me. She scratched idly at her temple and smirked as she answered. "Well anyone can dance if they wish to participate; however, I have not had the need just yet. It is also referred to as the Lover's Dance."

"What does that mean?"

She smiled as we watched a long line of cloaked figures approach the fire circle. "It is said that if you carry someone in your heart you should dance around the fire holding a token of your love for them. The hope is that our goddess will take note and give the two a special blessing in their union. Just watch, Kyri."

The drums started back up and the cloaked figures filed around the outside of the circle. Ori was the first one in the line because I recognized the cloak that I had made for her as a winter solstice present. After the drums had beat their way to a crescendo once again, they stopped completely. My mouth dropped open in shock when as one, all the dancers dropped their cloaks to the ground. The gleaming line of nude bodies spread around the large circle to where I could no longer see on the opposite side of the fire. As one again, they stepped to the inside of the circle save for the queen. When my eyes were drawn back to the nude shape of Ori's regal form I could see her staring right at me. In her left hand she carried an arrow. I was able to just make out the blue and green of the fletching when Shana nudged my arm. "Is that..." She trailed off but I knew what she was asking.

"Yes."

She shook her head in wonder. "Goddess, Kyri! This is serious business between you two, isn't it?"

I turned to look into my sister's amber colored eyes. They stayed bright in the firelight, despite the darkness all around. "It is everything." I turned back to the fire as Ori began her dance. The rest of the silhouetted line of women remained where they were, as the queen slowly made her way around the outside of the fire circle. She spun and stomped, then grasped the arrow in both hands and held it over her head. Her movements were alive, they were fire, and I felt myself heat up with them.

None of Shana's descriptions of the dance truly gave it meaning. It was one of the most athletic displays I had ever seen. At one point she did a series of forward flips without using her hands, all while continuing to hold my arrow. Ori made her way around the circle until I lost sight of her on the other side of the flames. Once she made a complete circuit and went to the back of the line of nude dancers, the next person stepped to the outside and made their way around. I turned to Shana and kept my voice low. "She is amazing! Has the queen performed the fertility dance many times?"

Shana continued watching the dancers but answered my question in the same hushed tone. "Yes. She dances every spring." I thought about what Shana said to me and what Ori had told me earlier about not holding another in her heart before. When the second dancer rounded the fire out of our view my sister turned to me with serious eyes. "Until tonight Ori has always displayed the symbol of Artemis on a thong around her neck. Tonight she declared her intentions in front of goddess and nation. Do you know what that means, Kyri?" I shook my head and tried my best to keep the fearful butterflies to a minimum. "It means you are well on your way to becoming the queen's consort."

There was a weight on my shoulders as my body filled with equal parts worry and awe. My voice was naught but a whisper as I opened myself up and let my fears spill out. "But what if they do not want me?"

Shana's eyes left the third dancer as she spun her head around to meet my anxious gaze. Involuntarily, I held my breath for a heartbeat at the fierce look in those honeyed amber depths. "You give yourself too little credit. It matters not what the nation thinks when it comes to choices of the heart as long as both partners are willing and safe. Ori is lucky to have you, just as you are lucky to have her. Artemis willing, your hearts will be as one sooner rather than later."

"What if the goddess does not will it?"

She smiled then and it caught me by surprise in the midst of all our serious talk. "Kyri, you're here aren't you?"

I was finally able to return her smile then because I understood what she was trying to tell me. In Shana's eyes, and most of those of the nation, I would not be with the Telequire tribe had Artemis not willed it so. I would be accepted because of that one notion alone. It would not take my belief to move a nation of Amazons, it merely took their own.

I turned my gaze back to the dancers and we watched for a bit longer. I had twisted to grab a water skin when Shana gasped beside me. Looking toward the dancers, I saw that another had started around the circle, leaving just two nude women left in line. The second to last dancer was Coryn. Squinting my eyes, I tried to see what she had hanging around her neck. I was unsuccessful until she shifted her body just a bit and the large circle of polished amber caught the light of the fire. I had to admit that it was a beautiful and valuable piece, not to mention a very discreet move on her part. No one save Shana and myself would know the meaning of her necklace. Too many times Coryn had remarked that Shana's eyes were like beautiful golden amber. All the women watching would wonder who the attractive First Scout Leader danced for.

"Why, Kyri? Why would she dance with that necklace on? What does it mean?"

I had seen the looks from one to the other when no one else was paying attention. I had also heard their stories separately. Owl friends they both had in plenty, but neither woman was want to let another into her heart. Maybe it was time they did. Clearly Coryn was the bolder of the two and I would let her continue being the bold one. It was not my place to explain the First Scout

Leader's heart or motivation, it was hers. I turned to look at Shana and kept my face calm, not wanting to give away any of my thoughts. "Sister, maybe it is time you took the herd beast by the horns, hmm? The only way you will get your answers is to ask the person dancing."

She looked at the ground, the beat of the drums filling the small silences around us. "But what if she is merely playing with me again, the way she plays with so many others?"

Her shoulder trembled slightly when I placed my hand on it. "The same way you play with others? Both of you with a pack of owls circling you each night. Think on this, Shana." I paused waiting for her to look up at me. "Think on why you have yet to settle down with just one person. Think about your motivation for not letting anyone close. Do you not wonder what her motivations are? And you should take into consideration that she is doing more than whispering her intentions into the dark. As you said about Ori, this is serious business if she is dancing to her goddess and nation."

Her eyes carried fear and something new, hope. "Maybe."

I nodded at her and stood. "Ask her." Then I pulled Shana to her feet and gave her a slight shove toward where I could see Coryn watching us. "Go." She gave me one last look over her shoulder and tentatively picked her way over to the tall blonde who waited for her.

"That was well done, Kyri Fletcher."

I spun around, only receiving a twinge from my side at my careless motion. "My queen!" In my desire to see two of my friends reach happiness I had completely forgotten about my own revelations of the night. I took in Ori's appearance and was relieved to see she was clothed once again. Relieved and disappointed. With thoughts that had turned to a decidedly warmer place, I could not stop the stammer that tangled my tongue. "I—I mean, Ori. I just—they both have so many secrets, you know? And the secrets they keep from each other only cause them pain." I sighed because I was unable to fully explain my actions without breaking the trust of either Shana or Coryn. "There is a lot of miscommunication between them. I just think that if they talked to each other for a while they would see they are not so different after all."

She stared at me for a heartbeat or two, as if trying to read the words between my words for understanding. "I think you're right. And what of you? Is there anything you wish to speak about on the night of this full moon?"

My mind flashed to the image of her bared body in the firelight, defiantly holding my forest fletch as she told the story of
her feelings with movement rather than voice. My heart pounded
in time with the remembered steps of her journey, nude and shining in the combined light of the moon and fire. Was there something I needed to ask? Were there secrets of hers that I should
know before going any farther down the path we tread? I took a
swallow from the water skin I had slung over my shoulder earlier. "Do you think it was wise dancing with such obvious intent
tonight?"

She stepped close to me and I trembled as she drew a finger
along my jawline. "I could not dance a lie."

There were days when I just had no understanding of her
words. "What do you mean?"

The trembling certainly did not cease as she moved the finger
to my bottom lip and gently caressed it. "What I mean is that the
queen is required to lead the Fertility Dance each spring equinox.
And I would be dancing false if I wore any but your symbol
now."

"But your goddess symbol—"

She pressed that warm finger over both lips to still my words.
Her smile was gentle. "While the goddess appreciates our love
and devotion, she appreciates the truth from us more. Artemis
put you in my path for a reason, Kyri. She would not begrudge
my love now."

She withdrew her finger and I licked my lips to see if there
was any taste left behind. Before I could think about anything else
I reached out my arms and drew her to me, mouth closing on hers
in a silent promise. I kissed her because I had no dance to give. I
kissed her because there was no Artemis in my heart to give me
such surety. Her mouth tasted like wine and honey as we
explored each other in the firelight. And her scent, leaf and arrow
but her scent was more intoxicating than Tanta spirits! She was
primal, earthy like forest loam and smelling of sweat and spices.

I lost track of the amount of time we stood in one another's
arms with the heat of the fire to one side and the cool night air to
the other. Eventually I pulled back to take a deep breath because
the pounding of the drums was matching my heart and a place
much lower.

It was amazing how just the faintest touch or taste of Ori
could affect me so. She stared at me as if I were the sun to her
moon. Her lips parted and I was torn to the very marrow of my
bones. I wanted to go someplace more private with her but at the

same time I was terrified for us to be alone together. I had no control when she was near, and I had come to suspect she had the same problem with me. As my heart pounded its own rhythm she took my hand in hers. "I would like you to stay the night with me." Her grip tightened as I trembled and fought the urge to run to the trees. She had seen me do as much on multiple occasions in the past, always when I was most overwhelmed. "Just to sleep, Kyri." I was reassured until I saw the smirk that followed those four words. "Unless you're ready for more. Are you ready for more, my love?"

My mouth was dry and the air in my lungs felt hot as I tried to answer. "I—I do not know what I am ready for."

"How about if we start by leaving the fire? If you want, I saw a good size group of scouts and others heading for the large bathing pool. We can go spend time with the group if you aren't ready to retire just yet."

I tried to gauge the sincerity of her offer, but it was getting too dark to make out the finer details of her facial inflections. "Is that what you want, my queen?"

She gave me a stern look that was easy enough to make out and graced my hand with a hard squeeze to emphasize her point. "It's Ori, gods be-damn you! I don't want to be your queen tonight!"

I cocked my head, finally understanding something of what she was trying to say. "And what do you want tonight, Ori?"

"I just want to be near you."

"Okay."

Her face registered surprise. "Okay?"

I grinned at her, no longer afraid. "Yes." As we made our way across the village to the bathing pools, I detoured long enough to grab more wine, water, and a platter of fruit and dates. I had been to enough of the gatherings in the big pool to know that food was always appreciated. When we walked through the curtains covering the entrance into the cave, I could see the pool itself was only about two-thirds full. The group of people was indeed large but the pool itself was much larger. We both received hearty greetings from the crowd, not all of which were sober. It was actually a good mix of people too, not just scouts. There were two council members, Kylani, a dozen different scouts, some of which were my own troop, plus the master fletcher for the village, a few of the cooks I recognized, and a double handful of people I did not recognize. More than a few appeared startled that Ori was joining them in the pool.

"My queen! It's an honor to have you join us tonight." I could see nearly all of them sported appreciative looks when Ori walked down into the water. She turned to the woman who had spoken. "Oh hush, Gerlani. It's just Ori tonight so pass me that wine, sister." I undressed as well, still shy, and found my way to where Ori was sitting. When I looked up I was surprised to note more than a few appreciative eyes turned my way as well. I wondered if they saw more than the reflections I had glimpsed over the seasons of my life. I froze at the first touch of fingers on my bare thigh beneath the water's surface. When I glanced to my right the breath caught in my throat. Ori was so near I could count her pale eyelashes in the combined lamp and torchlight. Water swirled ever so slightly around me as I leaned toward her, drawn by some force I could not control. The moment was lost when a voice cried out across the pool from us.

"Goddess bless, the queen and Kyri brought food with them!" The great pool was set down into the floor of the chamber so the tray was passed easily around the outside edge. I managed to grab a few figs and a handful of grapes before it made its way beyond me. Feeling playful I turned and held a grape near Ori's lips. She took it from me with straight white teeth and her eyes gleamed with mischief. My attention was diverted again when one of my scouts spoke.

"When are you returning to duty as Fourth Scout Leader, Kyri? It surely must be soon after the shot you made today." I had no idea the news of my latest impossible shot was already making the rounds. I could not recall seeing anyone near the field that morning but truthfully anyone could have been watching. Shelti was looking at me expectantly so I had to answer.

"I have not spoken with a healer yet, but I think I will probably be off another seven-day. My arm is nearly healed and my side is manageable but my leg is not safe enough to run the trees yet."

"Wait, what shot did she make?"

"Tell us the story!"

"When did she shoot?"

"Are you competing tomorrow?"

Voices clamored at me and were finally silenced by Kylani. "Quiet, you bow-heads! Kyri made the impossible shot again this morning, just after first meal." She paused to let her words sink in and I blushed at the news of my deeds.

Some expressed disbelief. "That's not possible!"

"By Artemis!"

The training master spoke quickly to enforce the truth of her words. "It's true, I was there to see it. I personally pulled the advanced target out and set the pendulum in motion. Even half healed from so grave an injury, the Fourth Scout Leader still has the truest fletch."

Ori vouched for me too. "I was there as well. Though it caused her pain to even string her bow, she shot truer than any I've seen before."

I lifted my hand from the water and scrubbed it over my red face. I think I was trying to wash away the embarrassment from all the attention. "Bow and fletch, but I am right here you bunch of feather heads! Can we discuss something besides my aim for once?"

More than a few laughed at my words which reassured me that they would move on with good humor. However my relief was short lived when Geeta spoke next. That girl always knew the best gossip. "Hey Ori, I noticed your Lover's Dance was different this cycle. Any particular reason why?"

"Oh gods!" Embarrassment was all consuming and I knew it well. I sank deeper into the water, perhaps hoping to escape their keen eyes and probing words. Ori chuckled beside me but answered honestly.

"As you already know, Geeta, the dance reflects what is greatest in our hearts. It is both a promise and a prayer, offering up the truth of both to our goddess, Artemis."

Another scout, pushed and prodded with her words. "But you weren't wearing your goddess symbol like all other dances. You've been wearing your Artemis necklace for as long as you've danced with a rite of caste feather in your hair."

Patient as ever, she continued to answer their questions. "No I wasn't. I carried an arrow tonight instead."

During the entire exchange there had been a few side conversations happening around the large pool. But slowly they quieted, understanding that the story they had always known was suddenly changing around them. "Whose arrow did you carry, Ori?"

"Yes, who?" People grew excited and whispers echoed through the chamber like wind. "Who has finally won the queen's heart?"

Finally tired of hiding and tired of quietly wondering in fear, I spoke up. "She carried my arrow during the Lover's Dance." And just like that, all the voices stopped. It was clear that some had suspected already, but I think most were surprised by such a bold and definitive declaration by their queen.

One of the council members, Vesichi, broke the silence from across the pool. "Truth?"

Ori nodded and gave my thigh another reassuring squeeze under the water. She had no idea that it was doing everything but calm me down. "Yes, truth. Kyri and I are courting." Breaking the silence seemed to give thrust to the new whispering voices that echoed throughout the chamber.

Dina, the Third Scout Leader, spoke from next to Kylani on the other side of the pool. "But Kyri walks in the footsteps of the goddess!" Ori raised a single pale eyebrow and gave her a look. Those that knew Ori best knew exactly what that look meant. It was proud innuendo, stating clearly to everyone in the chamber that my virginal status would not stay for long.

That was the moment it all came crashing down for me. The thought that everyone there felt no compunction about discussing such an intimate detail of my life, around me and over me, left me nauseous. I had done so well in the moons leading up to that moment. Large groups and too much attention rarely sent me to the trees any more. But in the space of heartbeats, with things so private brought out for everyone to see, with everyone's voices ringing so loud all around me, and with every bit of scrutiny placed on me by my sisters and tribe, I needed to leave.

Without another word being said I stood from the rock I had been seated on with Ori and rapidly made my way up the carved steps in the opposite end of the pool. I swayed with the heat and sounds became muffled, as though everyone was far away. I did not bother to dress, I merely donned my cloak and stuffed my feet into my boots. Then I scooped up the rest of my things and pushed through the doorway into the cool night air. I had to escape all the insecurities and the voices, especially the one that plaintively called my name as I left.

Chapter Seven

Will of the Goddess

THE AIR WAS cold indeed on my wet skin and I immediately regretted not dressing before racing outside. Goose bumps spread across my flesh and I picked up the pace toward my hut. I had no idea how long the drums had been quiet but the silence of the night made me shiver as much as the cold. While my hut was not very far away, the walk was much too long for my liking. Exhaustion from the day pulled at me and I fought it with every step. Try as I might, I could not silence the questions and voices in my head. My mind repeated the image of them staring at me, judging me for what I was and was not. It was too much. I was too small in the face of the greatness the queen's position demanded.

Other voices, more fearful ones, called from the darkest places of my psyche. They were quiet and frightened and told me that she could find another who would be more worthy, that she should find another who deserved her love more. I was so much in my head that I became deaf to all that was around me. At least until that deafness shattered into a million pieces when the voice of my queen split the night air. "Kyri Fletcher, your queen demands that you stop immediately!"

I froze at the way anger had made her voice so rough. Bent arrow and broken fletch, but how long had she been calling me? I did not hear her, I did not hear! I turned with arms still wrapped around the bundle of my leathers and dropped to a knee in supplication. I barely noticed the tears that tracked down my hot cheeks. My eyes stared down out of respect that was given when one was to face the queen for judgment, exactly as I had been taught during my initiation. "My apologies, my queen, but I did not hear you. Please forgive me." I stayed there for what felt like candle drops, shivering with the cold and my knee aching on the hard ground. Finally, I heard a long sigh and something in the sound of it made me look up at her. My queen was crying too.

Ori, no more dressed than I, but without the burden of her clothing, dropped to her knees in front of me. "Forgive me?"

Shock washed through my body. What had she done to demand forgiveness from me? I was the one who ran out. I was the one who could never live up to the expectations of the tribe.

"There is nothing to forgive. It was I who was in the wrong. And I am sorry if you were calling me longer. I truly did not hear." I dropped my gaze again because I could not bear to watch her tears, to see disappointment in her eyes. A hand came into view and tilted my chin away from my chest. Her worry was the only thing I saw.

"Kyri, do you not wish to be courted? I know it would be a hard path should you choose to walk it with me. Neither being queen nor consort is an easy job." Is that what she thought? Did Ori really assume that loving her would be too hard for me?

I had no choice but to vehemently deny her assumption. "No!" Her reaction was immediate and I watched broken-heartedly as her face crumpled in sorrow. It was then I realized that my words had been misconstrued. "Ori, you misunderstand, I do wish to be courted! It does not matter that our path is hard as long as I am walking it with you. I just worry. And they, um—"

"There were too many voices and too many questions, and it overwhelmed you. Is that it, Kyri?" I nodded, feeling like I had failed somehow. She placed a hand over mine. "I'm sorry, my love. I know you and I should have known it would be such." From one breath to the next, she stood and pulled me to my feet as well. "Well one thing is certain, the bird is hatched from the egg now. By this time tomorrow we will be hard pressed to find someone who doesn't know of the trail we are running together. That doesn't bother you, does it?"

I shifted my clothes slightly so I could continue holding her hand without dropping my things to the ground. "No, it does not bother me. I meant what I said. I really want to walk this path with you." My body gave a great shiver and I grimaced at her. "Can we take any more talk between us inside? I am freezing my feathers off here."

"How do you think I feel? Come back to my hut with me?"

In an instant I became aware of her naked body in front of me and a welcome heat raced through my blood. My tongue wet dry lips and I closed my eyes to the sight of her. "M—maybe it would be best if we did not visit Morpheus together tonight."

Ori smiled and stepped in close. Her arms were strong as she embraced me and I found it titillating that the only thing separating our skins was the feel of my day-worn clothes. "I want to kiss you right now, but it's much too cold to lose track of time out here like we have on so many instances before. Come." She took my hand and guided me as sure as the fleetest of foxes back to her hut. I joyfully noted that there was a low fire burning already and a few olive oil lamps lit, courtesy of one of the village runners.

I stood awkwardly, shyly, in the middle of her space while she put more wood on the fire and poured clay mugs of water for us. Luckily my feet were not cold because I at least had the fore-thought to shove them into my boots before running out of the cave. But the rest of me was still chilled as I continued to hold my clothes tight to my front. I was afraid, and when she looked me in the eyes she saw as much. "Is this our time then?"

She lidded the water pitcher and set it on the table before slowly walking toward me. "Do you want it to be our time? The choice is not mine to make alone. There are two of us on this path. What do you want?"

My eyes were drawn to the lines of her nude body and a shiver ran through me. "I do not know."

Another step closer, then one more. "Don't you?"

I desperately cast my eyes down so I could not see the beauty that advanced toward me. "I am afraid." Three words said aloud and I cringed expecting the fear that hovered over me at all times to crash down. I waited for the great eating darkness to press into me from above and buckle my knees. No such weight came. I star-tled slightly when sun burnished hands came into view and took my bundled leathers from me.

"Kyri, look at me." As if she were a goddess willing it so, my eyes tracked up to meet hers. Ori's smile was gentle. "Why are you afraid?"

I did not know the words for my fear. I only knew how it felt inside me. I tried, and stuttered, and tried again. "What if I do not—" Another sigh, but it was mine. She merely stood there patiently waiting for my windblown thoughts to come to her. "My queen, your experience is so much greater." I was unable to speak more but she still understood my intent. Before I could brace myself or protest she took that last step between us and pulled our bodies together. The feel of smooth skin where my cloak parted was almost too much.

"Can you feel that, Kyri? Can you feel me?" I drew in a rag-ged breath and nodded. "Outside this hut I may have more expe-rience than you in a great many things but inside this hut we are new. Do you understand? Together this is new for both of us. I want to be as one with you." She pulled me into a kiss that was different than all the others before. Instead of quickly becoming hot and hard, the touch of our lips stayed gentle and sweet. She pulled away with a sigh. "I'm ready to learn something new, Kyri Fletcher. Are you?" Her eyes spoke more words than could ever

fall from her lips. They promised challenge and passion, and I
wondered if I was ready.

I closed that small distance between our lips because I
needed another taste of her light. There were no questions left
and she knew that I was as ready as I would ever be. Clutching
hands made their way under my cloak and I felt them in the softest, most sensitive part of my lower back. Dull nails dug at me as
the kiss grew deeper and hotter. I lost track of time as we stood in
the center of her hut, warmed by the fire and our desire for each
other.

Eventually I came to myself when I felt one of her hands
move to the front of me and work its way up. Before I was aware
of her destination she caressed my breast in the full of her hand
and I arched toward her as my nipple hardened against her palm.
When she brought both hands up, caressing turned to more and I
moaned into her mouth. My legs grew weak as I panted her name.
"Ori."

It was both a plea and a supplication to my goddess made
flesh. I followed blindly as she led us to the bed. Shivering, I
stood there in the firelight as she removed my cloak and hung it
from a peg. She had grace in even the smallest things and my
heart ached for her. My mouth missed the taste of her lips. When
she bid me to lie back, I knew even then that I could still say nay.
But in truth I no longer held the meaning of such a word. In the
span of three kisses my body had cast it out into the night. The
fear was all but gone and I was ready for us to fly together.

"You are so beautiful, Kyri." Her voice surprised me because
I had been too long in a place of silence. Awe for me colored her
words, and in turn her words filled me with awe. Who was this
queen that worshipped me like a goddess? Was I even worthy of
such looks and devotion? I had no more words or thoughts
because her hands were in motion against my skin. Fingers gently
traced my most recent injuries causing goose bumps to march
across puckered flesh. Those same fingers moved on to trace the
scars that were left by Gata's mam, when the great leopard
attacked me the previous sun-cycle. Neither of us spoke as she
mapped my body's history with her hands. Before long, those
same hands grew bolder. My chest heaved with the sensation and
I was more than ready when she began kissing me again. I tangled my fingers in her hair and pulled her down to my right side.

My excitement grew when I found her breathing labored as
well, and I wondered if touching me made her body throb too.
Our mouths were torn apart when her pinching and rolling fin-

gers had me hissing out my pleasure. Goddess, but I did not know it could be like that. I could feel my need slick and ready and I could not help the whimper that escaped when she took my mouth again so fiercely. I writhed when her lips trailed along my neck at the same time her hand drew a line of heat down the center of my abdomen. Pain all but forgotten, I cried out at the first touch of something so holy.

I had peaked by myself many times but it was nothing compared to the mountain we climbed together. Ori was gentle and loving and all things I imagined a lover should be. And what I imagined would take way too long, in reality was much too short. At the height of it, when it felt as though the sun had burst forth from my eyes, emotion poured out of me. I sobbed on her shoulder, then afraid that my tears had ruined the beauty of the moment, I sobbed some more. Later, after she had reassured, petted, and teased me with gentle words, I became the explorer. I found all the soft and hard places that made her cry out. My hands worshipped at the altar of my queen's body and I was born anew. We were born together.

Morning came earlier than I previously remembered. Light from between the shuttered windows was precisely placed across the plane of my eyes. I could not bring myself to move though, for my queen had fallen asleep gentle in the crook of my right arm. My smile crept in slow as I remembered the candle marks before dawn. We continued to worship each other until exhaustion became a third presence in our bed. A part of me worried for Ori and her lack of sleep since she would be competing during the day. But the greater part of me could not help but be content. Happiness exploded in my chest and I unconsciously pulled the slumbering woman closer. I loved her. I loved the woman who held my heart so wholly, so thoroughly, that we both fell asleep full and cradled in each other. I was startled by a sigh that puffed air near my neck.

Even sleep rough her voice made me shiver. "You're squeezing me, love."

I immediately relaxed my unconscious grip. "I am sorry."

Her contented smile grew with each passing heartbeat. "Don't be. I have loved my first waking with you so far. I just need to be able to breathe." She raised fingertips to trace the rays of sun that painted stripes across my face. Though it was warm under the furs with her the rest of the air was chilly and I shivered as she traced my skin.

However, the scent on those fingers triggered an unexpected

flashback to the night before. I could not control the whimper that came from my lips as I remembered how those same fingers worked me from a tiny flame to a raging fire. Momentarily forgetting the day's duties and events I pulled her to me, crushing our mouths together in desperation. And the passion was not mine alone. She straddled my thigh and we moved together as our mouths battled for control. Her breasts were heavy in my palms and her strong thigh slid against me in a fevered rhythm. I crested first as I had done many times the previous evening. There was something about Ori that set my soul alight, and I could never slow the flames once they started to burn. But she followed soon after and slumped back down, panting even as our desire cooled. "Goddess, Kyri! I'm not sure how I'll compete today when your love has left me weak as a newborn lamb."

I kissed the top of her head, golden hair soft against my lips. "You could stay with me in this bed and I would give you a prize every candle mark." My suggestion fell to laughter because we both knew it was not an option for the queen to skip the day's festivities and events. She let out another great sigh and I tickled her ribs. The second round of laughter felt good but not as good as a warm hut. "We must rise, Ori. Your body needs food if it is to bring home the clay today, and I have to pee."

"Oh ho, so it's not really your concern for me but the state of your bladder!" She curved her fingers menacingly toward my good side and I gave her fair warning.

"If you tickle me you will be sleeping in wet bedding alone tonight!"

She smiled and lowered the threatening digits. "Fine, I will concede the victory to you this one time." I rolled my eyes at her competitive nature. Once a scout always a scout.

My side felt much better and I was able to sit up without any aid. Despite the cold air I felt warm and alive as the furs dropped away. I cast my eyes about searching for my missing clothing from the night before. Seeing them on the table across the hut drew a sigh from my lips. I did not look forward to putting on the crumpled items, and the dried sweat on my body made me feel less than clean. To make my decisions for the morning more difficult my stomach gave a loud growl. I clutched the offending part. "Bow and fletch but I am hungry! I also need another bath, or at least a wash in my hut." I looked at Ori because she stayed silent to my hungry chorus. The look in her eyes took my breath away but I remained acutely aware of the growing sounds of activity just outside the hut. My voice was a whisper as I tried to hold back the need that rapidly swelled with the heat of her gaze. "Ori."

She pulled her eyes away from my bare skin, swallowed thickly, and sighed. "The things you do to me, Kyri." She shook her head. "You really are my greatest temptation."

I prodded her side lightly. "Come on, the sun is up and there are things that must be done today. And I cannot get out of your bed around you."

"You absolutely can get out of bed around me." Her eyes were dancing with mischief.

"Oh, I am sure I can crawl over you but I do not trust your wandering hands this morning."

"You liked my wandering hands well enough last night. You also liked them at moon fall, and then again later just before sunrise."

My blush was instantaneous with her response. I scrubbed my face with both hands, willing the heat to fade. "Ori, please!" I tickled her ribs again causing her to jump away from me. Humor took me then and I continued to torment her until she had squirmed to the very edge of the bed.

"Okay, I yield! I'm getting up, you pushy scout!"

There was an unfamiliar soreness when I stood next to the bed but I wore it like an honor. Ori and I had finally given ourselves to each other and it made every single pain and missed candle mark of sleep well worth the experience. As I pulled on my leathers from the night before, I could not help watching her do the same. When she handed me a mug of cool water unbidden words tumbled from my lips. "You are beautiful, my queen."

She smiled indulgently with just a hint of blush to her cheeks. "It's Ori."

I set the mug down and pulled her close. "Ori is beautiful too." The kiss was nothing more than a slow and sweet exploration in the light of the new day. When we pulled away again, both sets of lips curved into a smile. Of course the moment was ruined when my stomach growled again. She swatted the offending part of my body.

"Hades take your yowling stomach! I've heard quieter field beasts at the end of the day."

I scowled as I grabbed my cloak from the peg but my mood quickly turned to laughter as her own stomach growled. "You were saying?"

Ori laughed too and made a shooing motion with her hand. "Oh, be gone with you!" When I moved toward the door she stopped me with a word. "Kyri?" Looking over my shoulder to meet her green eyes, they seemed as full of emotion as I felt. "Will you meet me for morning meal in a quarter candle mark?"

"Of course." I walked out the door before she could tempt me again with her expressive eyes or sweet red lips. There would be plenty of time to continue our explorations after the festival. During the walk to my hut, my mind was a whirlwind of thought. I felt a strange sense of symbiosis with the village around me as women rushed about in preparation for the games later. I was so in my head that Shana nearly took me to the ground as my feet carried me around the corner near my door. I surprised her as much as she surprised me.

"Kyri! Deh, but you're an early riser this morning. You've probably already eaten then..." Her words grew silent as she took in the state of my leathers and unbraided hair. As her gaze rose from the tips of my feet to my Amazon feathers I could feel the blush starting to rise as well. The look on her face was pure mischief. "Oh ho, where have you been, sister? I'm guessing it wasn't the meal hut."

The heat of my face and neck eclipsed that of the rising sun and I glanced around to see if anyone was watching. "Shana!" I turned and made my way into my hut and she followed close behind. I warned her before she could even open her mouth to speak. "I do not have time for your questions this morning. I have to meet Ori in a few candle drops for morning meal."

I turned to find my spare set of leathers and was abruptly pulled to a stop. "Halt that horse of yours." When I opened my mouth to protest she clamped a hand across my lips. "Something tells me that she'll wait for you." Shana moved her hand and stared at me for a few candle drops. I was not ready to discuss something so magical yet because I was still in the *feeling* stage. But I would have to try because I knew without a doubt that Shana would not let me leave my hut until I told her everything, or at least some.

Words were hard when everything meant so much. I could feel the heat as it rushed to my face but I did my best to ignore the discomfited butterflies flitting around my belly. Breaking away from her too curious eyes, I threw myself down onto the bed in the corner. There was a smile on my face that I could not break. "Leaf and bow, but she was amazing."

Shana moved to take a seat on the bed next to me. "And this came about how? The last I saw of you was near the end of the Fertility Dance."

"Hey!" Her words prompted interruption and I received only a small twinge from my healing side when I sat up. "Should we not be talking about you right now? What did Coryn say when you spoke with her?"

She looked at me with shadows in her eyes and I knew that whatever happened after the dance the previous night had affected her deeply. We waited for so many heartbeats in silence that I was unsure if she would even speak of it. Shana's voice was uncharacteristically quiet when it came. I knew then that she needed to talk about her own story more than she really wanted to listen to mine. "We spoke for a good long while last night. Coryn told me things that I wish I had known sun-cycles ago. She said she wanted to court me and I told her I didn't believe she was capable, nor did I think of her that way. Then she said..."

I was ecstatic but there was no way I could admit as much to Shana. I never wanted my involvement to come to the light so I had to school my face carefully so she did not see my excitement. "What did she say?"

The confident Telequire ambassador that I had come to know and love sighed and seemed to shrink in on herself. She did not raise her eyes from her tightly interlocked hands. Her knuckles had turned white. "She said that she would do whatever it took to make me look at her differently, even give up her owl friends."

I raised my eyebrows at her, all thoughts of schooling my face gone up like smoke from a fire. I had no idea that Coryn was so serious, though I should have guessed so when she did the fertility dance. Maybe getting to know my sister over the past few moons had returned that spark from so long ago. "What do you want, Shana? If you have no wish for that sort of attention then I think you need to tell her right away. Coryn is a good woman and she would not go through the Lover's Dance if she were not serious about this. Has she ever done the Fertility Dance before?"

I sat there while her face remained turned down. There was no fire going in my hut, merely silence, and I clearly heard her swallowing back cycles of pain and hurt. "No, she's never danced before. I don't know what I want, Kyri. She hurt me so much and I don't know if I can move beyond that."

She could not see my smile but it was there for a reason. I thought perhaps she had already moved beyond her pain of the past. Since the Confession of Stones at winter solstice, I had seen a change between the two women. Coryn and Shana had finally become friends. Maybe they were not best friends, but Shana was no longer indifferent to the attractive scout leader. "Shana." I kept my voice soft. Her gaze lifted and turned back to me. "Are you the same person that you were when you got your first feather? I have heard a lot of stories and sometimes I wonder how that jokester girl ever grew up to be the Telequire nation's first ambassador."

My thoughts to turn her to a lighter time worked well. "Goddess no. You've heard enough of my tales to figure out that I was a bit of a daemon back then. Why?"

I brought her back with a serious look. "You are not the only one who has changed, sister. You are not the only one who is allowed to change. Let Coryn prove herself. What is the harm? I do not think she would hurt you on purpose like some callous youth. Nor do I think you would be so conflicted if you felt nothing at all for her."

She stood and looked at me with real fear. "The harm could be to my heart! I don't know if I can risk that again."

I stood as well and grabbed her shoulders with both of my hands. Her eyes watered with emotion but I had to say what I believed was necessary. "Do you think it was ever just your heart at risk? Coryn's pool runs deeper than you think but you will never know unless you dive in."

Shana looked at me and I knew that she had returned. Just like that the twinkle was back in her eyes. "Swimming, Kyri? You really just compared Coryn to a pool of water?"

I released her shoulders and started dressing in my nearby spare leathers. "Hmm, she is nice to look at, and I hear she makes the Amazons wet."

"Holy Artemis! Where has my shy friend gone, the one who used to blush with the slightest bit of innuendo and who faithfully walked in the steps of the goddess? Did the queen keep her locked up in her hut for having such an impertinent mouth?"

I did not answer her cajoling for a heartbeat. Instead I finished sheathing my knives into each boot. When I stood I grabbed my bow and quiver from the pegs by the door and made to leave. "I happen to know the queen likes my mouth, impertinent or no. And I certainly would not object to being locked in with her." With that, I turned and walked out. But the look on her face, bow and leaf, but it was worth more than a pouch of gold.

Because I had surprised her so, she had no time to question me about the previous night's actions before we made it to the meal hut. Ori was already there, as was Basha, Coryn, Deka and Kylani. Ori moved to make room for me and Shana seemed torn since the only other seat available at the table was next to Coryn.

The handsome, feather-ruffling scout gave her a wary smile but did not say anything. I felt very exposed sitting next to Ori after the night of passion we had shared. It seemed as if every eye were on me, like everyone would know that I no longer walked in Artemis's footsteps. We were both aware that after the queen's words in the bathing pool most would know of our courtship. But that was not the same as knowing that I had bared my soul to her or that she had given me hers in return. She took my right hand under the table and I was forced to eat with my left because I was loath to let her go. After a few candle drops she noticed me not eating and called softly.

"Heyla Kyri, are you okay? What had you and Shana so late this morning? Did you need to talk with someone?" Her words were quiet and conversation in the busy meal lodge continued blithely around us.

I shrugged and gave her a smile. "Actually, Shana was the one who needed to talk. I am merely quiet because the moment I sat down with my food I realized that I wanted to kiss you more than I wanted to eat." She sucked in a breath and I was glad that I affected her so. She truly meant it when she said it would be new for both of us.

She licked her lips and kept her voice low. "You do?" I nodded. "So why aren't you?"

My whispered response was more for me than her. "I do not know." Almost against our will, our faces had moved closer than two people normally needed for quiet talk.

Coryn's loud voice cut through the conversation like a crack of thunder. "Kiss her already!" I became aware of the scores of eyes all around us and for the first time I did not care. The queen's face was a pleasant pink though admittedly her blush could do nothing to match my own. What made the embarrassment all the more acute was that like a single bird call in the woods, Coryn's words prompted a chorus from all the feather heads around us.

"Yes, kiss her!" "Do it, Kyri." Stomps and whistles also sounded all around the meal lodge.

I tried to focus only on Ori's lips and ignore the cacophony that surrounded us. Those lips formed a single word. "Well?"

Before either of us could change our minds, I threaded long fingers through her hair and crushed our lips together. One would think we had not just spent all the candle marks of the night together. One would think that I hungered sorely and that Ori was my only food. The world disappeared and there was only my queen. I lost track of time until the present crashed down on us as Ori pulled away. I whimpered because I could not help myself. The spell was completely broken when Basha cried out in shock. "Oh my goddess, when did that happen?"

Shana cracked up laughing. "Really, Basha? Always slow on the uptake, aren't you?"

I watched as Basha gave her a meaningful look, then flicked her gaze to Coryn and back to Shana. "I'm certainly not the only one." She smiled and gave Shana a wink. Though I had thought so on many occasions in the past, I was struck with the notion that there was more to the regent than met the eye. Basha was very quick and had a scholar's mind. Sometimes she missed the forest for the trees but most times she was on top of all the brewing news of the nation. I found it interesting that she had picked up on the thing between Coryn and Shana long before anyone else.

Morning meal continued as usual after that with people discussing their upcoming events of the day. I regretted that I could not compete in any of them. I think Thera may have given me approval for the archery event but I really did not think it fair to compete in something when my skill had already been proven on more than one occasion. Kylani would have to follow through with her promise to come up with a new challenge for me.

"Kyri, after you finish morning meal I'd like to show you something at the archery range." I had forgotten the training master was sitting at the opposite end of the table. She had remained so quiet through the ruckus earlier. I had no idea what she would need me for.

I looked at Ori, but she merely smiled in return. "The first event doesn't start for a candle mark. I'll need to oversee the Ceremony of Games, but other than that I can spend time with you 'til I compete." My heart gave an extra thump of excitement. Her company would be both a pleasure and a torment in the long day ahead.

I leaned forward so I could look down the table at the training master. "I can go as soon as I am finished here. I already have all my things I will need for the day." She smiled and while she continued to plow through her food, I felt a hand squeeze mine. The day was going to be amazing.

Thera found us just as we arrived at the archery field. "Kyri girl, how are those wounds doing this fine morn?"

"Heyla, Thera, other than my leg, the rest are coming along well. Just mild twinges from the arm and side now."

She looked at me shrewdly. "Have you been resting them like I said?"

I blushed as an image from the night before past through my mind. I was saved from further embarrassment when Ori answered for me. "No worries, Thera. I've been taking good care of her." The old healer cackled in response but started examining me anyway.

Luckily the weather had warmed enough that I was back in my leather strip skirt so she had easy access to see the mostly healed wound on my leg. "This one looks good, but if it's still sore some then keep your feathers out of them trees. No running either, scout. Now let me see the other two." My shoulder was easy. Other than the cloak it was left bare. I had to unwrap my top from the bottom for the last wound. She poked and prodded, muttering to herself and making little *hmm* noises. When she finished she bid me to fix my wrap and stepped back.

"Okay, let me see you string your bow. If you can do that and shoot easily, I'll clear you for everything but running and jumping. I'd say it will probably be another seven-day for the leg."

I pulled the bow from my back and strung it mostly with ease. I also took a forest fletch from my quiver, knocked it, and pulled back so she could see me hold my draw without pain. When I put the arrow away again she smiled and clapped me on the good shoulder.

"Look at that, you're practically good as new. Now don't be gracing my door again for a while, except when I see you in a seven-day to clear you for the leg."

She walked away and I looked at Ori and Kylani, who were both watching me with amused expressions. "Well that was unexpected. With my leg still not hale, there was no need for her to see me today."

"Actually, I asked her to examine you."

Ori and I turned to look at Kylani at the same time. I could only assume my face matched Ori's in confusion. "But why? There is nothing I can compete in with my leg still healing."

Kylani walked over and threw her arm around my shoulders. "Well, I was thinking you could compete in the archery contest—"

"No, you know I will not do that. It is not fair to everyone else." My shoulders stiffened under her arm and I shook my head vehemently.

The queen's look was one of dawning understanding. "Kylani, what have you done?"

Kylani pulled back and looked me in the eye. "I've been telling you for moons that I was going to give you a greater challenge. The fact that you made the impossible shot yet again yesterday morning really convinced me. I came to the conclusion that our advanced targets were much too predictable." With her free hand, she put fingers to mouth and gave a shrieking whistle. Cyerma, her Second, ran in from the side of the field carrying something in her hands. When she got to the target that was nearest to us, I saw that it had been altered slightly and sported a hole in the top. My mouth dropped open when I saw something that resembled the Tanta advanced target, only instead of a single wooden ring hanging from the pole, there were three suspended in line with the bullseye. Each ring spun merrily with the lightly gusting wind.

Ori started laughing and I swore. "Bent arrow and broken string! I am to assume that the arrow has to go through all three into the target?" Kylani nodded. I stepped toward the target, out of the circle of her arm and peered down field. "Woods weasel!" My gaze skipped to the queen when she laughed again. "Did you know about this?"

She regained control of herself enough to answer. "I did not, but I'm glad she's given you a challenge. Will you compete now?"

I thought about the difficulty of the new target and nodded my head. "I certainly cannot turn down a challenge, now can I?"

Kylani grinned and clapped me on the back with significantly more force than the old healer. "Such spirit. We'll make a scout out of you yet, Kyri Fletcher." I knew she was teasing. Her comments were only in reference to the scout's competitive nature rather than actual skill. She did not get a rise out of me but her words elicited peals of laughter from the queen.

I pointed at her mirthful reaction. "Oh, you think it is funny now but who do you think you will be competing against later?" Full of scout cockiness, I smirked at her. "I hope you liked your fall equinox archery win, because you will not be repeating your success."

Ori's laughter cut off and her mouth gaped open in surprise. "Son of a hissing snake, I didn't even think of that!"

"Care to make a wager, my queen?"

She licked her lips and I felt it come over me at the same time. I knew that in our heads we were both back in her hut reliving our waking dreams. She smiled, all-knowing and sly. "Perhaps I do."

We were interrupted when a runner approached. "My queen, you're needed to start the games." She winked at me and took off at a jog back to her hut. As queen, Ori would need her mask and all her weapons to start the competition. I watched her with a stupid grin on my face.

"So, you and the queen, hmm?"

I glanced at the training master, the old fears trickling in to still my breath. "Yes."

She did not say anything for a few heartbeats and my anxiety picked up. What if she did not approve? What would I do then? The training master was a very influential person within the Amazon nations. But she gave me no more time to ponder and worry. Instead she held out her arm for a warrior's handclasp. I took it and she smiled back at me. "Good, I'm glad for you both. You're a good person Kyri, and the queen has been lonely for too long. Take care of each other." With those words, she walked away.

Chapter Eight

The Archer

THE SPRING EQUINOX games started a little different than the previous one I had witnessed. During the opening ceremony the queen announced that she had received official news concerning the Festival of Nations. Many sun-cycles had passed since the Telequire nation last participated in the event, all due to the machinations of the previous queen. But when Queen Orianna took over she made diplomacy a high priority and pledged that Telequire would return to the annual festival. The Festival of Nations was a lot like the seasonal games, except on a much larger scale. Representatives from each Amazon nation would be sent to compete in the various events. Besides the different competitions, there were meetings among the queens, inter-nation trade, information sharing, and much revelry. It was an event that fostered general bonding between all the sister-tribes. Queen Orianna's announcement that Telequire had been chosen to host the next Festival of Nations had the entire village making noise.

The news immediately made me think of the friends I had made among the Tanta tribe and I hoped that some of them would be participating in the games, or at least be coming along. The festival always took place during summer solstice so there would be plenty of time to prepare the village for the hundreds of visitors that would come. Each Amazon nation would typically send anywhere between two and three score people and there were twelve nations total, including Telequire. Many things would have to be organized and built before the summer solstice arrived. Competition areas had to be altered slightly for more people to watch, temporary camps needed to be erected, and new cooking, hunting, and patrol schedules would need to be worked out.

I was disheartened to hear that in order to participate in the Festival of Nations games, you had to be one of the top three people in each event of the previous equinox. By the end of the queen's speech I was equal parts joyous and cursing my injuries that were keeping me from the tree race. It was then that I got a brilliant idea. While there was little I could do with a mending leg, there were still a few things I could do that did not involve running or jumping. I quickly found Shana and explained my plan then asked her what she thought of it. She looked at me for a few heartbeats with a strange expression on her face.

"Sister, you kind of frighten me sometimes. You really want to do all that for the skill event?"

I nodded. "It has to be more than what I did last time. They will expect it, and honestly I feel like my skill has grown so I have to do more to prove myself."

Shana shook her head but did not argue. "So you want me to what, shoot the arrows?"

I scratched my temple. My closest friend was many things, but a master archer she was not. "Actually, I was going to ask Ori. The shooting has to be precise for this to work. And she is the one that gave me the idea." Shana cocked her head in confusion. "It was on the day we argued and I shot her fletch from the air."

"Oh, that's right. But shooting at you as well?"

She was concerned for a reason. I had already been shot by three arrows. "I have already done it. In the morning of the attack I was catching the enemy's arrows and shooting them back the way they came. If she shot one at me and then shot one at the target, I could combine the two moves for the sake of the competition."

She put her hand on my shoulder. "Kyri, I don't know about this. Are you sure?"

"Have I been wrong when I said I could do something?"

My sister-friend sighed. "No, you have not. Fine, why don't I find Ori while you sign up? The event starts in a half candle mark and we still need to get a spare target from Kylani." We went in separate directions and I felt excitement build in my gut. My newest skill demonstration would be as good a challenge as my impossible shot of the previous day. Head councilor Gerta was in charge of competitor check-in for the skill event. I was glad to see her permanent scowl appeared to be missing as I walked up to the table, but it quickly returned when she caught sight of me. She raised her hand, palm out.

"Heyla Kyri Fletcher, I know for a fact that you are not cleared for duty yet."

I nodded at the truth of her words. "Councilor Gerta, while I have not been cleared for duty yet, I was cleared to shoot by Thera just this morning. And I will not be running or jumping for my demonstration."

She peered at me with eyes narrowed and lips thinned. The older woman was known for being cranky and a bit of a badger with most things so I hoped she would not cause me trouble. I waited for nearly a candle drop while she weighed my words. Finally she handed over the red competitor tie and I sighed with relief. She chuckled, knowing full well the discomfort she had caused. "You're the last competitor to go. Good luck today Kyri. I look forward to seeing what you do this time."

When I turned from the table, I smiled to see my friends approach. The queen did not look happy and Shana's face told me that I was going to owe her a favor later. Coryn was with them too and the charismatic scout merely grinned at me. "What are you up to this time, Kyri? Haven't you gotten tired of people shooting arrows at you?"

Before I could answer, Ori rounded on the taller woman. "That is no matter for joking, First Scout Leader."

Realizing that Ori was still very sensitive on the subject of the attack and my injuries, Coryn stepped back a pace and raised her hand palm up. "Peace, my queen, I meant no harm. Kyri is in no danger today. She would not have suggested this otherwise. She would not so foolishly risk her life like that."

Ori seemed to deflate and ran a hand through her short blonde hair. "You're right. My apologies, Coryn. I should not take my nerves out on you." She took a slow deep breath before turning to me. "What would you have me do, Kyri?"

"Well—" I got no further because Kylani strode up and interrupted.

"Yes, what would you have her do?" She pointed to the tree line side of the skill competition area. "I set the target over there so there would be no one near enough to get hit during your demonstration. Now what is the crazy thing you have planned?"

I smiled at the target placement because it was perfect. "While I was defending Maeza against enemy arrows I would catch them and then shoot the arrow back at the invaders. The problem only arose when they caught on to what I was doing and all started shooting at once. Also, the last time the queen and I took target practice together I shot her arrow out of the air before placing my own in her target center."

"But—" I held up my hand to stop Coryn.

"Patience please. I need someone who is a master archer that I can trust with her shot, which is where the queen comes in. My idea is for her to shoot an arrow at me, then shoot an arrow at the target. I will catch her first arrow and shoot it at her second to knock it out of the way. After that I will draw my own arrow and sink it in the target center. Three arrows, one kill."

"I don't like this."

"Neither do I." Predictably, Shana echoed Ori's concern.

"I think it's brilliant." Coryn was always up for a show.

Kylani was the only one who did not speak. We waited while she rubbed her chin. Finally her gaze turned to mine. "You say you've done this before?" I nodded. "Just once?"

"No, I shot a crossbow bolt from the air when we were traveling to Tanta nation. I also shot another from the air during Training Master Deata's test and I shot Ori's out of the air a few moons ago. It just seems to be something I can do, like catching arrows."

Won over, Kylani smiled. "Well then, I can't wait to see you meet your newest challenge."

Ori stepped close to me and the rest wandered away. It was obvious why they made themselves scarce. "Are you sure about this, Kyri?"

She was so close that I could easily caress her cheek with the palm of my hand. "Of course I am. I would not risk myself so, otherwise. I would not risk either my pain or your pain, for the sake of a competition. I can do this, Ori, trust me."

"Okay. I have faith in you." Hearing those familiar words from her lips, I knew then that she was truly okay with my plan. I grinned and took her hand as we walked over to stand by Coryn, Shana, Kylani, and Steffi. Some of the women displayed very impressive skills. The crowd cheered for each and the council of elders gave their ratings after each woman finished her skill demonstration. Because of my late arrival I was the last competitor in the event. I placed Ori so she was about thirty paces from the target, straight out from its center. I placed myself about forty paces from Ori, at a right angle from her line to the bull's-eye. It would be a longer distance than our traditional targets but no more than what I had done on the day of our argument. Shana and Kylani made sure there were no watchers directly behind me though Ori would not be shooting anywhere but the center of my body.

Apparently news of my late entry had spread and the crowd had grown in size in a short time. I noticed Maeza standing next to Pocori in the crowd and gave them a nod. Both women grinned back and made the Amazon sign for victory. Once we were in place the crowd hushed and waited for my demonstration to begin. I should have known that Ori would improvise. I should have remembered that she liked to test me on occasion. Instead of shooting an arrow at me, then turning and shooting an arrow at the target, Ori shot two arrows at me. My talking about Deata's test must have reminded her of all I could do. I caught the first then in a heartbeat of surprise I knocked the second to the ground with my bow. Before I could say a word she was aiming for the target so I did the same and was thrilled to see my arrow knock hers away. Then in a span of heartbeats, as fast as I could pull from my quiver and draw, I put three arrows into the center of her target. I was breathing hard from the rush of it all but still had the forethought to hold my bow away from me as Ori threw herself into my arms. "That was amazing!" The crowd roared, and the elder's marks clearly agreed.

Kylani walked up then and took my arm in a warrior shake. "Looks like you'll be repeating this particular trick at the Festival of Nations. And Kyri?" I looked at her in question, wondering what else she had to say. "I'd like to speak with you sometime about the course training you've been doing with the Fourth Scouts. I'd like to set something up at the village to get everyone used to moving through the trees while shooting. Let's talk more on your next rest day, okay?" I nodded and could not keep the smile off my face. I then turned to receive praise and congratulations from my friends and other Amazon sisters before making a detour to my hut and reverently placing my second clay Artemis statue on my shelf of treasures. It sat serenely between my first won statue and my carving of Gata.

Throughout the day I watched many exciting events. I think quite a few were especially competitive because they knew that only the top three in each event would be able to participate in the Festival of Nations. Ori handily won the sword statue, which no one was surprised to see. After watching another winning demonstration by my queen I was struck with the realization that she had a talent with the sword much like mine with the bow. Having witnessed her sword speed on many occasions I was sure she could knock an arrow from the air in much the same way I could dash one away with the wood of my bow. I was also acutely embarrassed when I caught myself wishing I could drag Ori back to her hut while she was in the middle of fighting for first place. It was disconcerting that simply watching her compete could start so fierce a blaze within me. At one point I was forced to take gulping swallows from my water skin and I heard Shana chuckling very clearly from my left side.

"What's the matter, Kyri, has someone started fire in your leathers? You're looking kind of warm all of the sudden."

I punched her in the arm for her teasing. Sadly, Shana missed taking the statue for knife. Deka, her longtime rival for the prize, won out in the end. Shana shrugged it off saying that as second place she would still get to compete against all the nations at the summer festival. I was also surprised to see Shana had entered the story telling contest and won a third place finish there as well, though Ori reminded me that Shana was made an ambassador for a reason. She truly did have a golden tongue. I asked her who she had been practicing her skills of oral persuasion on the night before which caused her blush deep red and to spit wine all over the grass next to me. I was learning, oh but goddess I was learning. Coryn won the tree race, and Dina and Deima took second and third place. Revelry and heartbreak went hand in hand throughout the afternoon. All of the competitors wanted to represent Telequire during the Festival of Nations.

The archery event was nearly last, with only the distance runners coming in after. I was both nervous and thrilled at the challenge of the new target. There was a palpable excitement in the crowd when Ori and I walked up. The news of a new impossible target had spread quickly through the competitors and watchers alike. Some had recognized the design as being similar to what a few other nations had, like Tanta. To others though, it looked as if only the goddess Artemis could make a shot to trap all three rings.

The contest was different from previous competitions in more than one way. Kylani had set it up in three rounds. First round everyone would shoot twelve arrows at a standard target. Everyone that put all twelve into the red center would move on to the next round. The second round utilized the old pendulum targets. The archers only needed to put one arrow into the red center, without having it dashed away by the pendulum. We were only allowed to shoot six arrows for that one. Everyone that passed the second test moved on to the final round. The third round was with the new target. We were allowed one arrow to pierce all three rings and hit the center of the target. By the time the third round arrived, there were only five archers left. Myself, Ori, Cyerma, who was the training master's Second, a warrior named Kasichi, and my veteran Fourth Scout, Malva.

We drew numbered bones to determine shooting order and I smiled to see that I was to shoot fourth, right before Ori. Cyerma shot first and was able to catch the front ring, but a gust of wind twirled the back two away. She was just a hair off center but it was still an amazing shot. I also wondered if she had been practicing on the new target since Kylani had thought it up. While Kasichi and Malva both had center shots with their arrows, neither managed to catch a ring. When it was my turn I briefly thought of my da. My mind always turned to him when I felt most challenged by bow and fletch. I thought of all I had learned and become since we parted ways and I knew with certainty that he would have been proud of me.

Knocked, drawn, and waited, I listened to the wind in the trees and the quietly shuffling crowd behind me. Then with one last glance at my blue and green fletching, I sent the arrow on its way. There was a little cheer as my arrow pierced two rings before burying itself in the center of the target. While the watchers all seemed pleased, I fought off a wave of disappointment at the fact that I had not hit all three. My arrow was removed and I graciously stepped out of the way so Ori could approach the shooting line. She winked as she passed and I called softly so that only she could hear. "Good luck, my queen."

I watched as she drew and sighted then timed her shot for the wind. When she released I was sure she would pierce all three. But a rogue breeze capriciously twisted the front and back ring just as her arrow came through. Kylani turned to her. "I thought for sure it was going to go through all three, my queen." I was sad for Ori which was probably why her good-natured laughter took me by surprise after the Training Master's words.

"Ah, it's only Artemis looking to keep me humble. I like the target though Kylani. It's a good one. Anything that stymies Kyri will always be a worthy challenge." The crowd laughed and I blushed at her backhanded praise.

Margoli was the one to hand out the clay statue for my win. I could not stop the pride that bubbled to the surface when I looked at the little clay fired statue of Artemis and traced the word "Archer" that was scribed into the bottom. The queen's Right Hand and Telequire military advisor took my arm like a warrior. "Congratulations, Kyri. I look forward to having you represent us during the Festival of Nations." It felt as though my smile was carved into the skin of my face just as permanent as "Archer" was carved into the clay.

CANDLE MARKS WENT by and I found myself in a very familiar place. I was seated at a long table surrounded by friends and faced with a clay-fired plate of excellent festival food. They even had honey cakes, a fact which Ori raved about. I made sure to snag a handful and hid them in my hut when I dropped off my second clay statue before the feasting got underway. I had a feeling they would earn me special favor later in the evening.

After the meal was cleared and the dancing began, I found myself in possession of one of Thera's spiced wine flasks. I felt warm clean through by the time Ori pulled me into the dancer's ring around the central bonfire. The drummers played a rhythm that was familiar but still unknown, yet I laughed and learned the steps as best I could anyway. After what felt like candle marks, I stumbled out of the circle and found an unclaimed water skin in an area lit by just a few torches. I also found the distinctive shapes of my two friends. They were sharing a cushion on the ground and appeared to be holding hands. Their voices were just a low murmur, but I did not really want to know what was said. It was no longer time for me to hold secrets for the two of them. It was time they shared those secrets with each other. I decided to make a detour on my way back to the drum circle and dancers. My delay was the reason that Ori found me just outside the firelight. "Sneaking away already?"

"No, my queen. I got thirsty and stopped to pick up a few other things on my way back." I held out the skyphoi I had filled to the top with figs, raisins, and a split pomegranate. Her eyes also flicked to the two skins I had slung over my right shoulder, one water and the other wine.

She smirked at me. "What's the matter Kyri, are you hungry or something?"

I took a fig from the bowl and placed it gently against her lips. "Actually, I thought you might like to find a place to wash off all the sweat and grime from the day."

Ori glanced at the small bowl then back into my eyes. "There doesn't appear to be enough for everyone this time."

I gave her a smile that felt straight from my heart. "Well it is a good thing I am not inviting everyone, is it not?" I held out a hand. "My queen?" She took my palm in hers and we made our way to the smallest bathing pool. By luck, or maybe the divine interference of Artemis herself, the pool was empty of visitors when we arrived. I set both skins and the bowl of fruit on the floor next to the pool then turned to remove my clothes. She was in the water first and my skin warmed with her gaze as I made my way down the steps into the pool proper. The heat felt amazing on my muscles and overall it was nice to know the dirt from the day was washing away as well. When I came to a stop in front of her, Ori's eyes roamed along every single finger's width of my flesh. One of her hands came out of the water holding a cake of lavender soap.

"Would you like me to wash your hair, Kyri?"

I nodded and gave her a shy smile, still amazed that such a beautiful and powerful woman could want me, a simple fletcher's daughter. She wasted no time lathering the soap into my long dark hair after I dunked down into the water. I found the act surprisingly intimate as her fingers massaged along my scalp. Hands smoothed their way down my neck and along the muscles in my shoulders. I groaned at the blissful feeling as my body began to relax. Ori was standing so close behind me that I could feel her breath tickling fine hairs at the back of my neck. Her breathing faltered as another groan bubbled forth from my chest. When she signaled me, I submerged myself to thoroughly rinse. The hands continued to move even as I was once again breathing air but they had become teasing in their motions.

Unable to take any more I finally gave in and moved her hands to where I wanted them. We both gasped as hard points met her palms and I shuddered at the caress of her. She moved closer yet, until the entire front of her body pressed into the back of my own. "M—my queen, as, as much as I like this, I want to wash your hair too." She gave a great sigh at my words and finally lowered her hands into the dark water next to me. I was able to breathe again when she stepped away from the press of our skin.

We reversed and I washed her in the exact manner that she had washed me. When she was rinsed and back above water, I did more than just lay my hands on her. I let my lips trace a path from the back of her neck around to the side and up to her ear. She whimpered and I thought for certain my legs would fail to hold me. I had no idea what to do in that position. I only knew that she felt good in the circle of my arms. The only sounds in the chamber were that of the flickering torches, soft mewling sighs, and the water trickling out of the pool through a channel carved in the floor. Understanding me and ultimately aware of how new I was to the intimacy between two people, Ori removed one of my hands from her breast. I was heartbeats from protest until I realized that she was merely guiding it lower. Her soft slippery skin was a joy to my fingertips as she panted out her pleasure. Heartbeats turned to candle drops and I lost track of who was more aroused.

"Artemis!" Her cry of release was like the joyful voice of a hawk circling the trees. I thought there was no better place in all of Gaea's domain than the one next to Ori. She was my queen and goddess, sun and moon, and I knew I would have given anything for her. A prayer, or maybe it was a pledge, slipped from my soul into the universe beyond. I would let nothing again stand between us.

The water was too hot to spend long in its depths but we cooled quickly on the way back to my hut. The drums were competing with the heart beating in my chest. Despite all that we had shared of our hearts, thoughts, and bodies, I still feared that everything within my grasp was merely a dream. I never imagined that life could hold so much pleasure.

When I still lived on the homestead with my da, my days seemed overfull of fletching, hunting, archery, and tree running. I never once assumed there could be more than those few simple things. Leaving home had ripped a great and gaping hole into the very fabric of my sky and for the first time in my life I saw the stars. Pinpricks of light that were as beautiful as they were infinite. That was how I felt when I looked into Orianna's eyes. We spent candle marks connecting and connecting again. I told her of my mother and all my childhood secret fears. She told me of her sister and her deceased parents and all the things she missed when she took up the Monarch's Mask. I would have given her back some of those things if I could. There was no other person that I would rather run the trees with, and I could bear no other sun in my sky.

Just the thought of another person caressing me as she had caused an ache deep inside, but the thought of someone besides me at the mercy of her hands brought the prick of tears to my eyes. We were cuddled on my bed under the warmth of the fur made from Gata's mam. Ori's back was pressed to my front and I could not keep her from feeling the sob that I barely caught in my throat. My breathing hitched and I pressed my eyes tight together to block out the sudden image I had of her with another.

"Kyri? Are you well?" My inhale was shaky and my exhale not much better as I tried not to acknowledge the tears that threatened. I shook my head behind hers but could not answer. I would not. Then before I could stop her, she spun within the circle of my arms. Her fingers burned where they traced the map of tears on my cheeks. "What's wrong?"

Emotions raw, I felt too far open. Like all at once she would see the things inside of me that should never meet the light. And fear, fear was the arrow that pierced my heart. "Please tell me we are not just owl friends. I..." I had to clear my throat to finish the thought. "I cannot bear the thought of you touching someone else. And the thought of someone else touching me twists me up inside. I want to be yours and yours alone."

"Oh!" Her surprised response sent a bolt of despair through me. My breath came faster as I started to panic. I wanted to run, to retreat into the trees like so many times before. But her strength was greater than I could ever have imagined. All it took was the barest of touches to pin me in place. Because my eyes were still shut I was startled to feel the press of her lips against mine. There was a smile that met me in the dim light and I felt my own lips responding in kind. Her words were soft but no less filled with awe and certainty. "You have always been mine, Kyri Fletcher. Just as I have always been yours. It took seasons and leagues to find you, but alas we are here together in this place and time. While I have no wish to rush the learning and growth between us, I also know that I'm as serious about you as I am about the welfare of this nation. I hold you in my heart as I have always held my goddess. You'll find my words always true to you, Kyri." I pulled her tightly to me, as if I could meld our skins together to become one being. Somewhere in the vast darkness of the spinning night sky, there must have been others out there who felt as I did. Images of eight-limbed beings with two hearts and one soul danced through my head and I kissed her temple with a sigh.

"My tree has flourished in these woods." As the fire burned low and our breathing evened out, I reveled in our easy slip into sleep. Before everything could fade completely, I heard Ori whisper into the night.

"My heart has flourished with you."

Chapter Nine

Mark of a Master

THE SEVEN-DAY PASSED much too fast and before I knew it I was back on patrol with my fourth scouts. I did not see Ori every night. She was queen after all and very busy. Before Thera declared me healthy enough to return to duty I spent many candle marks with Kylani discussing an archery obstacle course, much like the one my da had made for me. I mentioned that Amazons would only be able to use it in pairs because someone would have to count for the archer. She said it would not be a problem and implemented the new training routine as soon as the course was complete. It was a good course and I showed her how to subtly alter it each moon so that the Amazons in training did not become complacent.

My first night sitting around a fire with my fourth scouts was quite a trial. My courtship with the queen had become common knowledge by that point and more than a few teased me for being the focus of her Lover's Dance. Besides archery, blushing became a skill I most excelled at. Geeta, always the gossip, managed to surprise me with her poking. "I noticed that you and the queen left the dancers early on equinox night, Kyri. I also noticed that great cat of yours sitting outside the smallest bathing cave. Mayhap she was helping wash that goddess mark off your forehead?" The group of scouts burst out into muffled laughter.

I felt my face heat up once again and decided to surprise her right back. "Mayhap she did. Or, mayhap that mark was washed off the night before. It is really hard to remember."

Surprised laughter and comments echoed around the fire.

"Oh my goddess!"

"You wolf!"

"You rutting stag!"

I took their teasing and fun in good humor because they were all my friends and my people. The next morning I changed my schedule slightly and said my goodbyes to that scout troop. I decided that since I had been out of the trees for so long it would be good for me to make a run over to the next group that was located on the northeast quadrant. It was there that I saw more familiar faces. I congratulated Malva again on her shooting during the archery competition. She was quite a talented archer and I was lucky to have her on my team. Pocori was also on northeast quad for another day so I got to check her progress as well.

That night around the fire was nearly a repeat of the night before. I took plenty of teasing and was comfortable enough to tease right back. Since the evening that I had given myself to Ori, things felt different for me. I spent my entire life never really fitting in, never really comfortable in my own skin. But after bonding with the queen, after sharing every part of myself with her, I finally felt whole. What a strange thing fate was to allow me the wholeness I spent many seasons seeking, only after losing a part of me. And sure as the sun kissed the land each morning and again every night, I had lost my heart to Orianna, Queen of the Telequire Nation.

IT WAS STILL early the next day when the northeast scouts took to the trees. I had plans to move on to the southeast quad later but I stayed with my current group because they were headed that way as part of their rotation. A few candle marks into our day we were alerted by the forward tree runners that there was a rider on the path that snaked from the main trade road that crossed Macedonia, from the farther reaches of Thrace. Once we confirmed that he was following our path into the Telequire forest, we perched on the limbs above and waited. With masks down and leaves recently unfurled, we were well hidden in the canopy.

I studied the man as he approached. The horse he rode looked well cared for and the man himself seemed to be of middling age. His face was lined but some of those lines could have been from easy smiles and not an abundance of frowns. There was a mule tied behind him, much the same way I once tied Dan to the back of Soara's saddle. My trip with Shana seemed like a distant dream as I crouched in the treetops with my Amazon sisters. He wore a long knife on his belt and carried a full quiver on his back. The bow was strung and the reins of his horse were loose on the pommel, but he had no arrow knocked. That told me that while he was aware of possible danger, he posed no threat himself. Once he drew close enough I gave a whistling "watch" call and flipped down from the trees. The softly muffled thud of my landing did little to disturb the dry dirt of the path, nor did it seem to bother the man's beasts. My voice was clear in the mid-morning sun. "You are about to trespass on Amazon land. State your business or leave the way you came."

The man's voice was deeper than I expected, a rumble that would be hard to understand if one were not listening close. "Greetings, tree sister. I'm seeking the daughter of an old friend and I was told that she may have traveled this way last suncycle."

I felt a twinge at his words, a glimmer of something I had no name for. "And your name, traveler?"

"I am Master Fletcher Jordan. I'm seeking Kyri, daughter of Galen."

The mask hid my sudden sorrow. I could feel the eyes of my scouts above, knowing they waited for any word from me. I did not know what his news could be and for a heartbeat I feared that the king of our land had discovered my deeds against his forest patrol. What kept me from panic was the fact that the stranger said he was a friend of my da. That alone meant that I would heed Master Fletcher Jordan's words. I would need to know his purpose for seeking me out before I sent for Ori's permission to bring him to the village. "Why do you seek Kyri?"

He cocked his head curiously at me. "Do you know her? Has she been here recently? It was Galen's dying wish that I test the girl for her Master's Mark. I confess that I probably wouldn't recognize her now. I haven't seen the lass since she was naught but a wild thing running through the trees." He chuckled. "Such a sprite she was. That girl would ignore every word of caution that her mother Mira would yell to her."

I swallowed the lump in my throat at the thought of the time when I was so young and my mam still alive. I also grieved for the final knowledge that my da had really passed. Decision made, I swung my bow across my shoulder and chest so it faced the opposite direction as my quiver. Then I raised my mask so he could see the face beneath. "Well as you can see, Master Jordan, by the grace of Artemis I still run the trees like the sprite I was. I confess though, I do not remember you."

"By the gods, you look just like her!"

I could not help tilting my head in confusion. "Her?"

"Your mother, Mira. You could be her spitting image, though you seem to be as tall as Galen was in his youth. So you are an Amazon now? Why are you on the border all alone?"

His questions came at me faster than flies in the summer. I laughed and gave a shrill whistle. One by one my sisters came down from the trees behind me. "Oh I am not alone. Perimeter scouts flock together." One of the mandates of any Amazon

nation states that men cannot be brought into the village without
the queen's approval. If I wanted to spend some time with the last
man to see my da alive, I was going to have to send someone to
the village and wait for word to return. I turned to Degali, knowing she was the fastest distance runner in the group. "I need you
to notify the queen that we have a male visitor who wishes to test
me for my Master's Mark. Please tell her I am asking permission
for Master Jordan to enter the village and return with her answer
as soon as you can." Degali took off down the forest path and I
turned to the rest of the troop then. "You can continue with your
patrol. I will stay here until Degali returns, then send her ahead
to you after she rests." A chorus of "yes, scout leader" met my
words, then they all took to the trees and disappeared.

Standing on the bare ground in front of the man who last saw
my da, who last heard him speak, filled me with trepidation. I
was out of the trees and out of my element, with no clue what to
say to him or how to relate. I decided that simple would be the
best thing for me. "While we cannot travel far into Telequire
lands without the queen's permission, we can still take shelter in
the shade of the forest. Are you hungry Master Jordan?" I led the
way farther down the path into the sweet coolness provided by
the canopy above. He nodded and dismounted his gelding to follow. Surprisingly, he stayed quiet until I stopped at a nearby
stream. He let his mount and mule drink then hobbled them both
where the lush grass grew nearby. When he finally turned back to
me proper, I realized that he was older than I had originally
guessed.

"I could definitely stand for an early midday meal. So Galen
was right, you really did leave to become an Amazon. How do
you find things here?"

His deep voice was soothing, like the distant memory I had of
my grand da in the time of my youth. "I am doing very well here.
Everything he had wanted for me, I have found with the Telequire nation."

He nodded. "Good, good. I have to say that Galen was a fine
man and I'm very sad that he is gone. He loved you more than life
itself." Master Jordan gave a rueful smile. "And gods, but he was
so proud of you. In the last candle marks before he passed into
the Elysian Fields, he even joked that you would probably be
queen someday." I blushed at the stranger's remembered praise
but stayed quiet. The sudden visit and speaking with someone
who knew my da so well was hard. I found myself struggling for
emotional control. It did not take long for him to interrupt my

thoughts with his rapid questions. "How long before you get word of your request? How far away is the village proper? Do you still fletch? Are you a fletcher for this Telequire nation, or just a scout?"

I laughed at his exuberance and curiosity. Perhaps that was what I sensed under the surface when I initially thought him younger. "Master Jordan—" He cut me off before I could speak another word.

"Please, just call me Jordan. I am no one's master right now, just an old man who is fulfilling a good friend's dying wish."

The smile I wore was a sad one. "Okay, Jordan. When not staying in the canopy, runners can make it to the village in a candle mark. So I am hoping to see her back here in a little more than twice that. You can guess the distance based on the time it takes her to run." I paused to unhook and refill my water skin in the stream. "As for fletching, I do still fletch in my free time. The nation already has a fletcher and a handful of apprentices though I am not sure if any of them have the mark. There was more need for me here as the leader of the perimeter scouts."

Jordan's bushy gray eyebrows rose at my words. "Scout leader? So soon? You've been with them what, six moons?" I nodded. "Galen was right, you are a young lady with some skill. I've known a few Amazons in my time and scouting is no easy thing. You must have impressed them to become a leader so young, and so fast."

I could not stop the redness that worked its way up my neck and face. "I think I impressed them more with my bow skills than anything else."

"Aha, so you are his offspring in that too. Well done my girl, well done." He nodded to my quiver. "Are those yours?"

I pulled one out for him knowing what he was asking. "Yes."

The first thing he did was sight the length of the arrow shaft, then he inspected the fletching and the tip. "This is very nice work and certainly master quality. I'd say it's nearly identical to your da's, with the exception of coloring."

"Yes, our fletching was nearly the same. The only difference was in color and that I will use right or left wing feathers while he always preferred left."

Jordan laughed out loud. It was a rumbling noise that startled me at first. "That he did! Did your da ever tell you why he preferred the left?" I shook my head, curious at some new information about the man I had loved and admired. "Well, he used to swear that every single tournament he won were all done with left wing fletched arrows and the ones he lost were right. I personally think he was crazy but everyone has their beliefs and superstitions." He held the arrow up with thumb and forefinger in the center of the shaft. "Do you mind if I shoot this one?"

I waved my hand at him. "Not at all." He had slung his strung bow across his chest just as I had done. Once he removed it, he spun around looking for a target.

"What about there?" I pointed at a tree knot that was a little more than forty paces away. Will that work, or is it too far?"

He scoffed at my doubtful words. "Too far? I'll show you too far, young pup! Why don't we lay a wager on the shot?"

My curiosity was piqued and I could not help the grin that followed. "I am always up for a wager but what is the prize?"

He knocked my arrow but did not draw it back. Instead he held it and the bow in the fingers of his left hand. He held the right hand out to me. "The prize is that the one farthest from the center has to make lunch." I clasped the offered hand even though I truly did not mind the thought of cooking for us.

He shot first and it was a good solid mark. It was hard to tell the exact center of the knot we had picked out, but he was certainly close if not right on. He was good, just like my da was good. But I had finally realized in my six moons with the Amazons that I was better. When he nodded and stepped back, I took his place and knocked my own arrow. After drawing and sighting, I made a decision to do more than simply aim at the center. I released my first arrow, obviously to the left of his and off center. Then I proceeded to draw and release five more until I had formed a circle of my arrows around his. I grinned at my placement and turned to face the old fletcher. His low whistle told me just how impressed he was with my shots. "Galen's kid for sure! That is some grouping you made and it's no wonder you made scout leader." He peered at me as if he could see my very thoughts. Perhaps he could. "You strike me as a serious hunter and someone with a level gaze. I'm truly glad to see you doing well for old Galen's sake."

I think it was pride that warmed my chest and face and I did not fight the feeling. "I would like to think my da taught me to be as such, so I am honored to have you say those things." I shook free of my memories and jogged over to retrieve my arrows. "If you help me catch some fish, I will do the cooking."

The wrinkles on his face seemed deeper in the shade of the trees. "But you won the bet."

I shrugged and grinned. "Did I? I do not recall."

After catching more fish than the two of us could eat, I placed half a score of large rocks around the fire I had started to sear the fillets. Once the fish was cooked I sprinkled a bit of salt on them from my pouch. The meat went well with the roasted cattails. Jordan did not speak much while we ate but I did not mind the quiet though since I had never been much of a conversationalist. After we finished eating and burying the small fire, I carried the stones back to the stream.

"By the gods, Kyri look out!"

I spun around in time to see him raise his bow and I leaped to block his shot. "Jordan no! She will not hurt you." He lowered the bow but kept the arrow drawn. I was about to toss the fish scraps into the stream but set them on the ground for Gata instead. "Her name is Gata Anatoli and I adopted her on my trip here. She was pacing the scout troop earlier but wandered off before we met up with you."

"You really adopted a leopard cub? What prompted that?"

"Her mam attacked me and I was forced to kill her, which left the cub all alone. I could not bear the thought of leaving her behind so I took her with me. Luckily the queen let us both stay." I smiled at the image of Ori in my head. It truly was a lucky day that found me with the Telequire nation. My musings were interrupted by Jordan's deep voice.

"Ah, it looks good on you, lass."

Startled, I looked down at my leathers, wondering if he was talking about my skirt. "What?"

He chuckled. "Love! So who has finally caught your attention? Is it someone in the neighboring village, or perhaps someone in the nation itself?"

I blushed at the thought of discussing my personal love with a stranger, someone who felt like a father figure. "I, uh, it is one of my Amazon sisters."

Jordan cleared his throat. "Ah, I see. It's like that then?" I nodded. "Good for you, lass. Does she know how lucky she is to draw the attention of such a wonderful young woman?"

A strange feeling came over me, similar to the one I got when I last spoke with Torrel. It was almost as if he were taking personal responsibility for my wellbeing. I did not need his worry or responsibility but I appreciated it just the same. "She knows." I ducked my head in attempt to hide my returned blush. After that he seemed content to listen to my story while we waited for Degali to return. It hardly seemed possible that the running footsteps of my scout could occur so soon, but when I looked up to the sky I saw that the sun had indeed traveled a few candle marks across the blue expanse. The trees were not fully fleshed out and we were in a fairly sparse area in a glade next to the stream so it was pretty obvious how long we sat there. Degali's face was flushed but she seemed no worse for wear from her run to the village and back.

"Heyla Degali. Pull up a log and take a rest." I immediately handed her my water skin and took hers for refilling. When I brought it back I also dug out the leftover fish and cattails that I had wrapped in wide waxy leaves. She gratefully took the food and the added tree bar I handed to her. Tree bars were like a honey cake but they were very dense. Nuts, figs, and grain were pressed into bars that were filling and good to replace the energy used when running trees. "So what did she say? Can I bring Master Jordan into the village?"

Degali laughed around a mouthful of fish. "Goddess, Scout Leader! Do you think the queen would turn down a request from you?"

I caught Jordan's curious head tilt out of the corner of my eye and felt my ears heat up at what Degali so obviously implied. "I suppose not."

"She said that he could stay for the length of time it would take to do your Master Mark testing and that we would have a feast tomorrow night in his honor."

It was Master Jordan's turn to blush at my young scout's words. "Bow and fletch, you all don't need to go through any trouble for me."

I couldn't help the smirk that graced my face. "Sorry Jordan, but the queen's word is law." I turned to my scout. "Are you okay to continue on to meet up with the rest of the troop?"

She waved away my concerns. "I'm fine, don't worry about me. I did take second place in the distance race at spring equinox you know."

I actually did not know. "Oh, I am sorry that I did not get a chance to congratulate you then. I had no idea that any of the fourth scouts had entered that event. I just knew that you were one of my fastest. I look forward to seeing you compete at the Festival of Nations."

She smiled shyly as she stood to leave. "Thank you, Scout Leader." Jordan and I both watched her run off in the direction her troop had taken a few candle marks before. She would make good time on the ground until she caught up with them.

"She's got a bit of hero worship, doesn't she?"

I shrugged and slung my bow back across my shoulders, then shouldered my water skin. There was no need in telling him all that we had been through during the Western War. That was Amazon business. "Are you ready to see the village proper?"

He grinned at my refusal to answer his question. "I'm honored at the invitation. Lead the way."

WE WERE MET by an official escort just outside the training grounds where they brought Jordan to the queen's dais in the center of the village. I knew that the queen would assign guards to him for the duration of his stay and that he would not be allowed anywhere but the guest hut without those guards. My breath caught as we approached the raised platform. She was wearing her mask and ceremonial leathers and the flutter of attraction that skittered through my belly took me by surprise. There was something about Ori, a feeling that had been there since the first day we met, a sensation that shook me to my very core. It was a sureness of knowing that another spirit walked the path with me. My comfort came from knowing that spirit was Ori.

I stepped forward when we reached the ground in front of the dais and dropped to a knee, Jordan followed suit if only a little stiffly. When I looked up, the queen was too far away to make out the color of her eyes but her body language was easy enough to read. She looked tense and I had no idea why. Perhaps it was having a man in the village despite how harmless he seemed. "Queen Orianna, I present to you Master Fletcher Jordan. He has sought me out upon my father's dying request. He wishes to test me for the Master's Mark. I am petitioning for him to stay until my test is complete and I am petitioning for a reprieve from my duties until the time comes when I can escort him back to the edge of Telequire lands." The queen stayed silent long enough for murmuring to start, long enough for my stomach to twist with anxiety. I nearly jumped out of my feathers when she finally spoke.

"Both petitions are granted, Fourth Scout Leader. You have two full days from sun up to sunset, to complete your testing for the Master's Mark and after that your guest must leave the village." She turned toward Jordan. "My regent will go over all the rules you must follow for the entirety of your stay and we will have a feast tomorrow evening in your honor. Welcome to the Telequire Amazon nation, Master Jordan."

We both stood and Jordan did a graceful bow toward the dais. "Many thanks, Queen Orianna. I am honored to be welcomed by your nation. Wind to feather and leaf to foot, may the goddess bless your land."

I was surprised that he knew the traditional Amazon blessing, though I probably should not have been. Jordan was old enough to have traveled plenty and seen even more. The rest of the day and into that evening I spent talking to the old fletcher about my mam and my da. We took our evening meal in the guest hut and he told me many stories from before I was born and into my childhood. It helped ease some of the pain I felt at not being with da in his last moments of life. Jordan said that my da did not suffer at the end. He just had a fast pain in his chest one day and then he was gone. He made sure da was buried next to my mam and gathered a few more items he thought I would like to have. Afterwards, he went home to wait out the winter before coming to seek me out.

The next day I introduced him to the head Telequire fletcher and they were like two fish swimming the same stream. Achima showed him around her workshop then took him to meet our blacksmith, Iphigeneia. During my initial training I was told that as the size of the Telequire nation grew, the need for arrows grew as well. It made more sense for the blacksmith and her apprentices to supply all the arrowheads that the nation would need. I had used many materials for my own arrowheads, bone, antler, wood, flint, and even bronze. Iphi was very good at making the tri-lobate bronze. She told me once that she had switched over to the three-bladed bronze heads after being shot by a Scythian nearly twenty cycles before. She showed me the scar it left and I was not surprised that she studied the arrow enough to replicate the arrowhead.

I had to alter my fletching slightly to compensate when I started using her heads with my arrows. My da had always taught me that the fletch area should be three times that of the arrowhead cutting edge. I found that advice especially true through trial and error. I tried switching to smaller fletching so they did not take up so much room in my quiver, but my shots were not as accurate. Da told me that the larger the fletching was, the more it would resist the wind and would help balance a larger head.

Rather than work in my hut for the master test, Achima let us use a corner of the workshop. By law of the Fletcher's Guild, I would have to be tested in every step of the arrow making process and present a score of finished master quality arrows. I would also have to demonstrate all the different fletching techniques and use a variety of arrowheads. If Jordan was satisfied with my work, he would give me the Master's Mark on the inside of my forearm of my dominant hand. I would also be given a token as further proof that I had passed my testing. The first thing we did after leaving the workshop was head into the woods to cut a section of staves for the arrow shafts. It was necessary that I demonstrate my technique for seasoning and drying saplings, though not everyone starts with such young wood.

Because of the length of time it takes to prepare saplings staves, we were unable to use the ones I fresh cut for the finished arrows. I had some that were already dry in my hut, so I simply needed to cut the bundle apart and do my shaping and straightening. I did save a few of the new cut saplings to demonstrate the green method. Such was the only way a fletcher could work with fresh staves. For the most part, the shafts straightened the most while drying. As soon as the bark was removed I had to bend them until they look straight. The bending process was tedious because it had to be slow and gradual. Even then, some still did not take to proper bending while green and those ones I always set aside.

My preferred method is simple heat straightening. To do this I needed a candle, animal fat grease, and a straightening tool. I made my tool not long after my mam died. It was carved from antler with a single hole drilled in the large end for the shaft to go through as a leverage point. Making the hole was easy enough. Da showed me how to create a drill with an old arrow shaft and a proper size flint head. Then it was just a matter of rotating the shaft between my hands until it bit through the antler material. A fire can be made in the same manner with dried wood and tinder, minus the flint head. As with many parts of fletching, patience and light pressure were essential for success. By the time the feast started on the evening of the first full day, I had successfully selected and cut staves, demonstrated the different straightening techniques, and carved knocks into a score of straightened shafts. Jordan seemed well pleased with both my progress and my work.

"You know lass, I'm getting to be an old man. My boy went off to join the local militia and left me without an heir to my fletcher's shop. If you ever want to pursue the dream your da had for you, I'd be honored if you went into business with me."

Air rushed in and out of my open mouth and shock had nearly stopped my heart. "You do not have laws preventing women from running businesses or holding land and such?"

He burst out laughing causing Achima and her apprentice to glance toward our corner of the workshop. "Oh no, my kingdom is nothing like that. That's what happened in your homestead, right?" I nodded. "Galen told me that he would have worried for you if you would have stayed, and that you couldn't be a Master Fletcher there. But there is no such law in Macedonia." He paused. "Thrace has always been a lot more close-minded than its larger neighbor to the west. With your skill and attitude, I think you'd do quite well in my town."

I was flattered and very much honored that he would ask me to join him. For a hardworking man like Jordan it was no small thing to ask another, a woman nearly two score cycles younger, to take over the thing he had put his heart and soul into. And as much as I would like to say I was tempted, I really was not. I had already found my heart and soul and it was with the Telequire nation. It was with Ori. There was no way I could simply turn him down outright though. The gravity of his offer demanded the same level of consideration in return. "I am deeply honored, Master Jordan. Please allow me to think on the offer you have made me. It would be no small decision as I have made a home and family here with the Telequire nation. May I give you my answer tomorrow?"

He waved a hand through the air. "Of course, of course. I understand it would be a big decision for you. I just want you to know that the offer is open. I really have no one to leave my business to, and you seem to be a highly capable and talented young woman. And well, to be honest Galen once did me a large service and truthfully it's only half paid off by my testing you for the Master's Mark. Just let me know before I leave tomorrow."

I nodded. "I will, and thank you again."

After leaving Jordan and his guards at the guest hut, I went off in search of my own to get ready for the evening feast. It was not a real Amazon celebration, merely a way to show visitors to the nation that we were prosperous with food and joy. Shana caught up with me just outside my door. Everything had moved so fast from the morning before that I had not found a chance to talk with her at all. "Heyla Kyri, are you excited to finally get your Master's Mark?"

My smile came unbidden at the thought of finally achieving da's dream for me. I waved her into my hut. "I am excited. I know that it is not something that I will really need as an Amazon but it is just..." I was at a loss, unsure how to explain the reasons why I wanted the mark. It was not just for my da, and it was not because my role as an Amazon would be any different.

"You need to prove to yourself that you are indeed a fletcher, that you could live up to your family legacy."

I looked at her in surprise, though I probably should not have been shocked to hear the perfect words come out of her mouth. "That is it exactly. I want to do this in honor of my da, but I also need to do this to carry on the legacy of my fletcher roots. And perhaps if, um, if I ever have a child of my own, then maybe the legacy can be carried further."

Her hand felt warm on my bare arm and her smile was kind. "I understand, sister. Have you spoken with Ori since yesterday?"

The little worm of worry that had been in the back of my mind wandered toward the front. "No, I was with Master Jordan until late yesterday evening so I went back to my own hut for sleep. I thought she might come by today while he was testing me but I have not seen her. It almost feels as if she is avoiding me. Do you think she is angry that I brought a man to the village?"

Shana shook her head. "It can't be that. She's spent plenty of time at the Centaur village. Her sister is married to a man, after all. And it's not unusual to have the occasional male visitor here. Perhaps you should ask her before the feast."

"Maybe I should. I will do it after I clean up. I also want to share with her the news that Master Jordan offered for me to take over his fletching business since he has no heir trained as a fletcher. He said he owed my da a big favor but that it would be doing more of a favor for him since he did not want his life's work to disappear after he is gone. I am not going to go, of course, but I am still honored that he asked me. I promised to give him an answer tomorrow."

Shana smirked. "Well you probably don't need to tell her at all. I'm sure she already knows."

She was making no sense. "How would Ori already know? He only just asked me before I came back to my hut."

My sister rested her hand on my forearm. "Seriously, you don't know? Kyri, she's the queen. If there is a stranger in the village that is under guard you can bet that she knows every word that is said in their presence. Her guards would report on the different conversations, which means she already knows about his offer."

For whatever reason, her words did not stomp out that tendril of worry. If anything, her words made it grow. While I did not give an answer to him right away, she could not possibly think I would leave. She must have known that my heart could thrive no place else. Shana's look stopped my anxious thoughts from blossoming. I did not want to explain all my fears to her. Giving them voice would surely only make the anxiety worse. In the end I stayed silent. We agreed to meet up at the feast and I left in search of Ori.

I checked the council chambers first but the guard there said the queen had gone to spar with Kylani. At the training rings near the edge of the village, Kylani said I had just missed her, that Ori had gone to clean up before the feast. After more than a half candle mark of walking, I finally found her in the smallest bathing pool. I only knew she was there because Gata was sprawled on the ground outside the entrance. The half-grown leopard gave a stuttering purr as she rubbed against my legs and jumped up to put her front paws on my thighs. I could not help laughing when she nearly knocked me over. "You are getting too big for such cub love!" I pushed open the large sewn hide that covered the entrance to the small cave. The heat immediately weighed me down as I stepped inside. When I finally caught a glimpse of her in the pool I smiled at the way her short hair was slicked back from her face. I could see a bruise on her arm in the light of the flickering torches. I could also make out a thin cut on her shoulder. It showed enough red for me to know it still oozed sluggishly. "May I enter?"

She looked at me for a heartbeat, like she was trying to find out the answer to a question she had not yet asked. Before I could grow too concerned she gave me a nod and went back to soaping her skin. I stood there transfixed, marveling at the beauty of the one who could love me, of the person whom I could love more than any other. She broke my reverie with a soft voice. "Well, are you coming in?"

I suddenly felt shy again, like it was our first day meeting. "I, uh, did not bring a drying cloth."

"We can share." I swallowed and still hesitated. The look on her face was different and I did not understand it. "Kyri," Her voice was still soft, but more urgent. "I want to feel you."

With a throat so dry, trying to swallow my nervousness was near impossible. Instead I removed the clothes I had so recently put on and slowly walked down the carved stone steps of the recessed pool. She watched me like a panther watches a roe dear in the wood and I felt vulnerable. Shana once said that Ori was all fire and wind. She may have meant it in reference to her policies as queen, but it was true in other ways as well. My queen was not fire in the same way as Coryn and those like her. Hers was not a flame to burn you up, then move on to consume another as fuel. No, Orianna's fire was passion and it consumed us both.

Once I reached the center I dropped below the surface to wet myself completely. When I came up again she was right in front of me and the breath caught in my throat. I still did not understand the look in her eyes and she gave me no opportunity to ask. She slid against me, her hands stoking the flame in my body hotter than the water in which we stood. Her lips and teeth spoke to me in the silence of the cave and my moaning was needy in the wake of her touch. There was no time for worries or concerns. There was only Ori's passion, remaking me from the inside out. Much too soon the conflagration took me completely and I cried out into the humid air and flickering torchlight. After catching my breath I tried to return the attention she had given me but she stepped away.

"We have to go, Kyri. The feast will start soon." She waded through the pool toward the steps leaving me trembling in surprise. Was she serious? She had just shown me colored sky after a rain. She held my soul cradled in her hands and just walked away. Somewhere understanding had been lost.

"Ori? What is wrong?"

She did not meet my eyes. She simply dried with the cloth she had brought and began to dress. "There is nothing wrong but we both have to go. We can talk later." With that she left me in the cave, in the water, and in the sadness that confusion and anxiety had created. There was a sickness growing in my belly and it had nothing to do with the heat of the bathing pool. It was not even the fact that she had just left me, rejecting my returned love and touch. It was because she had broken her word to me. I knew every finger's width of Ori's skin. I knew her expressions and all the colors of her eyes for each emotion she had graced me with. But with her answer she did not show me her eyes, and when the words left her lips there was a tightness around her mouth that I had never seen. There was something wrong and she stood mere paces from me weaving false words instead of true. Queen Orianna had broken her promise and lied to me.

I finished washing, but nothing would remove the feel of her touch from my skin. Afterwards I dressed for our meal in Jordan's honor though the mere thought of food made me feel sick. The evening plodded on like tired oxen at the end of the day. I introduced Master Jordan to some of the other craftswomen of the village and to Kylani. He even showed Margoli some of the arrowhead samples he kept in a pouch at his side. Their shape was slightly different than the ones made by our own blacksmith. Jordan said they flew truer and held a better edge than the style used by our village. Eventually they struck up a bargain for him to share knowledge with Iphi, and in exchange we promised to buy two full shipments of the arrowheads he had in stock. His workshop was not so far away in Macedonia that the trade would be unprofitable. Everyone seemed happy with the deal.

Throughout the feast, no matter where I took Jordan, I could feel Ori's eyes on me. She never came down off the dais and I was immediately reminded of my Amazon confirmation. It hurt me enough then when she tried to pull away, but it was agony for her to do it again after everything we had shared. Eventually I wandered until the dais was out of sight. Before Jordan retired for the evening he came to find me.

"Kyri! Just the person I was looking for." I took in his face and wondered why he sought me out. "I nearly forgot to remind you that there is a fee for membership into the Fletcher's Guild."

My stomach dropped at his words. "I—I do not have any coins left. I was hoping to find the time to travel to the next village over and trade rabbit furs and arrows for coin."

He laughed. "Well that will work too." He continued at the confused look on my face. "If you trust me, your goods shouldn't be too much extra weight on my mule. I'll simply take with me what you need to meet the fee and sell them myself. It would save you a trip."

It seemed almost too perfect, like the gods were watching over me. "Really? That is very generous of you, Jordan. Thank you."

He gave me a sly wink. "Of course, if you say yes to my offer you can always come with me."

The heartbeat that my thoughts raced in circles turned into a candle drop and more. Finally I knew I would have to answer and follow my heart. "As much as I appreciate your offer, my heart and my life is here. I do not think I can follow my old dream of being a fletcher any longer. Since I left my da, since becoming an Amazon, my life has opened in new and exciting ways. I am more than a fletcher. I have become an archer when I was needed and I learned that I would give my life to protect the people around me, to protect my Amazon family. I can no more leave behind these trees than I could leave behind my own heart. So I am going to have to decline. I am sorry."

He nodded but gave me a smile anyway. "I had a feeling that's what you'd say and I'm sorry too, lass. I know what it's like to find your dreams shifting before your very eyes, and I wish you all the best." His disappointment was obvious.

A thought unfurled in my head and I put my hand on his arm to stop him from turning away. I was not sure if it was my place to say but I knew of someone who might be able to help him out. "Have you heard of Torrel, the Master Fletcher and Bower in Kozani?"

"Why yes, I met him and your da back in my tournament days. Why?"

"Well he has a handful of apprentices working for him. Some he said were studying to be a bower and fletcher, but a few were only studying one or the other. He mentioned having so many was more than he could handle but also said something about owing his cousin a favor. Maybe you can stop by Kozani after you leave here and see if he would let one of them apprentice to you."

Jordan scratched at his head for a few heartbeats then his craggy face broke out into a solid grin. "That's a wonderful idea. I think I'll do just that. I'm actually not too far from Kozani so any apprentice he has wouldn't be hard put to switch to me. They'd still see their families often." With a clap to my shoulder he seemed genuinely relieved at my suggestion.

I knew he was ready to head back to the guest hut for the evening and I could see Ori approaching from the direction of the dais so I wanted to wrap up our conversation. "Before you go, I just wanted you to know that I will have my things packed on the mule tomorrow afternoon. I know you said you wanted to leave as soon as my testing is complete so I thought that would be a good time."

"Yes, yes, that's fine. Okay, it's off to bed for this old man. I'll see you in the morning Kyri."

"Morpheus soothe you, Master Jordan." I watched him walk away and turned to speak with Ori, but she was gone. Once again, she had run from me and my heart was getting tired of the pain.

Chapter Ten

Bond and Brand

WITH BOTH THE queen and Jordan gone from my sight, there was nothing left at the celebration for me. I needed some time to myself so I took off for the trees at the edge of the village. I could no longer bear Ori's looks and indifference and I had been unable to clear her false words from my head. The darkness was growing and the moon just rising so I was careful when I entered the forest. My faithful leopard friend joined me not long after. I had found a large branch to perch on, one that gave me a good view of the bonfire in the village center though it was hard to make out more than dim shapes dancing around it. Too many thoughts crowded my head and I needed the comfort of the trees to ease my aching spirit. Gata had stretched out next to me along the length of the branch of the great oak I was seated in.

Ori's behavior unsettled me. The only explanation was that she must have thought that I would accept Jordan's offer and leave the Telequire nation. I wanted to find her and explain but two things stopped me. The first was the thought that maybe she did not care whether or not I left, that she had changed her mind about our courtship. Why else would she stay silent if she thought I was leaving? The other concern was that even if she still wanted me to stay, she had lied to me. She had broken her oath and word to always speak true. How could I reconcile that with the pureness of the maxim I had always known from her? How could I trust her to always speak truth in the future? As queen, she held all the power and prestige between us. The only thing that made us equals was the honesty in our hearts. Without that honesty, what did we really have? I was startled from my thoughts by a voice higher in the canopy, to my right.

"I'm sorry."

I immediately knew the reasons for her earlier actions with me, by the tone of her voice and the fact that she sought me out in the trees. When she had done so before, it was because she felt sorrow and guilt for being drawn to me, not wanting to pull me from the path I was on when I first became an Amazon. She did not want to pressure me into returning her interest and at the time I simply thought that she regretted the fact that we were so drawn together. It seemed like an entirely different life when I looked back and saw how I had no proper sense of self-worth when it came to my place in the nation. I had no idea how bound we both were to each other.

As I looked up at Ori my stomach seized with the knowledge that things were different from that last time. I was stung by her lie and the hurt swelled inside me. "You lied to me. You hid behind your stoicism and silence and when I asked what was wrong you treated me to untruths. I have no wish to be in a courtship where we cannot speak honestly to each other."

Though I could not see the expression on her face in the darkness, I heard her gasp at my words. "Kyri, please. I was afraid. I was afraid that you would leave."

I stood abruptly, my anger making it impossible to keep still. Gata jumped to the forest loam below, perhaps deciding she did not like the tone of our voices. "What possible reason do you have to be afraid? I have always spoken truth to you. Since our courtship began, I have given everything to you, my heart, my body, and my future! And to have you pull away from me physically and emotionally, to have you lie—" I could not stop my voice from breaking on those painful words, and I could not stop the sob that followed them. But I spoke what was in my heart because she needed to know, even if the words felt heavy like crushing stones. I did not want to cry. I did not want to be nothing more than a hurt girl. I wanted to rail and scream out my pain but I knew that would not solve our problems. I waited for a candle drop in the silence and when she did not speak I decided to just go back to my hut. I swung down from my branch to the ferns below and had taken only a step when I heard her land behind me.

"Kyri, wait!"

I did not bother facing her. "Wait for what, more untruths? I am tired and I would rather just go home to my bed." I took another step and was surprised to be forcibly turned around and pinned to the trunk of the oak next to me.

Ori's strong hands were on my biceps holding me in place and her eyes were wild. "Goddess, no! Please, Kyri! I pledge that there will be no more untruths from me."

The rough bark stung where it dug into my bare skin and I shivered at the sensation of her holding me in place. I liked it and I did not want to. She had hurt me and I wanted to stay angry. I was unsure if I would be strong enough make her see that it was not okay to treat me so poorly. I was afraid that it would only take a single look to make me forget about the pain in my heart and become a slave to her desires. I tried to let anger color my voice, but that was not the emotion that caused my words to come out sounding more like a pained growl. "Let me go." My heart raced and I needed to get away in order to maintain my balance.

"Hera's tits, but you're stubborn! Please, listen to me! You can't do that if you run away."

Ori was so close to me that I could feel the heat from her body against mine. The hammering heart in my chest told me that if I did not get away right at that moment I would be lost again and I was not sure I could survive more lies. "Please, just let me go—"

She cut me off and her anger only made my situation worse. "That's what I'm trying to tell you if you'd only listen. I can't let you go, Kyri!" Her grip in my arms increased as she drew herself closer and her words came out in a desperate rush. "You are as much a part of me as the blood in my veins or the limbs on my body. To lose you would be to lose a part of myself and I was afraid of losing you! But instead of saying anything I stayed quiet. I've been so used to keeping my own council in such personal matters that I was unable to speak my fears aloud. And when you called me on it, I panicked. I knew it was a mistake and I knew that I should have talked to you about what I was feeling but I also knew how important that childhood dream of being a fletcher was to you. I can only say I'm sorry and hope you don't leave."

We were both breathing hard, hers triggered by the fight reflex. I had seen it in hunted animals many times. And I know that mine was all about flight. I wanted to escape. I wanted to not feel all the emotions that were coursing through me. But I could not run. Instead, I stared down into her stormy green eyes and pulled her closer. Our lips met hard as we both fought for control of the kiss. It was not a battle to be won or lost. It was about communication of the most basic kind. It was about one heart speaking to another and coming to an understanding. When lack of breath forced us apart she leaned her head against my chest, panting. "Ori, I could no more leave you than I could leave my heart on the forest floor at my feet."

"But I heard—"

I cut her off before she could tread any further down the road of worry and assumption. "You heard a small part of a much larger conversation. Jordan asked me if I wanted to return with him and take over his shop since he has no heirs who are fletchers. I turned him down, Ori. I suggested he speak with Torrel from Kozani, who has apprentices to spare. He also said I would need to come up with my mastership fee for the fletcher's guild. Since I had no more coins he agreed to take equivalent value of my furs and arrows to sell in the next town, to cover my fee." I took a deep breath and forced her back slightly so she could look at me. "You keep assuming at every turn that I do not know my own heart, that I will simply change my mind like some sort of irresolute child. You either love the woman I am or you do not. But stop making assumptions about me!"

In a move that nearly stopped my heart, one that dropped my stomach down to my knees, she stepped away from me and out of my arms. My body mourned the loss of hers and I feared the worst. Shana had warned me that Ori could have a stubborn temper when her honesty or motive was called into question and I could not read the look she had on her face as she cast her eyes skyward. Night had finally fallen full and the woods were dark with the exception of the three-quarter moon that had risen high above.

I waited as she reached for me, wondering what she could be thinking, afraid of what she was feeling. When she moved her hand to the thong of my rite of caste feather I thought for sure she was sending me away. I wanted to scream and run from those questing hands. Willing the night to swallow me whole, I was frozen and unable to move. All I could do was close my eyes and resign myself to the lot the fates had woven for me. It seemed like an eternity before she moved her hand away again, taking my future with it. The trembling began at the realization that I no longer had a home or family, that I no longer had my heart.

Heartbeats lingered for an eternity before her voice broke through the fearful pounding in my head. "Goddess, Kyri, but hold still. You'll make it impossible for me to tie this."

Her words made no sense. I opened my eyes then because confusion was a black thing and I needed to see. Why was my feather tied into her hair? Why was she holding her own rite of caste feather out to me? While very similar bird of prey feathers, the main difference was obvious. Each right of caste feather had at least one bead strung onto thong that held shaft to hair. The bead was always the color of the Amazon's eyes. The feather in her hand was corded with the most beautiful green bead, which was then topped by three bravery beads. I could not actually see the true colors in the darkness but I knew it as well as I knew my own. "Ori?"

She stared at me in the moonlight, looking so serious. "Kyri Fletcher, will you accept my feather as you have accepted my heart?" Her feather. She wanted to exchange feathers with me. As I tried to process her intentions a slight trembling of her bottom lip caught my eye and I knew she waited on me to answer.

"Yes, yes, yes!" Then I stood there while she tied her feather into my hair with shaking hands. My surety returned with the weight of her commitment to me. It was more than a simple pledge between us, it was her acknowledgment that she accepted me for all that I was and all that I was not. I did not care that she was the Telequire queen nor that she was my queen specifically. It was not the queen's feather in my hair, it was Ori's. My heart had been made whole again. We kissed with our feathers reversed and I swore then that it felt different. We kissed until the cooling night air forced us apart to seek warmer comforts. In her hut that night I lost track of how many times we traded favors, of how many whispered words of love were spoken, but I never lost track of her. With the exchange of our caste feathers, our futures were even more bound together. Our paths were as one.

THE NEXT DAY went faster than I expected. Ori was with me when Jordan passed me into mastership and I received my bronze guild token. She also held my hand as he seared the arrow brand into the skin of my inner forearm. I clamped my teeth onto the wood of an arrow to deal with the pain of it. Afterwards he rubbed a numbing salve on the mark and wrapped it gently with some cloth. I rode Soara when I escorted him from Telequire lands later that afternoon and I found myself sad to see him leave. Before he continued up the road toward the main trade road of Macedonia, we both dismounted to say our goodbyes. I embraced him just as I had done with Torrel so many moons before. I felt a kinship with the two men who reminded me so much of the family I had lost. Perhaps it was the fact that both of them were fletchers like the man I had grown up with or perhaps it was their air of responsibility, but I felt kinship nonetheless. It was because of that familiarity that I sincerely hoped he found the apprentice he searched for within the town of Kozani.

As I turned to ride back into the forest and back to the village, the wind kicked up. Out of the corner of my eye I caught the familiar green glint as Ori's rite of caste feather danced with my hair in the breeze. I temporarily forgot about the throbbing pain in my right arm and thought only of my life as an Amazon. For the first time I was glad I had meetings the next day with Margoli, Coryn, and the other scout leaders. I wanted a chance for my arm to heal a bit before heading back out into the trees. But more importantly I wanted to spend another night with Ori and bask in our bond. No one had noticed the fact that we had exchanged feathers but I knew it was only a matter of time until more questions would be asked.

The next morning dawned gray with a fine mist soaking everything in the village and trees. The rain made me even happier about the meeting that would keep us inside the scout hut for a few candle marks. Ori and I showed up together in the meal lodge, which was no longer an uncommon sight. We sat down to eat first meal with Basha and Coryn who already had full dishes of food. A quarter candle mark later we were joined by Steffi, Shana, and a very sleepy looking Deka. I imagined that Dina probably just stayed awake in order to make the meeting with Margoli but Deka, being the Second Scout Leader, probably did not get to sleep until late after her shift was done. Shana, who was seated next to her gave the woman a light jog with her elbow. "Heyla Deka, I don't normally see you with the early birds. What has you up before the worm?"

The tired woman accepted the ribbing and stifled another yawn with her fist. "Scout leaders have a meeting with Margoli this morning." She glanced over at my amber-eyed friend. "Question is, Ambassador, what are you doing here so early? Did you flap that diplomatic yap in your sleep and get kicked out of bed by one of your owl friends?"

The large table erupted with laughter and Shana shot me a look of consternation. "Kyri Fletcher, don't you dare laugh! That phrase is all your fault and everyone seems to have heard of it now. Thanks a lot, friend." Her words only made us laugh even more. Shana turned to Coryn and tried to pretend that she was not the butt of all our laughter. "Is this about the annual trade caravan to Preveza?"

The attractive leader of the scouts nodded. "Yes. Margoli wants to put together teams for escorting the wagons to the coast."

"Oh goddess! I forgot about that." Deka set her eating knife down and thumped her forehead with the heel of her hand. "Everyone hates caravan duty and we're going to be forced to recommend people as guards."

The Second Scout Leader's words lifted my spirits even more. "Wait, there is a trade group going out? When does the caravan leave? How long will they be gone, and who can volunteer?" I felt Ori stiffen beside me but she did not say anything.

Deka threw her hands in the air. "Goddess, Kyri. Only you would be interested in such dull stuff." Chuckles went around the table and it was Steffi that answered my questions.

"Every sun-cycle the Telequire tribe sends a caravan to the great agora in Preveza. It's a port town and we do good business there. The nation sends community produced goods for sale, to fill the nation's coffers. We also carry personally produced items to sell for the sisters. There is a percentage that the nation taxes for the goods since it adds expense and drains resources to allot extra space for those personal items. You understand so far?"

I stuck my tongue out at her. "I did not do so poorly in my training with you. Yes, it all makes sense, thank you."

She continued when the laughter at my comment died down. "Anyway, it's about five days of travel there by wagon and we spend a score of days at the market before returning. Are you interested in sending items for sale, Kyri?"

I nodded because I actually had quite a few items I was hoping to sell. Not only had I been amassing supple rabbit furs over the previous few moons, but I had made two more basic leaf-type cloaks and ten score of plain fletched arrows. As a master fletcher I was free to sell the arrows at market for full price. That was one of the reasons I was able to give Jordan arrows as part of my guild fee payment. "I have some furs, plain stock arrows, and a couple cloaks I want to try out at market. I also would like to go and see the agora for myself. How are the guards chosen?" Deka snorted again and mumbled something about crazy featherheads.

Coryn set her eating knife down. "We take volunteers first, as long as Kylani approves of their bow and sword skills. After that, it's up to us and Margoli to submit the names of good guard candidates."

"Kyri—" I turned to my right to look at Ori and Shana practically exploded across the table from me. I had forgotten about the new feather I wore in my hair, but the green bead had become quite obvious to my sister-friend once she saw my profile. Whatever words Ori had for me were lost to Shana's exclamation.

"Holy Artemis!" Her mouth dropped open as she pointed at my feather, then at the queen's. "They've traded feathers!" The rest of the table all craned their heads to look, and even some tables beyond. Being the center of attention was something I did not enjoy and Shana knew it. I kicked her under the table and shot her a displeased look for good measure. As she leaned down to rub her shin she looked contrite, but still shocked. The rising volume of voices threatened to drown out all other conversation.

I was not sure if I was happier or more horrified when Ori stood and turned to address the entire lodge. "For all of you that have been living under a rock for the past moon or so, Kyri and I have been courting. And yes, last night we exchanged feathers. End of story." She sat back down to silence. The tone of her voice let the rest of the meal hut know that they should take their questions and speculations elsewhere. Unfortunately the table of our immediate friends had no such intentions.

Steffi spoke first. "My queen, you know the council will want to meet on this." Her words trailed off and I had a sinking feeling in my stomach as Ori nodded in agreement. It was then that my floating, flitting heart was brought back down to solid earth. Sometimes it was easy to forget that the love we held so close between us affected more than just two. Ori was queen, and with that came a lot of responsibility for both her and her future bond mate. By exchanging feathers with me she had pledged more than just a casual affair. While we could not actually be truly bonded without a proper period of betrothal and ceremony, the council would see us heading in that direction. And it was the council that would bestow official Consort status on the queen's chosen one. There was no denying that I still had doubts of my worthiness. My fears were assuaged somewhat when Ori squeezed my hand beneath the table.

"I'm well aware of what the council will want to meet on Steffi. I'll take care of it." Her tone indicated to the table that the matter was closed, for now. I was glad of that because I wanted more time to deal with the implications and ramifications of her decision, of our decision. She leaned toward me once the attention of our sisters wandered elsewhere. "Are you sure you want to go on the trade mission? You would be gone for nearly a moon."

I felt a pang at the thought of being away from Ori for so long but I was also resolute in my decision. "Though it pains me to say yes, I really do want to go. I wish you were going too but I understand that you cannot. Now that I am a master fletcher I can sell my goods on the open market and get more coins for them. And I know that I could just send my things along to be sold for a small tax, but I need more material than what I have here if I want to make more cloaks. I also want to walk through the agora and see if some of the goods there will give me ideas for what to make next. You know they can use my bow on the way there and back.

Please say you understand."

She smiled but there were lines of pain around her eyes even as she spoke positively. "Yes, I do understand. But I will miss you every day that you're gone."

Before we could discuss more we were interrupted by Coryn. "Kyri, we have to leave now if we're going to be on time for the meeting."

I looked up, startled that so much time had passed. "Oh, sorry Coryn. I just need to take care of my dish." Before I could rise Ori pulled me into another tender kiss. We both sighed as the touch of our lips ended, but I had to go. "Can we talk more this evening?" She nodded and I walked toward the door with the other two scout leaders, depositing my dish in the collection basket on my way.

In the meeting I learned that the caravan was set to depart in a fortnight. We had some names of women already interested in guard duty and the scout leaders would go through their ranks looking for more. I thought about how different caravan guard duty would be compared to that of a scout. I was not surprised that many were loath to volunteer. Amazon scouts were most at home in the trees, not on the hot dusty road on the back of a horse or wagon. I hated the thought of leaving Ori for so long but there was a big part of me that was ready for an adventure. Another reason I was glad to go was because it would allow me to get some good riding time in on Soara. I knew she would be good on the trip because she was dependable and fairly unflappable. She had proven herself to be a good one to stay calm in tense situations.

I did not see Ori after the meeting but she had sent a runner to me asking if I would take evening meal in her hut. Because I was so often living on the edge, we tried to take advantage of all my nights spent in the village. Our relationship was still new and every opportunity we had to reconnect and renew our bond was the greatest of treasures. There was a tiny bit of worry that tightened my gut at the thought that she would not be happy about me going away on the trade mission. But we had both come to agree that I needed to live fully in order to feel as though I were a contributing member of the tribe, to feel as if I truly deserved the honor of the queen's love. Well, maybe it was just me that had come to the agreement and she humored me because she truly wanted me to be happy.

THE NIGHT BEFORE the caravan was scheduled to leave, I made my way to Ori's hut and could not keep from smirking when I saw the new addition to the side of her dwelling. She opened the door and immediately wrapped me in a fierce hug. The kiss that followed tightened things all over my body and sped my heartbeat beyond what it should be for a simple dinner. When we pulled back from each other I grinned and looked toward the new door that had been cut into the wall. "I see you have finally seen the benefits of the 'Gata door.'"

Her laugh was full of light and melody and it was a sound that I knew I would miss the entire time I was gone. "Yes, I have finally accepted the notion that we are both a pair of fools for giving in to that spoiled leopard." She hesitated for a heartbeat as a shadow seemed to pass over her eyes. "I wish more than anything that you could take her with you. Actually, I wish I could go myself. I have a bad feeling about this trip, Kyri—"

I gently covered her lips with two fingers. "Shh, it is going to be fine Ori. I really need to check out the agora and see about making some extra coins with my wares. And I also want to see the things that are available at the market to find new ideas for my cloaks. The benefit and my own usefulness cannot be questioned. Neither can my safety. You've said it yourself, Telequire makes this trip every cycle so there is nothing to worry about, my queen."

She growled, and it came out as a cute sound rather than menacing. "God's be damn you, it is Ori—hey, why do your fingers smell like honey?" Taking a page from Shana's book, I wiggled my eyebrows at her and she swatted me in the stomach before heading over to the table to lay out dinner.

"Well, it may have something to do with what is wrapped in cloth in my pouch." She spun around and her eyes lit with a surprised gleam.

"You brought honey cakes?"

I shrugged, pleased to make her happy. "What kind of going away is it if we do not have some sort of treat?"

She crossed the short distance between us and once again wrapped me in a fierce hug. Her words were soft and serious and I knew immediately there was no innuendo intended. "My treat is you. I'm going to miss you desperately."

With hands as gentle as I could make them, I cradled her face. The words came straight from my heart. "A moon is nothing but a drop in the sky. You realize that my heart will be back soaring through the Telequire trees before you even know I have been gone."

She pressed my hand to her cheek, eyes shutting out the world around us. "My love, every single heartbeat of every day that you are gone from me will be an eternity of loss. I don't think you realize just how much of my heart you've claimed."

The air went out of my lungs and I closed my eyes in the face of such love. "You honor me."

We stood there for a few heartbeats longer before she slowly pulled away. "We should eat."

Her abrupt mood change baffled me. "Why the rush?"

One look from those green eyes of hers brought it all into focus. "Because I have plans for you and I'd like to get to them sooner rather than later, fourth scout." I chuckled and nearly swallowed my tongue when she spoke again. "Tell me, have you been practicing your knot work like I suggested?"

"Ori?"

She merely gave me a mischievous smile in return and my heart raced with anticipation. Dinner was tasty, if fast done, and our honey cakes became a sticky mess of teasing expectation. Candle marks later, after we had sated both our bodies and our hearts, I lay in the bed watching Ori sleep. She maintained her worry lines even while in Morpheus's realm and I knew that my pending absence was going to affect her sorely. We were both aware that it was nothing more than a trade trip but it would still be the longest we had been apart since equinox eve.

Even though our love felt older than the language we used to speak the words, it still had the shine of newness about it. My heart sorrowed for my absence and my body ached for her as if she were not lying next to me in the night. It was because of my need and the pending ache of loss that I could not still my hands through her hair. It was because we balanced on the precipice of separation that I had to tell her goodbye one last time. With lips and the practiced hand of soft caresses, I roused her to wakefulness once again. In the dull light of the dimly flickering oil lamp her eyes held sleepy confusion before registering the insistent touch of my questing fingers. It was there, when the moon was high and sleep the last thing on our minds, that we connected again. Like flame to fresh candlewick, we burned bright and longer into the night than good sense dictated. But the morning's ride would be an easy one for the first part of our journey and I had done more on less plenty of times before. The solace of sleep was a worthy sacrifice for a few last moments with my queen. I knew that if the world ended with the rising sun we would die content.

Chapter Eleven

The Promise

THE AIR CHILLED our skin at first light and I was glad for the cloak my mam had made for me sun-cycles before. I decided to leave the fall pattern behind and take my familiar green because I knew it would blend better with the spring leaves. I had packed the few completed cloaks, rabbit furs, and all my finished master quality arrows onto the supply wagons the previous day, so all that was left to do in the morning would be to saddle Soara and say my goodbyes. My mare stood placidly nearby with saddle and bags in place. I hung my spare fourth scout quiver from the pommel for easy use though I sincerely hoped we would not need such an extreme amount of arrows for the trip. But living on the edge taught me to be prepared. I had both daggers in my boots and sword in a sheath down my spine. Finally, my quiver and bow were slung crisscross against my back in their usual manner.

Shana was already mounted nearby, waiting for the rest to move. I had been pleasantly surprised to learn that she was going on the trade trip as well. I questioned Ori to see if she had sent Shana along as the Telequire ambassador, or as my friend. She assured me that Telequire had to renew their trade agreement with Preveza and that as ambassador, Shana was the correct one to represent the nation. Either way, I was excited to have my closest friend and near-sister along for the trip. I thought perhaps the moon's absence away from my queen would not be so bad with the right company.

I turned away from my horse and gear and sucked in a breath at the nearness of the one person who cradled my heart so tight. My gut clenched at the sadness in Ori's eyes and I ached to take that anticipated pain away. I held out my arms and that was all it took for her to throw herself into my embrace. We perhaps held each other too long, and yet it was not nearly long enough. I meant to give her the softest of kisses to remember me by but our mouths and hearts demanded a greater sacrifice. When we were forced apart by the need for air, I blushed nearly crimson at the catcalls and whistles that cheered our desperate behavior. With a shaking hand, she cradled my cheek and I could see all the emotions reflected in her watery green eyes. "Promise you'll come back. Swear to me, by leaf and by arrow, that you will return."

I laughed, hoping to diffuse some of the sadness of my departure. I also recognized the very words I had said to her moons before as she rode off to fight in the Western War. "My queen, it is a harmless trade mission and less than a moon."

She shook her head, refusing to be bated from solemnity. "Promise me, Kyri. Promise."

As I met her gaze with my own, I knew that the words that left my lips would be important, perhaps more important than the promise I had made to my da to live free, or my pledge as a Master Fletcher, and possibly surpassing my own pledge to honor queen and nation when I received my rite of caste feather. I knew that the words I spoke to answer her were more than a few words that meant something to some people. What came from my mouth would also come from my heart and the words would mean everything to just one.

I smiled and deposited featherlight kisses to her brow, her cheek, and the corner of her lips. "By leaf and by arrow, I will return to you just as I left. As Artemis is my witness, I will hold you in my heart every moment that I'm away." I paused after reciting her own words back to her. "I will always return to you, Ori. Always." She nodded once then turned and walked away. I did not take it personally. I knew she had to deal with my absence in her own way just as I dealt with her departure the day they all went to war. Gata also waited nearby, looking like she was ready to come with us. I shook my head and pointed in the direction that Ori had gone. "Gata, stay with Ori. Stay Gata." With one last look at me, she too disappeared around the corner of the nearest supply hut. Watching my lover and dear leopard friend walk away left me feeling curiously alone.

Shana rode next to me as we made our way down the road leading south toward Ioannina. She let me sit in silence until we broke from the forest proper and her quiet voice snapped me from my reverie. "This is hard for her. Ori has always been the independent one, keeping her own council on most things close to her heart. I think your leaving so soon after exchanging feathers has really cast a shadow over her days." I shot her an angry look for making me feel guilty but she quickly waved it away. "I'm not trying to make you feel bad about leaving, Kyri. This trip will be very good for you on a lot of levels. I'm merely trying to explain why she is so very sad about you going on a relatively short and harmless journey."

"I am coming back."

She smiled. "She knows that too. But I think she worries, much the way a mother will worry when her child takes their first steps alone. I'm not saying she thinks of you as a child but rather she sees how new and fragile your bond is and worries for that."

I thought for a few heartbeats and nodded. "I guess that makes sense. We both have our fears and insecurities about the shape and strength of this love between us."

She caught my attention again with a tap to my foot from her own. "But hey, at least we're on the road together again. We made a pretty good team last time, right?"

Shana's mood proved infectious and I smiled at her upbeat comment. "Yes, we did."

The first leg of the journey was mundane. Each day we traveled with guards wary and alert. There were enough scouts to rotate every two candle marks at night, so no one had to be without much sleep. The entire group took turns setting up camp, taking care of the horses, hunting, and cooking meals. Our group was fairly small, two score in total, half that being scouts charged with guarding the traders and merchandise. It was no wonder few brigands chose to mess with us on the road. Not many would want to confront a force of Amazons with bows in hand.

Besides Shana and all the scouts, we had waggoneers, two cooks, hostlers, and a few other specialists. Semina, a second level healer, had come along to provide support for the group as well as to look for more medical supplies and scrolls to bring back to the nation. Kylani sent along her second in command to check out the new weapons. Cyerma had instructions to bring back anything that looked promising for the weapon master's perusal. Steffi's Second, Iva, was also along as the money and record keeper as well as help negotiate the best deals for nation's produced goods.

We made good time along the southerly route and reached the outskirts of Preveza before sundown on the fifth day. Shana, Iva, and six scouts went into the city proper to negotiate for our agora space and the rest of us set up camp in the allotted area just off the road. As ranking scout for the trip, I went over the rules while the others were away. The agora was open from sunup to sundown each day. Anyone going in had to stay in pairs since no edged weapons longer than a small eating dagger were allowed in the market place. There would be two scouts posted at the exit closest to our camp and all Amazons were to check in with those scouts at the end of the day. Iva and Shana were slotted to have three escorts each at all times, and the rest of the scouts would be split between guarding our stalls in the agora and guarding the wagons.

I set up a rotation for the scouts since no one wanted the same duty every day that we would be in Preveza. Our small camp was actually near the top of a hill, just before it sloped toward the buildings and harbor below. If I shaded my eyes from the sun I could make out the abundance of ships sitting in the glittering blue waters of the Ionian Sea. The breeze was steady and smelled strongly of salt and fish. Pocori was first to mention the heavy stench of the city and rotting sea life.

"Ugh, how can they stand to live here? Give me the clean trees and streams of the forest any day."

More than a few agreed with her and I grinned knowing they would be in the heart of it the next morning. Despite the heat and smell of Preveza, and despite the seething mass of travelers I could see moving up and down the road, I could not wait to visit the giant market. I had never been to a city or market so big before. "Well I for one am excited to get into the city and see the agora. They say it is the biggest one in Epirus. I should get some good coin for my arrows here." Someone groaned and another threw a grape at my head.

"Goddess, Kyri! Only you would be excited to be inside such a foul smelling city." Sheila waved at her herself and the others that were seated around the fire. "None of us volunteered for this duty."

"I volunteered and I'm excited to do a little shopping for myself." Mitsah, Geeta's cousin, was nibbling on a bit of dried meat. Geeta had mentioned that her cousin volunteered for cara-van duty every sun-cycle and all the other scouts thought she was a bit touched in the head.

I noticed Shana and Iva returning with their escorts and addressed the remaining scouts around the fire. "You all know the duty roster for the next fortnight and I do not have to tell you that the sun rises early near the sea. But I will tell you that anyone that is late tomorrow will get extra drills for the next three days." Kylani and Coryn told me what would be expected as the scout leader for the trip. While the trade trip was considered relatively easy duty, we all had to be attentive because we were entrusted with the bulk of the nation's wares. The money made and items purchased would help carry Telequire through the seasons until the next cycle's trip.

Shana walked up as my scouts dispersed and I handed her a

skyphoi filled with *psarosoupa*. The fish soup was made with local meat and had the rest of the vegetables rationed for the trip there. Shana took the bowl from me and one of the departing scouts snatched a couple pieces of flat bread that had been warming on the rocks by the fire. "Here you are Shana, and I have first two candle marks duty tonight. After that I'm free, if you're interested." Herem, one of Dita's scouts, left her offer open and walked away to start duty.

I raised an eyebrow at Shana as she started eating, and she raised an eyebrow right back. "So, are you going to thank her for the warm bread later?"

Rather than answer me, she met my question with one of her own. "Are you going to wander off to your bedroll tonight and polish the bead of your Amazon feather while thinking of our queen and her talented hands?"

The large swallow of water I had just taken sprayed across the fire in front of me. "Shana!" I was glad for the near darkness that hid my blush from the few left around the fire.

She chuckled at my discomfort. "That's what you get for asking such a personal question. Now that I know you've got your own personal answers in return, you can bet I'll be prodding you the same way."

I scrubbed my hot face and wondered at her change in attitude. "That is not fair, sister. Those questions have never been personal before. Everyone knows that you're a very popular owl friend." I waited in silence as she made short work of her savory broth. She wiped the bowl clean with the last of the bread before she sighed and turned to answer me.

"You're right, it's never been a secret that I like to share pleasure with my owl friends, and it's never been personal." She set the bowl aside and turned to me in the firelight. "The truth is, I've given up owl friends for a while."

Shana was a beautiful woman and nearly as much a feather ruffler as Coryn. For her to abstain for any length of time was big news. "Does this have to do with Coryn?"

She nodded. "If she's willing to make that level of commitment with merely the hope of something possible between us then I can do no less."

I prodded a little, a gentle push between the closest of friends. "And how has it been? Have you..." I trailed off, unsure how to ask to what level the waters of emotion had risen between them.

"We are taking things slowly. I cannot spend the night with

her again until I'm sure that she will not break my heart." I gave
her a warm understanding smile. The path they had begun to
walk was no simple tryst for either of them.

We let the subject drop after that. The night quickly wound
down and I took to my bed role on the hard ground, not far from
Shana. However before I let my eyes drift shut into dreams, I
looked at the stars high above and whispered my heart to the
heavens. "Good night, my love. I am counting down the days 'til I
return."

OUR TIME IN the city went by as fast as waters in a swollen
stream. By the end of the first seven-day I had sold all my wares
and had a nice pouch of gold to hit the shops though I left nearly
all my earned coin with the guarded nation's coffers. With only a
couple days left in Preveza, I picked up a few bolts of promising
fabric and some small gifts for Ori and my friends. Remembering
Shana's lesson from our previous trip together I managed to steer
clear of the delicious smelling meat skewers for sale along the
way. It was near dusk when Binalla and I came through the exit
nearest our camp. I stopped to check in and relieve the guards
that were posted there for the day. As far as I knew, we were the
last two in the agora from our group so I called out as we came
through. "Heyla scouts! It looks like we just barely made it. You
are free to walk back to camp with us if you would like."

Seifa gave me a worried look and butterflies flitted through
the deepest part of my belly. "Scout Leader, Iva and Pocori are
still inside."

"Still? And just the two of them?"

Carah, the other exit scout, nodded. "Yes, scout leader. Iva
sent her two senior scouts back with the money and ledgers but
she forgot something in the Telequire stall. She went back in with
Pocori about a half candle mark ago. She sent the other two on to
the camp where the coins and scrolls would be more secure."

Worry swamped me with a cold sweat. It did not take a half
candle mark to cross to our stall and come back. I quickly handed
my goods and money pouch to Binalla. "Take these back to the
camp and let Shana know what is going on. I am going in to see if
I can find them." I turned to the two scouts still on duty. "Stay
here and wait for Iva and Pocori to come out or for Shana to come
here from the camp." Before they could say another word I turned
and pelted back into the nearly empty agora, hoping that nothing
dire had happened to Steffi's second in command and my most

junior scout.

Even though there were torches lit to help brighten the streets and walkways, darkness was quickly creeping in. The cool air was barely noticeable with the setting sun. Even through my boots I could feel the bricks below my feet still held the heat of day. Our stall was in the southeast corner near the dock exit. There was no one at our reserved area so I looked to see if maybe they went out the entryway that was closest to the stall. Two sentries were lounging nearby, looking very little like they earned their keep. "Excuse me, have you seen two Amazons come through this gate?" One spit on the ground near my feet and the other leered at me. I tried to ignore their dark looks.

"We ain't seen nuthin' like that come through here. Just a few bilge rats and their baggage." Both chuckled as if they were in on some private joke that I had no ken to.

I shook my head and pushed past them. "Never mind." As I turned the corner closest to the gate I heard a sound coming from an alley nearby. I nearly walked past, attributing it to the vermin that teamed the streets near the docks. It was the faintest of whimpers that brought me to a standstill. Even though I had no weapons on me I rushed into the dark alley, both hoping my sisters would be there and hoping they would not. What I saw cost me valuable heartbeats of attention. Iva was lying in a heap on the ground and a rough looking man in sailor garb was tying her hands and feet. Pocori was wrestling with two more men, one trying to catch her violently kicking feet. The other man had stuffed a rag in her mouth and was holding her tight from behind. Just as I moved forward she worked the rag free and called out a warning.

"Kyri, behind you!" I never saw what was behind me. I only felt intense pain to the back of my head and everything went black.

THE FIRST TIME I woke it was dark. My head throbbed with a sickening intensity and my stomach roiled and heaved with the motion of whatever floor I was on. All I could do was roll to the side and vomit. The pain was so intense I blacked out again. The second time I woke it was dark but I felt slightly better. My head still ached fiercely but at least my stomach had calmed. Despite the darkness I tried to get a feel for what was around me. Someone was softly crying nearby and the sound of clinking metal told me that I was not the only one in shackles. I tried to think, to remember anything that happened after I was hit from behind. But it was an impossible task. Instead I called softly into the darkness. "Iva, Pocori."

The crying cut off and I heard someone shift to my right. "Oh, thank Artemis! Kyri, is that you?"

I cautioned the younger woman, though I knew why she was so scared. "Shh, Pocori. We have to be quiet. Is Iva with you? Do you know where we are?"

"Ye—yes. But she's still unconscious. We…" Her words trailed off and she started to cry once again. Her words came out watery around her tears. "They've taken us onto one of the slave ships. We set sail candle marks ago." Fear seized my heart and she started to wail louder. "How will we get home?"

Before I could answer there was a scraping noise and boot falls sounding too loud in our space. I could only assume we were in the hold below deck. Based on the shifting chains around me, I figured the hold was full of people also bound for slave auction across the sea. I could smell the man that came below with us long before I could make out his outline from the torch he carried. My vision was still blurred slightly but it was enough to know we were in serious trouble. He spoke Greek but his voice carried a distinct Roman accent. "I told you earlier to shut your mouths down here! The next one I hear is gonna get the whip. After that, I guarantee that our buyer won't notice if one of ya disappears up top to service the boys." Silence met his words but I couldn't keep silent in the face of so much uncertainty.

"Where are you taking us?"

He peered through the gloom in my general direction. "Who said that?"

I stood with difficulty, swaying as much from the blow to the head and movement of the ship as I did the weight of the chains binding my wrists and ankles. "I did. We are free people. None of us are slaves."

He laughed and the sound grated on my nerves. "Oh, but you are slaves now. You and all the filth around me are nothing more than human cattle. You're being taken to the slave auction in Tarentum."

Rage filled me as his words filled my ears. "You cannot just take us from our homeland when we have committed no crimes!" Someone pulled my shackles from below, willing me silently to sit, but I would not be dissuaded. Fear and anger prodded me to irrational action. "You are a soulless Roman pig!"

I knew as soon as the words left my mouth that I had gone

too far. He called up the stairs behind him. "Berren, Gnichi, get down here. We've got someone who wants a taste of the whip!" Before I could say another word two more men came barreling down the steps. Once he pointed me out they forced their way across the hold. A chain connected my wrist and ankle shackles, and another chain connected me to a metal ring in the floor. Once they unlocked me from the ring they alternated between dragging and pushing me across the hold and up the stairs. I fought them as best I could while chained with a head knock but only received a few well-placed blows for my trouble. The fresh air was but a brief respite when they took me across the deck and chained me chest first to the main mast. I tried to fight again when we were halfway there but another blow to the head had me seeing spots of light across my vision.

The first crack of the whip surprised me because it took a heartbeat for the pain to hit. Fire blazed across my back and I bit my lip hard enough to make it bleed. The man doling out my punishment crisscrossed the lashes on my back so that no part hurt less than another. He gave me ten and by the time they came to unhook the shackles my knees were weak and my voice was raw from the hoarse screams I had forced out. Someone called off to my right.

"Hey Drusus, I heard she was one of them Amazons. Doesn't seem too tough if'n ya ask me."

Drusus, the man with the whip, came up behind me and pressed himself against my bloody and torn back. I cried out at his touch. It was not merely the agony caused by his action, it was the smell of him and the hardness that told me he enjoyed the pain he had given to me. I shuddered with revulsion as he leaned closer and ran a tongue along one of my bloody rends. "Oh, she'll toughen up just fine. If'n she can keep her smart mouth shut, she'll do quite well at auction." I was unable to walk when they tried to take me back below so they were forced to drag me by my arms. The motion only added to the fire that seared the muscles and skin of my back. Once into the hold proper, they threw me onto the boards at their feet and reconnected my chain to the ringbolt. Laughter and crying were the melodies that sung me to sleep as I passed out once again.

HOT AND THROBBING pain woke me to the new light of day. Stripped to the waist, I found myself lying face down on a rough covered pallet. Clearly having made it to land. I could feel strips of something on my back, material of some kind. The only thing in my line of vision was the wall next to me. Low murmurs and shuffling feet told me that the space I was in was large and contained at least a few people. I tried turning to face the room but the pain was too much. The sound that came from my throat was less than human but it still caught someone's attention. She spoke Latin but her accent was as Roman as the men on the slave ship. Romans and most Greeks spoke Latin but it had been a while for me. I tried to answer her best as I was able. My throat was so dry I could barely form the long unused words. "*Aqua*, water, please."

Whomever it was disappeared but she came back within a candle drop. An arm reached over me to press a dipper of water awkwardly against my lips. I drank some and spilled more but it was enough to sooth my throat. I tried once again to turn my head and she immediately reached down to help. The pain of such a simple movement left me shaking with sweat dotting my forehead and upper lip. "Thank you." The woman helping me was older, maybe twice my age. She wore a slave collar around her neck and I shivered at how worn it looked. "Please, can you tell me where my friends are? I came in with two other Amazons. They are my family." I had no idea whether or not she would know such a thing but I had to try. It was my duty to protect them and I had failed.

She looked furtively toward the door and then turned back to me. "If they are uninjured then they are in the slave pens. Yours was the only ship to come in today so the barracks should be empty save you Greeks. You must rest now and worry about yourself. They will only give you three days here, then in the pens you too will go." She pulled one of the strips of cloth from my back and hummed to herself. "I will be back in a little bit. I need to mix more salve for your back but it should feel better fast. Next time do not provoke the men with whips." As she walked away my mind reeled with thoughts that were dark and foreboding. I knew that slavery existed, everyone did. As Greeks, there was always the fear of being at war and being conquered by soldiers of another land. I also knew that criminals were occasionally sold into slavery. But I had no idea that people could be stolen and forced into it so blatantly, that they could be carried away in the night from the families, friends, and homeland.

I immediately thought of the Amazons who were taken from Kombetar and Ujanik during the Western War and wondered if they too ended up in the land of Romans. I wondered if any of them spent time in the same city or on the pallet I found myself recovering on. They never came home and there was that blackest part of my fear that thought we would not make it home either. Despair pulled my heart into an abyss that seemed greater than the world around me. Would Shana know what had become of us? Would they search or would they return to Telequire and accept us as lost?

Just the thought of Ori's face when she learned that I had not kept my promise to return to her was enough to hitch the breath in my chest. Tears flowed freely down my face to soak into the rough material below. The pain was greater than anything I had faced before. I had known plenty of hardship and loss. I could say with certainty that I'd had a taste of some of the physical pain that life had to offer and none of it was what frightened me the most. There was no bodily pain and suffering that could surpass the torture of my soul if I never saw her face again. Orianna was my heart, my hope, and all that brought me to life. Without her I would be dead inside.

I had to think. I had to find a way to prevent our new misfortune from becoming my future. Who did I need to become to get myself and my sisters back home? While I waited for the healer my mind was awash with all I had done and become in my two decades. It was not the fletcher with her placid precision that would see me through. It was not even the archer with her calm focus and competitive spirit. There was an emotion that was building slowly within me, burning my gut and singeing my heart from the inside out. My da would have told me that rage was not the way to go either. Rage would make me sloppy and imprecise. Rage would leave me vulnerable at the worst time and I could not afford any of those things. My anger would have to be shoved down deep if I was to survive. While it made for great fuel, it was not the motivation I needed to get home.

Before I could travel further down the path of thought and planning, before I could lapse further into sorrow and self-pity, the healer returned. She removed the rest of the loose strips of cloth and gently bathed my back with a soft rag and cool water. After that she applied more numbing salve but otherwise left it bare. She wiped her hands on the loose dress she wore and met my eyes once again. "I will have some food for you in a little while. I'll help you sit up to eat at that time. For now, let the salve numb you up good."

"What is your name?"

For a heartbeat she looked as if she would not answer.

"Della." She stood and walked away before I could ask another question. I knew then that three days recovering would be too much. I had to get back to where Iva and Pocori were being held. Most of all, I had to get home.

Chapter Twelve

The Price of Freedom

DESPITE MY WANTS and needs I was three days in the healer's area after all. Della told me that my age and health made me valuable enough that they wanted me as healed as possible for the auction. When the time came to leave I was given a rough tunic and re-shackled, then marched through the bustling compound to a long low building. It looked like the army barracks at Preveza from the outside but the inside felt like Hades. Men, women, and children were chained the same as I was and most were spread around the walls. It was dark and stifling inside. Despite the fact that we had not yet met with summer solstice, the heat stole the very breath from my lungs. I was shoved roughly from behind, causing me to stumble painfully to my knees on the dirt floor. They did not bother locking me in place as they had below deck on the slave ship. None of us were going anywhere.

"Kyri!"

I looked toward the source of the voice and just made out the familiar faces of my Amazon sisters in the gloom. Standing slowly, I shuffled toward them and tried to get a better feel for movement with the chains on. They were leaning shoulder to shoulder and I sank into a squat in front of them, thankful they were both still alive and relatively well. "Heyla sisters, I am glad to see your faces this day."

Iva placed a gentle hand on my shoulder. "How is your back?"

I shrugged, not wanting to talk about the injury my recklessness had cost me. It could have been much worse. I swore to myself in the healer's hut that I would not be so foolish again. "It is better. Are you both well? Do you know how long we will be here?" They looked drawn with dark circles beneath their eyes but Pocori's gaze seemed especially haunted. She was young and attractive and had much to fear as a slave. I hoped that I would be a little too tall for the men looking to buy slaves as concubines, and while Iva was not unattractive, she had at least ten sun-cycles on me and walked with a limp.

Pocori remained silent to my questions and her arms stayed tightly wrapped around her drawn up knees. Iva answered for both of them. "We're okay so far. They give us two meals a day and we get a dipper of water every other candle mark, probably because of the heat. There were a couple people here before our ship came in. They said the auction is held every seven-day and that the next one is due tomorrow."

I slapped the dirt floor in anger causing my chains to rattle loudly in the large space. I cursed and abruptly lowered my voice so I did not call attention to myself. "That does not leave any time at all."

The bookkeeper tilted her head. "Time for what?"

Frustration colored my words and I covered my eyes with the palms of my hands. The weight of responsibility seemed to press me lower with every passing heartbeat. How could I save us from the horror unfolding before our very eyes when things were happening so fast? The shackles dug painfully into my cheeks. "Time to make a plan, time to learn more about where we are and what is to become of us. We cannot stay here." My furious whispers sounded like insects in the hot dark and I fought the urge to let the threatening tears fall. I lowered my hands and met Iva's resigned eyes. "Tell me everything you know."

With a quick glance at the door and the others around us, she began whispering all the things she had learned since coming off the ship. "We've all been collected by one of the regular slavers. Right now we are in Tarentum and as I said earlier the next slave auction is tomorrow. Over the past few days the quaestor has taken down all our names, ages, health, and skills." She cleared her throat before continuing. "I was worried because there's not much I can do with this leg of mine but apparently bookkeepers are very valuable so I may get a decent placement." We both cast our eyes toward Pocori but neither of us said what was at the forefront of our thoughts.

I nodded in understanding for what she had told me to that point. "Yes, I was also visited by the same man. What else do you know?"

She grimaced. "Not a whole lot. At the auction, we'll all be stripped nude and forced to stand on platforms with our information on plaques hanging from our necks. The woman who was here when we arrived, Gaell, said that we could be sold into a handful of different occupations. Domestic, public, service, agriculture, or mining. In case you wondered, I listed them best to worst. Well, according to the opinions of most."

My gaze was as serious as any I had felt. "You have seen more than I outside these walls, what are our chances of getting away from this place?" She gave me no answer, just shook her head and closed her eyes. I pretended like I did not see the tears that glittered in the sputtering light of the stinking torches.

The next morning we were each given small loaves of emmer bread and two dippers of water. We had a half candle mark to eat and relieve ourselves in the latrines that ran along the back of the barracks. After that they connected our chains together in lines of ten and marched us out to large troughs of dirty water where we were stripped and administered a good scrubbing. There was no quarter given for my recently healed back and I felt the blood trickle from a few re-opened wounds. I never said a word though, merely gritted my teeth to the pain and endured.

After the quick wash we were marched naked and shackled through the dirty streets, humiliation coloring our skin with every step. The slave market was an open space similar to any other agora, but with humans as the only ware being sold. I scanned the crowd of buyers to see that most appeared to be men. I wanted to reassure the two women who were chained ahead of me but we were already warned that talk of any kind would result in swift punishment. I could not bring the whip to them as I had for myself, so I was forced to leave my sisters with a sympathetic look as cold comfort.

We were not the first line to go up, nor were we to be the last. I tried to gauge each of the prolific buyers and the types they seemed to be looking for. Many walked right up to the slaves, poking, prodding, and checking the merchandise. They read the plaques around each one's neck, and I even saw one check a man's teeth. It was as if he were no more than a horse for sale, a beast of burden. I guessed to the people at the slave market, we were.

One of the richer looking buyers had been bidding on all the tough and sturdy looking men and I suspected they would be destined for the harder physical labor of fields or the silver mines though I supposed they could be made into gladiators. One of the other Greek slaves said that many captured soldiers were bought by the gladiator schools. Another man, bloated and corpulent with his lust filled gaze, was specifically buying the most attractive young women and the breath seized in my lungs out of fear for Pocori. My heart hammered at the thought of one of my sisters being sold for sexual favors, let alone one who was barely sixteen summers in age. From the many moons I had spent as her scout leader I had doubts that she would survive such an occupation.

It felt like an eternity that we stood there as the sun rose high

above. Dry Roman air pressed around us and the tender parts of
our skin turned red under the unrelenting light above. But the
worst was the way the stone streets grew hot beneath our bare
feet. You could only shift so much to alleviate the pain but escape
was not an option. Even so, I would have gladly taken the burning cobbles to going up on the pedestal in front of the gathered
crowd. I had started to tune out my surroundings by the time my
line began to move. Bile rose in my throat when it was Pocori's
turn to stand in front of the group of slave owners. Nothing could
have prepared me for her actions. I had always known the girl to
be strong but our brief captivity had left its taint on her soul as
deeply as the whip had stripped my back. My greatest fear for her
came true as the fat man immediately bid on my young sister and
eventually won over all the others.

Iva gasped in front of me and my heart sorrowed. I could see
desperation in the young scout's eyes and I knew what she would
do. "Oh, Pocori, no." My words were but whispers, but either
way they would not stop her rage and fear. The young fourth
scout gave a ragged scream and leaped for the nearest armed
guard. Sadly enough for him, he was lax in his attention. She
broke his neck just as we had been taught and stole the man's
dagger before the rest could intervene. The crowd immediately
backed away from her thinking she would attack again, but I
knew better. I could not keep quiet any longer in the face of her
dead eyes. "Pocori, no! We will find another way!"

She looked at Iva, then moved her gaze to me. "I'm sorry,
Scout Leader. Artemis forgive me!" My sweet, brave scout drove
the long dagger up under her ribs and straight into her heart. She
was dead before she hit the ground. Iva gave a gasping sob and
her hand immediately went to her mouth to stifle the noise. They
did not even give us a candle drop to mourn. Someone hauled her
still bleeding body away and then it was Iva's turn to be
unchained from the line and taken up. As she limped toward the
pedestal many lost interest. One man though followed with eager
eyes as they read her skills. He was of average height with curly
black hair going gray, and he wore his robes well. With him was a
boy who could only be a few cycles past his first decade. He
sported dark curls and even darker eyes. I suspected they were
father and son as they walked around Iva together speaking in
quiet tones. Only a few ended up bidding on my fellow Amazon
and the man and his son were victorious. As I watched the two
interact I could see the father had kind eyes and hope soared
within me for the Telequire bookkeeper. I could not even get a

word of encouragement to her as she was taken away in the opposite direction from where I was chained. And then it was my turn.

I shivered on the raised pedestal with so many eyes on me. Many men came into my personal space, touching my skin and scars. They noted my master fletcher mark, the blackened claw marks on my shoulder, and the other puckered flesh from when I was attacked by Gata's mam and more recently from when I was shot by three arrows. The man and his son were also back to look me over though I wondered what he could want with me.

As they circled around to my side near the man who had bought Pocori, a cry rang out in the crowd. One of the slaves had stolen a crossbow from another lax guard and appeared to aim it at the corpulent man with the evil leer. Unfortunately he ducked behind the older man and his son, which is exactly where the crossbow bolt flew. I did not think, I could only react. Despite the weight of shackles and chains, the boy was so close that I had no problem grabbing the arrow from the air in front of his chest. The guard that was standing nearest to us saw the arrow in my hand and immediately tackled me to the ground. My barely healed back screamed with pain as I slid on the hot cobbles with nothing to protect my skin. He drew back his fist and I shut my eyes to the blow.

"Wait!" The expected blow never came. When I opened my eyes once again the man whose son I had saved had his hand wrapped around the guard's wrist. "Let her up." The guard slowly pulled himself off me and I was left to try to stand on my own. "How did you do that?"

As I looked back at him I noticed that his eyes were light blue, lighter than anyone in my own family, or than any I had ever seen. I shrugged. "I do not know. It is just a skill I have."

He cocked his head curiously as people murmured around us. "You've done this before?"

"Yes, many times. I have caught arrows and fired them back at my enemies. I have caught arrows to save my friends and fellow Amazons. I have won contests with both my ability to catch arrows and my skill in shooting them." One of the guards frowned and I thought perhaps I had said too much. We had been discouraged to talk beyond the bare minimum required to answer the buyer's questions. I saw the *quaestor* approaching from the side of the crowd and knew they wanted to get on with the auction. However, the man was not to be rushed.

"The two women before you, how do you know them? The one who died called you Scout Leader?"

I swallowed thickly remembering Pocori's sacrifice. "We are sisters from the same Amazon tribe. We were captured at dusk when we were making our way back from the agora in Preveza. Iva, the one you bought, was our bookkeeper and in charge of the finances for our trade mission. Pocori—" Pain flooded me but I had to answer. "She was one of my scouts. I was her scout leader." The man nodded once and led his son away without another word. The bidding started right after and apparently my stunt with the arrow had made me very popular. Fear coiled in my belly when I saw Pocori's buyer offering for me as well. When the man with kind eyes ended up as the top bidder I felt light-headed with relief. The auctioneer announced that C. Caecilius Isidorus had won my bid and I was led from the platform. Iva and I would be kept together but beyond that, the future was unknown.

After being escorted out of the agora I was given a poorly made wool tunic with a belt, but my feet were left bare. Once clothed I was taken to another building nearby and shoved inside. A score of people who had been sold before me were milling about the room, including Iva. "Kyri!" She rushed over as much as her chains would allow. "Who bought you and what happened? Someone said a slave attacked one of the buyers right after I was led out and I was afraid that it was you."

I shook my head. Others gathered around wanting to hear the tale as well. I grabbed both her hands in mine. "I was purchased by the same man who bought you, C. Caecilius Isidorus. While the buyers were all milling around me, poking as if I were nothing more than a lo beast, the slave at the end of our chain line managed to grab a crossbow from the guard next to him. He fired at the man who bought Pocori but nearly hit Isidorus's son."

A man crowded close to my right side. "What happened then?"

I spared him a glance then turned my gaze back to Iva. "The boy was right next to me and I caught the bolt before it could take him in the chest."

"Liar! No one is fast enough to catch an arrow!" I did not know who spoke but it prompted murmuring around the group.

Iva held up a hand to interrupt. "No, it's true. Kyri can catch arrows and she's the finest archer my nation has ever seen." Even with the circumstances as they were, I still found it in me to blush at her praise. The bookkeeper gave my arm a little shake. "What happened then, Kyri?"

"Well, he asked some questions about where I was from and

how I knew you and Pocori. He made no mention of the fact that I had saved the boy but my bidding was a lengthy process and he had no problem coming out on top."

The young woman behind Iva stepped forward. "How high?"

I gave her the answer though it had no meaning to me. "I do not know anything about Roman coins but it was four thousand *denarii*." More murmuring followed my words.

"Are you to be his concubine for that price?"

"She saved his son."

Iva held up her hand again. "Hush, all of you. Leave us be now." She grabbed my arm and led me toward the back of the small building. "While I'm cheered by the news that we will remain together. It worries me not knowing what your job will be."

I sighed and ran a hand through my hair out of habit. It was in that moment that I nearly came undone. "My feather, they have taken our feathers!"

Iva looked at me with concern. "Kyri? They took what little belongings we had back on the ship."

I grabbed her arms, frantic with worry. "You do not understand, it was not my feather!"

"Scout Leader, you're not making any sense. What's wrong?"

I sank to my knees, legs unable to hold me up any longer. "No Iva, they did not take just my feathers. The rite of caste feather was Ori's!"

When I turned watery blue eyes up to hers, understanding skittered across her face. "The queen?" I nodded. "You two exchanged feathers? How did I not hear about this? Oh, Kyri, I'm so sorry." I looked away and buried my face in my hands. Her love, her precious gift to me, I had lost it just as I had lost myself. I felt Iva take a seat against my right side even though I knew it was a motion that pained her bad leg. Silent hidden tears slowed as she gently rubbed my arm.

I had no idea how long we waited in that dark and reeking cell. Occasionally a guard came by to bring in another slave or to take slaves away. I assumed the building was a holding area for the slave owners until they could come and take their property home. After a score of such comings and goings the door opened and our names rang out. I helped Iva stand, for her leg had stiffened while we waited. The guards escorted us to an area just outside the agora. Isidorus and his son sat on horses while two men wearing slave collars took up the bench of a wagon. One held the reins and the other held a crop. The guard was gruff as he bolted us to the rings set into the wood floor of the wagon's cargo area.

"Watch these ones close. Word is they're Amazons and you know how crazy the Greeks are!" He eyed me up and down and I bristled at his unwelcome leer. "And the tall one looks like a runner."

My new owner laughed at the guard's words. "Ah, that may be true but they're not going anywhere. The tall one may be a runner but the short one is not, cannot. I don't think our fletcher friend would leave her sister behind, do you Allecte?"

The boy answered his father with a serious look. "No, *mi pater.*"

"Good then. Now let's be on our way. We have candle marks to go and I want to be home in time for a good night's sleep." He gave his gelding a little kick to the side and started down the road with Allectus and our wagon falling in behind him. Iva was sitting across from me. Neither of us spoke. I could see in her eyes that she was leagues away from the wagon and our circumstance. I knew that she had no hope of escape because of her lame leg. And I could no more leave her behind than I could leave my right arm. Regardless, I could not help the bit of glimmering light inside me that while we were together we had a chance. Just as the *dominus* promised, we rode throughout the day until late afternoon, only making brief stops to rest the horses and relieve ourselves. Iva managed to doze off with the rocking of the wagon but I was not sure how. The bread we had eaten for breakfast was long gone and my stomach growled its displeasure. I felt a pang of homesickness as I remembered how Gata used to growl back at the sound. As Allectus began eating a bit of dried meat from the saddle, I could not help my hungry stare. He looked at me curiously then called out to C. Caecilius.

"Mi pater, do they feed the slaves before auction?"

The older man pulled his horse to a stop which forced the wagon and his son to stop as well. The dominus looked at me and Iva, who woke with the abrupt cessation of the wagon's motion. "Well, did they feed you two?"

I was unsure how to address him but I answered anyway. "Just some bread and water at first light, sir." I winced at the immediate slap to the back of my head by the man with the riding crop.

"He is our *erus*, you will address him properly!" He turned to our owner. "My apologies, *ere*. These Greeks are naught but savages." I glared at the man and rubbed my head gently. The spot was still tender from the blow I had received when we were taken captive.

Our erus laughed though I found no humor in the situation. "That's well enough for now, *serve*. Time will teach her more than you. Now, give them some food and a skin of water so we can be on our way. I wish to delay no longer." He seemed to think of something and paused while looking at his son. "And Allecte, do not be too soft with the slaves. They are our property to do with as we wish. If I wanted to buy someone to beat to death or to watch starve, it is my prerogative. You understand?" The boy's face darkened perceptibly, but he nodded assent. "Good. I'm not saying that is how I do things. After all, you get out of your slaves what you put into them, but I am the dominus here."

"*Ego intellego, pater.*"

THE SUN WAS low in the sky when we started down a long narrow road. In the distance I could make out the sprawling buildings of an estate. Canals branched off from a nearby river before the estuary emptied into the sea. Out beyond the fields and villa, the water glittered deep blue and was dotted with the occasional vessel. I thought back to the lessons with my mam, then the ones later with Steffi, trying to fix the geography of the region in my head. The water north of our Ionian sea was the Adriatic. Guessing by the sun, we had been making our way steadily northward from Tarentum. My heart was weighed down by the thought that we were even farther from home than when we started. Eventually the wagon rolled to a stop next to a now familiar looking barracks style building. I was awed by the fact that there were many such buildings in a row. How many slaves could one man own?

Light was fast being pulled over the horizon by the setting sun and we were met by two guards and another slave with a torch. The slaves with the wagon pulled away after we were unloaded and the dominus dismounted and handed his reins to his son. Our new owner watched in silence as Allectus followed in the same direction as the wagon. After a few candle drops passed he finally spoke. "My name is Caius Caecilius Claudius Isidorus and I am in the consulship of Gaius Asinius Gallus and Gaius Marcius Censorinus. I am a former slave, now freedman." He paced with his hands clasped behind his back while he spoke. I sensed that his speech was one he gave often. I was not good with numbers but even I had figured out that he must have had thousands of slaves to fill the barracks and tend to his vast tracts of land. "I have expectations of everyone, not just my slaves, but most find me a fair master. If you work hard for me you will not be treated poorly." He turned to the slave with the torch. "Lock them in the cell for tonight. At first light I want to speak with both of them to sort out their duties personally. Bring me the smaller one first and when I send her back, bring me the tall one."

The man gave a short bow. "Yes, ere." The guards allowed us no choice as to whether or not we would follow the slave through the nearest barracks door. I could feel his eyes on us as we walked away. There was no understanding left for the world around me, for my entire life had been shattered and remade over the space of days. My soul felt battered and thoroughly lost.

When I woke the next morning it was still dark. Even though we were in a cell with bars, the entire barracks was fairly open and I had a good view of the cots lined up in neat rows. We appeared to be in a female only building but it was hard to tell from the snores that filled the night air. It sounded more like a den of wild animals. I remembered how loud my da was and it brought a small smile to my face. Oh Da, what would he think of me in such a place? Would he have despaired or would he have fought to see me free? But my da was not with me and I had only myself and one other Amazon for counsel. A sound came from the other cot and I glanced over to find Iva staring across the space between us. I had questions and there was no one else to answer save her. Iva was at least ten sun-cycles older and I hoped she would have some wisdom to share. My voice was low to prevent being overheard. "Do you think they know what happened to us?"

She did not feign ignorance, nor did she fill me with false reassurance. "I don't know. I've prayed to Artemis every night since we've been gone but maybe she doesn't hear my prayers while we're across the sea." She shrugged her shoulders in the dark gloom of early morning. "Shana is smart. She may figure it out. I heard her commenting on the fact that there was a slave ship in the harbor the morning after we arrived."

I nodded and swallowed down the thought that I would never see my sister-friend again. "D—do—" I sighed and already knew the answer to my question but I asked anyway. "Do you think they will search for us, come for us?"

She did not respond right away and eventually we started hearing the sounds of people waking and going about their day. Finally she gave a sigh that was easily as great as my own had been. "No, I don't think they will come for us. As much as I hate to say it, it goes against everything we stand for to risk an entire nation in order to go against Rome itself and its filthy slave trade. The queen will have to think of the nation first. This is our life now, Scout Leader."

My vision went gray for a heartbeat then cleared again. I would not let the anger take me to a place of uselessness, nor would I let it steal my focus. Though my voice shook, my resolve remained solid like the stone beneath us. "No, this is not our life. This is merely a detour between where we were and our home. And I pledge to you before Artemis and all others, I will get us home!" The sun had begun to filter through the shuttered windows near our cell. While it was not the brightest of mornings it was still enough to make out Iva's unshed tears. She did not believe me but her belief wasn't necessary. I was the one who was going to make sure we got home and I only had to believe in myself. The previous night's torchbearer came to get us mere candle drops after my last spoken words.

We were allowed to eat and use the latrines then I was put back in the cell and Iva was taken away. She was gone long enough for the barracks to finally clear out, all the slaves having moved off to their duties. Since it was impossible for me to keep idle in the face of such uncertainty, I began doing drill exercises that Kylani had shown me. They were what she referred to as resistance exercises and used my own body weight to build muscle. It pained my back greatly but I was getting better at dealing with pain. I was halfway through my second set of drills when the slave came back for me. Iva was nowhere around and his voice was gruff when he unlocked my cell. "Come on now, we mustn't keep our erus waiting."

Worry for my sister had started to creep upward from my gut. "Where is Iva? What have you done with her?"

He shrugged with indifference but I did not get the sense that he was cruel. "She's been taken to the other bookkeepers for training. That will be her job from now on. You will find out your own job as soon as we get to the erus's office."

I followed, still in shackles and chains. I had already surmised that keeping Iva and I separated would be the easiest way to control us. Our erus was right in assuming that I would not run without her. We did not enter the main villa but rather another good size house off to the side. The architecture was unlike anything I had seen in my homeland, except for maybe some of the places outside Preveza. My simple hut in the Telequire village seemed very plain indeed compared to the rich villas of the Romans. The dominus was eating his breakfast at a small round table. Despite the bread and porridge I was served in the barracks my stomach growled at the sight of the food before him. No slave fare sat upon his table, but rather he had a selection of eggs, cheese, honey, and fruit. Food seemed to be an obvious sign of class separation in the lands of Rome. It was certainly an injustice to my belly. My shackles and chains were removed by the slave before he took his leave, shutting the door behind him. My erus did not stop eating nor did he look at me as he spoke.

"So you're an Amazon, yes? What is your name, serva?"

Remembering my lesson of the previous day, I was careful with how I addressed him. "Yes, ere. My name is Kyri Fletcher."

"And from what I know of you Greeks, the mark on your arm means you are at master level. Yet you say that you were a scout leader with the Amazons. Why?"

I tried to puzzle out what question he was asking. Why I was a fletcher, or why I was a scout leader? "My apologies, ere, but are you asking why I am a fletcher or why I am a scout leader?"

He looked up while he chewed his food and intelligent pale eyes met mine with a curious glint. "Both."

I stood stiffly in front of him and tried to condense my reasons into a simple answer. "I was raised as a fletcher by my da. When I became an Amazon last sun-cycle the nation had no great need for my fletching skill. But they did have great need of my skill with a bow and my ability to run the trees. I was offered the job as perimeter scout leader because of those skills and my level head."

He grunted. "You're young for such responsibility. How old are you, eighteen, maybe nineteen?"

"I will be twenty-one the day before fall equinox."

I waited as he cast his eyes back to the remainder of his breakfast. Candle drops went by while he finished eating. Eventually he pushed the plate away and stood to come near. "So you've only recently become an Amazon. Perhaps that is why I don't sense the same wildness in you that I did the others. You're trained though, right? What weapons?"

I nodded. "Yes, ere. In all Amazon weapons. I am master with the bow, good with sword and knives, proficient at chobo, staff, and unarmed combat."

He walked around me as he spoke and I did not try to follow him with my eyes. I stared vaguely toward the floor as I had seen many of the other slaves do. "I wasn't going to purchase you yesterday, Kyri Fletcher. I only went to the market to bring in another bookkeeper. I took Allectus because he is at an age where he needs to start learning such things if he hopes to someday take charge of my land and property." He stopped in front of me and continued to speak. "I expected to find someone that either knew bookkeeping or that could be reasonably trained. I expected to see a variety of transactions and people in the agora. And I expected for my son to gain an understanding of both the bidding process and the basic workings of slave trading in general." He paused and took a deep breath. "I did not expect you. Look at me, serva."

I moved my eyes upward at his command. "I bought you yesterday partly out of gratitude and partly out of surprise. Perhaps I was a sentimental old fool because you have hair very similar to my late wife. But I regretted my purchase almost immediately. Not because I couldn't afford it, but rather because I simply don't need you. I thought to myself as I lay in bed last night, what can I do with this Amazon who can catch arrows? What can I do with someone who clearly has honor beyond that of an ordinary slave? A few answers came to me." He started pacing with his hands behind his back and I grew nervous with his speech. "I saw your muscles and your speed when you stopped that arrow and I thought perhaps I could have you trained as a gladiatrix. As a woman you'd be more a novelty than anything else. But I didn't immediately take to that idea. Do you know why?"

His question caught me off guard and I scrambled for an answer. "No, ere. Because I would be killed?"

He laughed at my answer but it was not cruel. "All gladiators die eventually. No, while I think you would possibly do quite well physically, I don't think it would suit your temperament. I saw your face as you begged your Amazon sister to stay the knife yesterday. You pleaded with her to find another way. I also watched as you stood on an auction block uncertain of your fate and saved the son of a slave owner. There was no thought in it for you, no hesitation. You simply acted. No serva, your tender heart shows quite clearly through those striking blue eyes of yours." He gave me a curious measuring look. "Have you killed, serva?"

I schooled my face from emotion. "I have killed many with my bow and fletch."

He nodded, as if he expected my answer. "But have you killed up close, with your sword or knives, with your bare hands?" I shook my head no, immediately discounting the raider I stabbed with my forest fletch on the road to Telequire. I knew what he asked and it was not the same. He stepped back and walked to the table to grab an eating knife. When he held it out to

me handle first I was cast adrift by confusion and fear. "Take it."
I hesitantly took the knife in hand and he smiled at me. Just when
I thought he could not surprise me more, the dominus suddenly
lunged forward and I was forced to pull the knife away from the
both of us so he would not be hurt. Then as quickly as he moved
forward he stepped back again to stand in front of me. "There!
That is exactly the reaction I expected to see."

As he laughed my mind whirled in circles. Bent arrow and
broken string, but nothing made sense any more. Hesitantly, I
handed the knife back to him handle first and he took it from me
before giving a great slap to my shoulder. "Well done, serva!" He
suddenly turned and flipped the knife around so he held it by the
tip, then threw it at the table. The blade sunk into the wood top,
perfectly spearing a date that had fallen out of a nearby dish.
When he turned back the grin slid off his face and he became
deadly serious. "The arrow yesterday was not an accident of an
escaped slave and it was not aimed at that swine, Galianus, like
many would have thought. No, I have enemies because of who
my friends are in Rome and because of who holds my consulship.
It was not the first time that a slave has been sent to kill me, but it
was the first time that anyone has targeted my son. I want to have
you trained as a gladiator. Your primary duty will be that of a *stipator* and you will be in charge of Allectus's personal safety. Most
employ gladiators for such duty but my son is tenderhearted like
you. I do not think he'd do well being guarded by the usual rough
sort. What say you?"

I thought on it, though I did not really need to. Could I protect the son of the man who had become my owner? Could I
honor my creed to protect the innocent from harm even though
Allectus was neither a woman nor an Amazon? Yes I could. He
was just a boy still and he did not deserve to suffer for his father's
actions. "I will do my best, ere."

He shook his head. "No, you will do better than that because
failing me is not an option where my son is concerned. In return I
will make a deal with you. Because I see the honor you possess
and because you saved my son's life, I will make a pledge to you.
Besides the guardianship of my son, I will allow you to earn a
wage while in my service. Not only that, but I will compete you
as a gladiatrix once I am satisfied with your training. If your skill
with a bow is complimented by an ability to shoot from horseback
then perhaps I'll have you fight as *sagittarius* instead. Either way,
we will split the winnings for all gladiatorial contests. And when
the time comes that you have earned enough to pay double what

you and your Amazon friend are worth, then I will set you free. You will both get your papers of manumission and enough coin to see you back home to Greece."

My vision blurred but I refused to let the tears fall. How was it possible that we could get such a reprieve from what was certain to be a bleak and lonely future? I did not know how long it would take to earn our way to freedom but I was not going to let such an opportunity slip through my hands. I gave a short bow and crossed my right hand over my heart. "I pledge to you that I will protect your son's life with my own and that I will honor this bargain you have offered me."

He smiled but his eyes had a dangerous look about them. "Good. The captain of my personal guards is a former *tesserarius* with the Roman army of Pompeii. He is highly skilled and will be your immediate commander. You have two months to learn everything Aureolus has to teach you. At the end of those two months you will be tested before you can begin your service to Allectus. Until then you will train every day from sun up to sun down. The only time your training will be interrupted is if I choose to have you accompany my son to any functions away from our lands or when I host visitors here at the villa. During those times you will guard him with your very life. If you fail me for any reason, if harm comes to my son and you are still alive, I will send you and your friend to the silver mines. There you will spend the rest of your days keeping the men company. Have I made myself clear, serva?"

"Yes ere." It was not as if I would say no.

"Good. Come with me and I'll take you to Aureolus myself. I have a meeting with him next so there is no point in summoning Lucius again." He turned to leave and I paused while glancing at the discarded shackles and chains off to the side of where I stood. The dominus merely waived a careless hand toward them. "You can't wear them if you are to guard my son. You'll be fitted with new clothing and a slave collar when I turn you over to my captain."

He made to leave the room but I had to know one more thing before I set foot into what was to become my new life. "Please, ere," He stopped and turned his piercing gaze back to me, nearly making me lose my nerve to speak. When he merely looked at me expectantly, I took heart again. "Will I be able to see Iva, the other Amazon?"

He thought for a candle drop, clearly weighing something heavy in his mind. "I'll arrange for you to share a room since I do not want you sleeping at the barracks with the other soldiers, nor do I want you staying with the gladiators. It is because you have honor that I place my trust in you, serva. Don't make me regret it."

I nodded in acknowledgement. "No, ere. You will not regret it."

Chapter Thirteen

(A Prayer for the Dying)

MY FIRST TWO moons as a slave were even busier than my time spent as an Amazon initiate. At the beginning I was fitted with clothing and boiled leather practice armor as well as my slave collar. The captain also tested me in all manner of weapons. He seemed pleased with my skill at sword and knife and clucked his tongue at me when it came to unarmed combat. He scolded me and said I was too weak to be of use that way without more training. But he also said he would have me do exercises to build muscle and he would teach me better ways to move.

On the dominus's recommendation, he also tested me with bow and arrow on and off the back of a horse. The bows were very different than any I had seen in Greece. They were short and reverse-curved. Captain Aureolus said the design made it much more powerful than you would ordinarily get from a short bow. I had to admit that they did not tangle on the saddle as easily as the longer Amazon bow did. Despite my misgivings about using such a small thing, my shots remained true whether I was on the back of a beast or not. Just as I had told my fourth scouts, running while shooting translated very well to horseback.

When I first began my training Iva was thrilled to hear that we would be sharing a sleeping room and that I was given the opportunity to earn our freedom. But she was not so happy to find out about my stipator and gladiator training. "Kyri, I'm glad you accepted his offer but I don't think you should risk entering any of the gladiatorial events. Just focus on doing your job guarding Allectus. I'd rather it take longer to get home than have you be killed and not make it home at all. Be safe, sister."

We argued on it often but in the end the choice belonged to neither of us. "I will be safe, but I cannot wait for the length of time it would take to earn twice our slave cost. It would take—" I stopped to do the math in my head but numbers were never my strong suit.

"It would take nearly twelve sun-cycles." Her face was sad, resigned.

I would never willingly wait so long to return home if I had the slightest chance to go sooner. "No, I have to get back to her!

I—I promised. Besides that, it is not my choice. If he wishes me to fight as a gladiator then I have to do it. We are slaves, Iva. We are no longer free people to live as we choose." I swallowed back the tears. There would be no more tears for me until I saw my queen again. Until then I would have to become someone else, someone harder.

At the end of my training period I was given my own weapons and told my final test would be in official combat. After much discussion between the dominus and my captain, it was decided that I would make my debut as the first female sagittarius. A roman senator, Caecina Severus, was to host a gladiatorial show in honor of his late father. Caecina Severus had his rural villa near Venusia, which was a day's ride away. Aureolus explained how we would travel and what would be expected of me once we arrived. The dominus showed up while I was being fitted for my competition armor.

Most *sagittarii* fought in pointed helmets and scaled armor, however women were not allowed to wear helmets. Instead I was given two lightweight tunics of rough blue cotton. They were the color of the shallowest parts of the Ionian Sea and looked nice beneath the silver armor. Greaves were fitted to my legs and I requested bracers as well. Aureolus was convinced that the bracers would jeopardize my shooting but the dominus told him to test me. I was given the smallest set of leather bracers they had in storage and sent through the obstacle course.

The horse I rode, Aethon, was a lively fellow and I had spent more time on his back during my instruction period than I spent in my own bed. While the horse was well trained, I had to be taught how to ride without hands. Steering by the pressure of my legs alone while trying to hit a target was difficult on the best of days. My erus clapped enthusiastically when I displayed proof that the bracers would not interfere. I also requested a pair of *pugiones*, though most gladiators only wore one. A *pugio* was the roman version of a dagger, though it had a wide leaf shaped blade compared to the much narrower ones I had trained with as an Amazon. When I dismounted from the horse, I gave my erus a deep bow then turned and bowed to Aureolus as well. The captain still seemed skeptical of all my extra requests.

"Serva, your requests make it seem as though you are preparing for the eventuality of being dismounted. But if you are dismounted you are as good as dead. No dagger or bracer can save you that fate. As a sagittarius, you will either be fighting another mounted archer, or you will be fighting multiple men at the same time."

I nodded to show that I understood him. "I have faith in my skills, captain. I can handle myself on foot as well as I can on the back of a horse. And no fighter is perfect. I want to be as prepared as possible for all eventualities." He merely cast a worried look toward the dominus, and walked back toward the center of our training arena.

WE LEFT EARLY the morning before Senator Severus was to have his spectacle. It was tradition for the Romans to hold gladiatorial events as part of their funerary process. I had even heard the other slaves say that the amount of gladiators involved was directly representative to how important the person who died was. At first light I found myself dressed in a simple tunic and sandals, which was typical of what Iva and I wore each day. It was the only similarity between our lives as slaves. My competition clothing, armor, and weapons were all packed away. I knew I would be riding a different beast to the funeral than my precious Aethon. It would have been disastrous if he went lame on the way there and I was left without a mount.

After I dressed and braided my hair, I fingered the single feather that was tied just above my left temple. Iva had given it to me the night before as a symbol of luck. I was not sure where she found a bird of prey feather so similar to the ones we used to represent our rite of caste. I also had no clue where she got two wooden beads to lace onto the thong. One was painted green and the other was painted blue. She smiled when I looked at her in shock. "I know you miss her. I hear you calling to her every night when you think I'm asleep." She shuffled her feet shyly. "I just wanted to give you something that might help you remember what you're fighting for."

A warm sadness filled my body and heart with her words. She reminded me of just how precarious our positions were as slaves and she also reminded me that I could not give up. "Iva, I—" I had to swallow the lump in my throat to speak because I would not, I could not, cry. "You do not know how much this means to me. Thank you." I knew I would be allowed to keep the adornment, despite my slave status. It was just another thing that separated me from the others.

She nodded once but stepped away from me. "Just come back safe, okay?"

I smiled back. "I will do my best."

After traveling all day we finally arrived at the senator's estates. The gladiators were to compete in a large open area near the farthest slave barracks. Besides the dominus and his son, we were accompanied by Captain Aureolus, ten guards, and a handful of slaves. The erus and Allectus went up to the main house and two of the slaves followed with their bags. We set up the large tent where we would be housed for the duration of our stay. It was the biggest of such things I had ever seen and the captain laughed at my wide-eyed awe.

"Aye serva, there are even larger that travel with the armies." The big tent was partitioned into four sections. Rather than put me with the slaves, I was given my own corner. I was confused as to why and he patiently explained. "All gladiators, even slaves, are treated better than the others. Even though Isidorus depends on his soldiers and slaves to make his estate run smooth, the gladiators actually bring in money and notoriety. He is hoping that you will win at least two events tomorrow and get his name out in the gladiatorial circles."

My breath caught in my throat. "But Captain, he said I was only going to be in one event, that this was merely a test to see if I was worthy to be a stipator for his son."

Aureolus's look of discomfort had me uneasy. "Aye, serva. That may be mostly true, but he did enter you into two events and I know that he has hopes of competing you again after this. You have displayed unexpected skill as a sagittarius and he means to capitalize on it. I suspect you will spend more time in the arenas than by Allectus's side." His normally rugged gaze turned kind for a heartbeat. "I know of the bargain he has with you. If it helps, think of this as your way to make enough money to go home sooner rather than later."

I scrubbed my face with a sword calloused hand. "It helps not if I am dead."

The loud sound of his laughter startled me as he gave a great clap to my shoulder. "Well then, don't be dead!" He walked into his own partitioned area and left me to place my things beneath the cot. The horses had been picketed with all the others and the single wagon we brought was behind the tent. There was nothing more I was required to do before we had to be at the feast. I had enough time to wash up, re-braid my hair, and change into one of my matching blue tunics. Aureolus came to get me shortly after and we walked together toward the *convivium* while he spoke. "I nearly forgot to tell you that after the meal you'll be taken to the bathhouse for cleaning. Two slaves and a soldier will accompany you. If you wish a partner for the night, that will be provided as well. We have both male and female slaves with us to satisfy you."

I could feel my jaw drop as the shock of his words rolled through my mind. I ignored the extravagance that was to be provided me and focused on the last few words. "S—satisfy me?"

Aureolus's brow shot up with his own surprise. "Surely you're not untouched, a woman of your age and *appelatio*?"

I could not help the blush that heated my face. "No, I, um—"

His laughter was great and loud. "She's shy! The woman who shoots like Diana herself is red as a berry. No worries, serva. As a gladiatrix, you are entitled to a lavish last meal before competition as well as the other services provided to those who will be fighting. I offered the services of the other slaves because I thought it might make you less nervous and possibly help you relax before tomorrow. You do not have to partake in sexual favors if you are against such things."

In an instant all humor and embarrassment left me. Pain came down with his jocular words to split me asunder. There was no one that I wanted to touch me in such a manner, save my queen. The thought of giving myself to another, to share what I had shared with her and promised to her, filled me with anger and revulsion. Through gritted teeth I formed the calm and quiet words. "I am against such a thing. There is no one here I wish to share myself with." I closed my eyes hoping to block the misery and attempted to regain my balance.

He did not give me the respite I longed for, pushing instead. Perhaps it was part of his job to poke and prod me physically and emotionally to ferret out all my weaknesses. "But there is someone, that much I can see. Is it your fellow Amazon, the one you share a room with?"

I opened my eyes and my face felt tight with anxiety. "No. I have exchanged feathers with someone else in the Telequire nation." We had stopped, or rather, I had stopped when things became too difficult to walk and remember all that which I had lost. He placed a hand on my shoulder in a strange show of sympathy.

"Your lover, this Amazon back home, will she come for you?"

I shook my head and my vision blurred with unshed tears. "No. She is the queen and cannot leave on a hopeless mission into another land."

"*Futuo!*" Strangely enough, his curse fit the way I felt and I was not even sure what it meant. It was the emotion behind it, as if he knew that without her I was merely half a person. Strong hands connected to great and muscular arms forcibly turned me to face him. His brown eyes were intense. Before he spoke he glanced around furtively, then the words came out low and urgent. "Kyri Fletcher," He startled me with the use of my name. I had grown accustomed to simply being called serva, or slave as it is meant. "You will need strength to do this kind of fighting. It is hard and sad to go against noble opponents and make the decision to end their lives. And if you are called to kill them you must not hesitate. Even I can see that while you are an excellent sagittarius, you're no killer. Your best hope is to win the crowd over and to make sure you are the only one standing when the gold laurel is handed out. And if you need something to fight for then fight for her. Fight for that queen you wish to see again. Don't lose yourself tomorrow. Don't let it break you. But most importantly, don't forget about her!"

I nodded and continued to stare at him. He had frightened me with his intensity and worry. I had killed before and while I did not enjoy it I was still fully capable of defending myself. How much worse could fighting in a forum or arena be? How much worse would I feel if my life and death struggle were nothing more than an afternoon's diversion in the rich lives of the Roman people? Time would tell. "I will fight for all of us, captain. Failure is not an option."

He gauged my sincerity and resolve, then nodded and started walking again. The convivium was not far from us because I could already hear the revelers and smell the amassed people and food. Romans had a stink about them that I did not care for. I followed Aureolus as he made his way unerringly to my master's side. Allectus was standing next to him looking as uncomfortable as a boy could be at such an event. When the dominus saw me his voice cut through the crowd of nobles in his circle. "Ah, here is my gladiatrix now! Kyrius will compete as a sagittarius tomorrow and I will be going home richer."

A commotion went through the group at his proclamation. "What is this, Isidorus? You would send a woman in to fight against men?"

"This is a joke!"

"You are a fool, Isidorus! Women cannot shoot as men. Everyone knows it as fact."

The dominus raised his hand to bring the crowd of onlookers to attention. "My gladiatrix can outshoot any man I've known before, and you will see that as the only fact tomorrow."

The murmuring began again, most of it sounding displeased. "You will make a travesty of the funeral!"

Suddenly the crowd parted as a well-dressed and well-poised man walked through. The dominus bowed to him and called a greeting. "It is good to see you again, Severus. It has been much too long."

The roman senator did not attempt any sort of pleasantries. "What is this about making a travesty of my father's funeral, Isidorus?"

Isidorus shook his head and smiled at the powerful roman. "There will be no disrespect. I promise you that my gladiatrix is highly skilled and will prevail tomorrow." When the senator continued to look skeptical, the dominus's grin got even bigger. "Perhaps you'd like a demonstration right now?"

Someone guffawed and yelled out. "We have no need of a concubina with our dinner!"

My erus ignored him and cut his eyes to me. "What do you say, serva? Would you like a chance to prove yourself to these fine Romans today?"

The collar around my neck reminded me that the word "no" was a luxury I was not accorded. "Yes, ere." At my reply he gestured to one of his nearby slaves and whispered something in his ear. The slave took off at a run back toward our tents and I assumed that he was going to fetch my bow and quiver. I was confident in my skills for I had spent two moons working with strangely short weapon. When the slave returned the senator and my erus had cleared a length of space in the open area.

The senator had a loud voice, or maybe his voice was just pitched loud to carry through the crowd. "Okay Isidorus, you've turned this into a spectacle now so what are you willing to wager?"

The dominus genuflected to him and the crowd then held up a pouch of coins. "I have ten *aurei* that says she will hit her target with ease." The people around us shuffled their feet and I tried to remember how many denarii were in an *aureus*. I gave up realizing that I would just have to ask Iva when we returned to the villa.

Caecina Severus smiled and it did not feel like a good one. "Since you have chosen the wager, why don't I pick the target?" The senator didn't wait for a reply before he stalked over to a nearby feast table and snatched an apple from the centerpiece. When he turned back to us his smile was even larger and more troublesome. "Now, if your son would be so kind as to hold this on his head the wager can begin."

I could hear Isidorus sputter in rage but my gaze was solely focused on Allectus. He turned his wide fearful eyes toward me. I smiled and gave him a subtle nod. He had spent a lot of time watching me train when he was not with his tutors. I tried to convey to him that all would be well, that he could trust me. After all, I had saved his life once before with as much skill as anyone he had seen. Before the argument could go any further the boy stepped forward. "Mi pater, I can do this. I have watched Kyrius often over the past month and there is none better with a bow. I will not be harmed."

The dominus's eyes were that of a torn man. He feared for his son but he could not acknowledge that fear in the face of such young bravery. He also knew that the senator had trapped him sure as a spider traps a fly. He made the wager and he would have to follow through with it. "Fine. Allecte, count out thirty paces and stand and place the apple on your head." Thirty paces was nothing for me to cover. I had found the short bow to be very powerful. Before Allectus could take a step, Severus's voice interrupted.

"Sixty paces!"

The crowd gasped and Isidorus's face turned nearly plum. Allectus gave his father a look of terror then turned his fearful gaze to me. I nodded again and smiled to let him know that all would be well. Before my dominus could launch another protest the boy strode briskly away from us counting aloud. At sixty he turned and placed the apple on his head. The senator stood directly to my right and the dominus stood to my left. I thought perhaps they did not trust me, a slave, with a weapon at such a gathering. I hung my quiver across my back where it was most logical. When everything was in place there was no longer a reason to delay. I knocked and drew the Roman fletched arrow and after some deliberation, released. The apple was taken abruptly from his head by the arrow where it tumbled comically onto the cobbled stones behind him.

Allectus smiled and gave a noticeable sigh of relief. Unfortunately, I had no time to celebrate my success. A familiar tingling ran up my spine and I heard a rustle to my right. My empty hand reached out instinctually to grab the bolt before it could pierce flesh beneath the senator's breastbone. Another sound to my left and I knocked that bolt from the air with my bow. It grazed the leg of another nearby noble but was otherwise rendered harmless.

A motion caught my eye and I looked up toward the roof of the villa. A man was on his feet running across the baked clay tiles, his feet slipping with every step. I quickly drew another arrow and took off running to sight him in. I purposely waited, timing my shot exactly to his position on the roof. Just as he was passing across the tiles above a balcony, I loosed my arrow. It struck him true in the lower leg and he lost his footing, falling and sliding onto the balcony below. Guards went running into the villa to apprehend the man that I had brought down.

"Kyrius!" The dominus bellowed my name and I dropped to a knee, certain that I had overstepped my bounds. I carefully set the bow and quiver aside as he and the senator approached. My eyes stayed on the ground in front of me.

"My apologies, ere. I was concerned for your and the senator's safety." His sandals entered my line of sight first, and I felt a tap to the shoulder.

"Rise serva, and pick up your weapons." I did as he asked and waited calmly for direction. The senator stood staring at me curiously but his guards returned with the injured man before he could put voice to his thoughts. Severus looked at the man who was slumped between his guards. He had an arrow sticking from his lower leg. The fletch end had broken off in the fall but the stub still remained with blood oozing around the wound. He was clearly in pain but his lips did not utter a sound.

With a weighted glance to the guards, the senator waved them away from the courtyard and turned back to his guests. "My apologies to all of you. Now that the commotion has died down, let us feast!" As one, the crowd meandered back to the center of the large courtyard where the long tables of food remained. The senator cast one more curious look at me then addressed my dominus. "She is magnificent, Isidorus. Where did you find her?"

"Yes, she certainly is. She is one of two *Amazone* I picked up in Tarentum two months ago. Now you understand why I have entered her to fight as sagittarius?"

Severus glanced back at me with a glint in his eyes that I did not enjoy. "I've heard of the Amazone. Gaius Claudius Marcellus purchased somewhere near a dozen about three months ago. He informed me sadly that their spirits were already broken by the time he received them so he sent them to work as basic laborers on his farm outside Brundisium. But by the look in this one's eyes, I'd wager she is still quite wild. I'll give you tri-fold what you paid for her. Such a woman would be a most fierce concubina to tame!"

I did not look at the dominus to gauge his reaction to the offer. I would not have seen anything in that very moment. Thoughts of the sisters stolen in the Western War whirled and raced through my head. But in the wake of the senator's words his intention set in. My heart pounded in my chest and my stomach was full with the heaviest weight of dread. Three times was more than he had asked me to pay him for my freedom. And Romans were a notoriously greedy sort. Finally my gaze flicked up to the man who could buy and sell my fate with impunity, but his face gave nothing away with its impassive mask. Then, as if he switched from one role to another, he gave the senator a leering grin.

"With all respect, Severus, my Amazone is not for sale at this time. I have not yet discovered all her many *virtues*." I shivered at the way the words rolled from his tongue. There was no mistaking the innuendo and it confused me. Was he to use me as other men used their slaves? Worry gnawed at my mind like a beast gnaws a bone. While it was good to know he would not sell me to the senator, I could not help recalling Aureolus's words on the way to the convivium. What more did the dominus have in store for me? And would he honor his word to let us go in the end? The two men walked off together with the rest of the crowd all around.

"He doesn't mean it."

Startled, I glanced behind me, having completely forgotten about Aureolus's presence. "Does not mean which, that he will eventually put me up for sale or that he has interest in sampling me as all other Romans seem to sample their female slaves?" My fear was slowly fermenting into anger and I was hard pressed to keep a civil tongue. Though to be fair, Aureolus had always done right by me over the previous moons.

The captain shook his head. "He still mourns his wife who died five years ago and has touched no woman since her. And he is not a fickle man to make so serious a promise to you then take it away." I briefly wondered at his deliberate phrasing but it was not for me to judge the dominus's predilections. We began a slow walk toward the food and gathered people. "You have nothing to fear from him, serva. It's just that he must put on a certain face in this crowd. Because he is a freedman, no amount of money will make him feel equal in the eyes of the Roman nobles. So he must talk as they do, act as they do, and participate in their little games and intrigues. But underneath it all he is a man who misses his wife, he's a father, and he is a consummate businessman."

He led us to the end of a great table of food and gestured that we should fill plates and take a bench in the courtyard. He waved a hand around us. "Normally we Romans would have a convivium inside the great dining room. There would be male and female attendants and maybe flute players, while the wine and food flows copiously. However, this is no ordinary gathering. It is much larger due to the funeral and gladiatorial events being held tomorrow. I suspect Senator Severus had to compromise a bit."

Unsure of my surroundings, I stayed very near to the captain. I declined all offers of wine and drank both water and fruit juice. Compared to what I knew Iva and the other slaves ate every day, the meal was beyond extravagant. Oft times I felt guilty for the privileges that training as a gladiatrix allowed me. Iva told me that I should be happy for it because I was doing twice the work and it was significantly more dangerous than the bookkeeping she did as her own slave duty. I still smuggled fruits and other fresh items to her as much as possible.

Once I had managed to eat my fill I was summoned back to the dominus's side. He seemed to take great pleasure in showing me off to the other Romans in attendance. Though I saw many gladiators strutting about, I had yet to see any other women competitors save myself. Candle marks passed and before I knew it Aureolus was leading me to the bathhouse for cleaning and purification. Two female slaves came in to attend me though I protested their presence. The captain seemed steadfast in his decision.

"No serva, they must accompany you. It is tradition to be washed and robed the night before you compete. Enjoy the pampering for tomorrow is sure to be brutal." He nodded toward a guard named Calumus. "I'm leaving you a guard to see you back afterwards. *Carpe noctem.*" He walked away and I was left staring at the guard and two slaves, unsure of what to do.

One slave girl, Aelia, opened the door for me while the other one guided me inside with a hand to my lower back. The bathhouse was made from stone block and featured a large tub set into the floor. I relaxed a little, thinking of how similar it seemed to the Telequire bathing pools. On more familiar footing, I undressed and hung my tunic from a nearby peg then stepped into the hot water. My muscles relaxed almost immediately. It was the first bath I had been treated to since leaving the nation. Both slave girls stripped and entered the water with me. One had a lump of scented soap and the other carried a large piece of sea sponge.

Aelia spoke first, holding up the cake of soap. "If it pleases you, Amazone, we can wash you now." The Roman land was strange and it held many strange customs. I just wanted to wash myself but I was afraid of what would happen if I did. Would they have to report back that I had refused the traditional service? Would I get in trouble for it? More importantly, would they? I could not take the chance that I would bring punishment down on them by catering to my own comfort.

I addressed the one I was most familiar with first. "Aelia, have you been directed to help me with the cleansing and purification?"

She nodded. "Yes, Amazone."

I looked at both of them perplexed. "Why do you call me Amazone? I am a slave, just as you both are." The second slave shook her head no so I turned my attention to her. "What is your name?"

She flicked her eyes down shyly. "Cassia."

"So tell me, Cassia, how am I any different than you? We are all slaves here, subject to our master's whims."

Aelia, the braver of the two, answered. "No, you are more. You are a gladiatrix. You are Amazone."

I had no idea that the society was so complex, even amongst the slaves. Rather than fighting with her about who was worth more I tried to find a compromise. "Would you concede to use my name in private, at the very least?"

Blonde hair cropped short bobbed with the movement of Aelia's head. Nearly all the slaves I had met wore their hair cropped, even Iva. It was common practice for slaves, and apparently that was just another exception that had been made for me as a gladiatrix. Her smile seemed genuine as she stepped nearer to me and I was put at ease. "Yes, Kyrius, but only in private."

I wanted to argue with her, tell her that my name was not that which the dominus had settled over my shoulders at the convivium. But the words died on my lips. Perhaps Kyri no longer existed in Rome. The person I had known since childhood was certainly not standing in the bathing pool with two slave women, awaiting their attention. The daughter of my da and mam was no slave flaunting a leather collar and whip scars on her back. The queen's lover certainly never fought in the bloodiest of arenas for only the sake of men's entertainment and pleasure. No, Kyri was no Roman slave. Kyrius was the gladiatrix they wanted. Kyrius would compete as Sagittarius for the gold laurel. And it would be Kyrius that would take us back home. I closed my eyes and shivered with the acceptance of such cold logic and reason. Standing in the large pool of Roman water with the slaves of my master, it was Kyrius who submitted her will to tradition and ceremony. Heart closed and mind intentionally blank.

MORNING CAME EARLY and I was surprised to find myself refreshed. Aureolus explained that there would be the funeral ceremony and after that the competitions would begin. Temporary stands had been erected for the spectators. After eating I was taken to one of the holding areas for the other gladiators. I carefully checked over my mount to be sure he had no injuries or sore spots. Aethon was brimming with energy, almost like he could sense that we would finally be put to the test as a team. I could see trees and other obstacles in the temporary arena where we would be fighting. The captain told me that sagittarii often fought against each other or against a handful of unmounted men. The items in the area would provide valuable cover for all fighters.

I was unsure who I would rather face. Part of me thought it would be easier one on one because I had confidence in my shots. But I feared injury to Aethon from the arrows of another sagittarius. The sun had barely traveled across the sky when I was instructed to mount up. Aureolus had already checked my gear and with a final slap to Aethon's rump I cantered into the makeshift arena. The size of the crowd took me by surprise. A roar went up as my dominus's name was called out, and another roar went up when they called out my name. I was an unknown, a slave, and I wondered what all the noise was for. Perhaps word of my actions the day before had spread. More names and sound washed over me and I saw the four men that had entered before me from the opposite end. Upon noticing me they immediately went for cover in the surrounding area.

I checked my bow, and with one arrow knocked and another clenched tight in my teeth, Aethon and I galloped across the open space. All four men ducked down as I neared but one was not fast enough. He got the first arrow from my initial pass. Just like that, I was only left with three. The competition hardly seemed fair but I was not about to stop and complain. As I came around one of the trees a man jumped out and cast a net in my direction. It was only by the grace of Artemis herself that I kept from being unseated when Aethon suddenly shifted away. I knocked the arrow in my teeth but he was already under cover again. Two more suddenly charged me from behind, one with a spear and another with a *gladius* much like the one I wore on my back. Seeming the greater danger, the spearman received an arrow, but I was forced to spin away from the blade of the second. I had two left.

The familiar tingling sensation was not something I expected to feel but I grabbed the arrow anyway just as it nicked the base of my throat. Before I could think about the fact that the rules had changed, before I could grow angry at how close I had come to losing everything, I fired the arrow back toward its owner. I watched as a fellow Sagittarius fell from his saddle. Neither armor nor his pointed helm had saved him. Unfortunately my attention had lapsed at the worst time. The swordsman had gotten too close and a quick thrust lightly pierced my thigh above the knee. My arrow was fueled by rage and desperation and took the man in the face at close range. As he fell I could see the shaft protruding from the back of his skull.

Before I could get my bearings again I became tangled from above as a heavy net settled over me. The final gladiator gave a triumphant yell and pulled me from the saddle. Aethon skittered away as I hit hard on the packed dirt below. Both my bow and sword were useless to me while trapped in the net and the man knew it.

He approached with his three-pointed trident outstretched as I scrambled to my feet. The crowd grew even louder as they chanted a name, Faustus. The word came out in two syllables as the blood-hungry Romans yelled it over and over. Faustus leered at me as I crouched a mere ten paces from the tip of his trident. The *retiarius* was tall and well-muscled but barely armored with only an arm guard and a shoulder guard. He wore a loincloth held in place by a wide belt, and a lightly padded short tunic. As I watched him edge nearer I stared intently at the confident look on his face. I thought back to my training with Shana and Kylani. The overconfident man was the man you should get closest too. I surmised that he probably would not be prepared for a close attack since he wielded such a lengthy weapon. I knew I would have to time it just right to win.

While he slowly approached, I had been busy discretely searching for the edge to the net. I purposely did not draw my pugiones because I needed to get out from under the net first and I did not want to give away the element of surprise. When the tip of his trident was only five paces away I threw the edge of the net backward over my head, releasing me. A rush of energy ran through my body then and before he could attack I drew my knives and dove forward under the tip of his weapon. Up close he had no defense against my blades. One took him deep in the stomach and the other I slashed at his neck. Hot blood washed over me in the two heartbeats it took his body to fall.

In a half crouch, I remained frozen and panting. I was vaguely aware of the pain in my leg and of the crowd cheering into the hot day. Blood pounded in my veins, pulsed and rushed through me just as Faustus's blood had rushed from him. I felt empowered, angry, and exhilarated. But under it all I felt a part of me die with the man at my feet. Until that moment, bow and fletch had been responsible for every death by my hands. Kyri had always fought to defend against the darkness. The same darkness that rapidly rose from within. His blood coated my hands and arms and sprayed across my armor and blue tunic. I felt his life's fluid drying on my forehead and I was thrown into the memory of when I last received the mark of Artemis.

I shook my head in denial of the unwanted vision. No, Kyri had received that mark. Kyrius did not walk in the footsteps of the goddess. She was a slave who danced to the bloody pleasure of Roman pigs. Slowly, calmly, I looked up to where I knew the dominus to be seated while the crowd around me began chanting a new name. "Ky-ri-us. Ky-ri-us!"

He stood then, perhaps afraid of what I would do. Did he wonder if I would hold to my honor and play out the performance as they expected? Was he concerned that I would fall on the blade of my pugio as Pocori had done at Tarentum? Or perhaps he thought I might take up the bow I had dropped under the net and shoot him in the throat as I had done to so many other men before. In a daze and riding the wave of my victory, I stared at him from across the open space, my soul fractured. The pugio was still clasped tight in my right hand. The left blade had been lost when the retiarius collapsed to the dirt at my feet, its bloodied edges buried deep within a sheath of flesh.

Slowly and without breaking his gaze I brought the blade to my lips. In the haze of rage and battle lust I had finally submitted to the mantle of Kyrius. I had accepted that blood was her lover and death her only friend. And in the back of my mind, cringing and cowering with emotion, that tenderhearted girl pleaded and prayed. "Please Ori, do not let me go." I whispered a prayer for the dying, then welcomed my new life with a stranger's smile.

About the Author

Born and raised in Michigan, Kelly is a latecomer to the writing scene. As an introvert with self-taught extroversion, she has traveled to nearly every state in the US and draws from her experience with everything she writes. Over the years she has loved playing a variety of sports including volleyball, bowling, softball, and most recently, roller derby. But then bad knees became worse Kelly returned to the comfort of fan fiction to fill the void. Reading the amazing tales she found prompted her to try her hand at writing again. The ability to turn out an engaging tale was discovered and a bittersweet new love affair began.

Kelly works in the automotive industry coding in Visual basic and Excel. Her avid reading and writing provide a nice balance to the daily order of data, allowing her to juggle passion and responsibility. Her writing style is as varied as her reading taste and it shows as she tackles each new genre with glee. But beneath it all, no matter the subject or setting, Kelly carries a core belief that good should triumph. She's not afraid of pain or adversity, but loves a happy ending. She's been pouring words into novels since 2015 and probably won't run out of things to say any time soon.

OTHER YELLOW ROSE PUBLICATIONS

Be sure to check out our other imprints,
Blue Beacon Books, Mystic Books, Quest Books,
Silver Dragon Books, Troubadour Books, and Young Adult Books.

VISIT US ONLINE AT
www.regalcrest.biz

At the Regal Crest Website You'll Find

- The latest news about forthcoming titles and new releases

- Our complete backlist of romance, mystery, thriller and adventure titles

- Information about your favorite authors

- Media tearsheets to print and take with you when you shop

- Which books are also available as eBooks.

Regal Crest print titles are available from all progressive booksellers including numerous sources online. Our distributors are Bella Distribution and Ingram.